Praise for

Gluten for Punishment

"Nancy J. Parra has w... ...o delight!"

—Peg... ...f

"A delightful heroine, ~~cherry-filled~~ plot twists, and cream-filled pastries. Could murder be any sweeter?"
—Connie Archer, national bestselling author of
the Soup Lover's Mysteries

"A mouthwatering debut with a plucky protagonist. Clever, original, and appealing, with gluten-free recipes to die for."
—Carolyn Hart, national bestselling author

"A lively, sassy heroine and a perceptive and humorous look at small-town Kansas (the Wheat State)!"
—JoAnna Carl, national bestselling author
of the Chocoholic Mysteries

"This baker's treat rises to the occasion. Whether you need to eat allergy-free or not, you'll devour every morsel."
—Avery Aames, Agatha Award–winning author of
the Cheese Shop Mysteries

"Romance novelist Parra takes the cake with this cozy romantic suspense title . . . A very clever twist makes small-town Kansas positively sinister." —*Library Journal*

"Boasting a great cast of characters and engaging conversations, this is a fantastic read and I can't wait for the next book in this delightfully charming series." —*Dru Ann Love*

continued . . .

"A winning recipe for success! As a delicious cozy mystery, it is filled with quirky characters, handsome romantic interests, and at least a baker's dozen of unusual happenings, capped with a twist at the end. *Gluten for Punishment* is a witty and wily read that will appeal to both gluten-intolerant and gluten-tolerant readers alike! Enjoy!" —*Fresh Fiction*

Berkley Prime Crime titles by Nancy J. Parra

GLUTEN FOR PUNISHMENT
MURDER GONE A-RYE

Murder Gone A-Rye

NANCY J. PARRA

BERKLEY PRIME CRIME, NEW YORK

THE BERKLEY PUBLISHING GROUP
Published by the Penguin Group
Penguin Group (USA) LLC
375 Hudson Street, New York, New York 10014

USA • Canada • UK • Ireland • Australia • New Zealand • India • South Africa • China

penguin.com

A Penguin Random House Company

MURDER GONE A-RYE

A Berkley Prime Crime Book / published by arrangement with the author

Berkley Prime Crime Books are published by The Berkley Publishing Group.
BERKLEY® PRIME CRIME and the PRIME CRIME logo are trademarks of
Penguin Group (USA) LLC.

For information, address: The Berkley Publishing Group,
a division of Penguin Group (USA) LLC,
375 Hudson Street, New York, New York 10014.

ISBN: 978-0-425-25244-4

PUBLISHING HISTORY
Berkley Prime Crime mass-market edition / May 2014

PRINTED IN THE UNITED STATES OF AMERICA

10 9 8 7 6 5 4 3 2 1

Cover art by Patricia Castelao.
Cover design by Rita Frangie.
Interior text design by Laura K. Corless.

This book is for my sister, Mary.

Thanks, Chief, for your twenty years of service in the navy and for going all the way to DC for a visit.

ACKNOWLEDGMENTS

This year has been one filled with meeting and hanging out with the best readers, writers, bloggers, and reviewers. Without your support and care our books would be no more than black ink on paper. Your kind comments, loving praise, and requests for more are what pushes me to keep writing.

Thanks to Paige Wheeler and the great staff at Folio Literary for their help and guidance. Thanks to Faith Black whose insight makes the book better every time. Thanks to the support staff at Berkley Prime Crime. The work you do is so important to our process. Thanks to the people in the gluten-free world for helping with recipes and comments. Celiac disease is not easy, neither is gluten sensitivity. May this series bring you a little sunshine and a few smiles.

CHAPTER 1

For most people Thanksgiving is synonymous with football and shopping. Let's clarify. Most people, that is, who don't live in Oiltop, Kansas. In Oiltop, Thanksgiving is Homer Everett Day. Who is Homer Everett? He was the only football player from Oiltop to ever make the pros, and to make matters worse, he was also a Congressional Medal of Honor winner. A war hero and a sports figure—what small town wouldn't be happy with that? As for Homer, he was elected mayor in the 1950s and had a bronze statue replica of himself created and erected in the center of town square right in front of the gazebo. Someone polishes it twice a day. Even the pigeons won't dare roost there. Even though he died in 1975, people still speak his name in hushed tones, with an awe usually reserved for Sunday mornings.

And so it was declared way back in 1977 that Thanksgiving was Homer Everett Day—complete with parade and carnival at the county fairgrounds.

This year I decided that I needed to enter a float in the Homer Everett Day parade. Not that I needed a float, but it would be good advertising for my gluten-free bakery, Baker's Treat. It would also show the Chamber of Commerce that I was a team player. I hoped that it would make me more legitimate and somehow replace the image of the man who drowned in the horse trough outside the bakery last month.

The hot pink tissue paper flower in my hand was one of two hundred my best friend Tasha Wilkes and I'd made. We'd worked every minute of our spare time for the last month. Now it was Saturday. Only two weeks left to work on the float. I didn't know anyone who waited until the day before Thanksgiving to work on their float unless they were hiding from their relatives. Hiding from my family was not even an option. I twirled the flower between my fingers and studied the float. It was one of several trailers lined up inside the 4-H building on the county fairgrounds.

It felt as if the entire town was crammed inside the aluminum building. In reality it was maybe fifty dedicated float builders all working feverishly to create a prizewinning display.

"Do you think the *Gluten-Freedom* sash across Homer's chest is a bit much?" I asked over the noise of drills and forklifts.

Tasha stepped back from her life-sized, papier-mâché copy of Homer Everett's statue. She tilted her blonde head, her always perfect curls bouncing in response to the movement. Her simple outfit of jeans and a pale blue tee shirt refused to wrinkle despite the heat of the building. "Actually, Toni, I think it's wonderful." She reached over and took the flower from my hand. "Better than the one Stuart's Hardware had last year, and they won."

"What did they have?" I drew my eyebrows together and chewed on the inside of my mouth, trying to remember.

Tasha smiled and showed off the dimples in her porcelain-skinned cheeks. "They portrayed Homer pardoning a turkey while holding a pig under his left arm."

"Oh, now I remember the float. It seemed a little silly, but Aimee Everett loved it." Aimee was Hutch Everett's wife, and since Hutch was Homer's only child, Aimee had married into Oiltop royalty and was proud to let everyone know it. It didn't help that Hutch was the marshal of the parade every year and one of three judges for the floats. Aimee made it perfectly clear that her favorite usually won. "Okay, so I'll bite, why did a hardware store do a float about pardoning a turkey?" I repinned a group of flowers that had slipped from their bonds at the corner of the float. Tasha was trying as hard as she could to make it perfect, but in the end the float, like me, was a little rough around the edges.

"That's easy. Avery Stuart's son lives in Iowa and owns a hog farm. So they wanted to remind us that pork is the other white meat."

I wiped my hands on my sturdy black cotton pants. They were a staple in my closet and served me well as a baker. My long-sleeved shirt was white and smelled faintly of pumpkin. Not that anyone could tell in the dust that was kicked up around the floats. "Pork is the other white meat. That's reaching, isn't it?"

"Not really. Stuart's Hardware had purchased fifty hams. They gave one away with every one hundred–dollar purchase." She placed the flower in the colorful garden at Homer's feet. "I heard they drew more shoppers than Kmart did with their twenty-dollar DVD players. Rumor has it Hutch got the biggest ham of all."

I pursed my mouth in thought. "Who doesn't have turkey on Thanksgiving? I mean, it's called Turkey Day for a reason."

"Lots of people don't eat turkey. One year my parents served trout."

"Seriously?"

"Seriously."

"How did Kip like that?" I put my hands on my hips. Kip was Tasha's son. He had Asperger's and hated changes in routine and ruined expectations.

Tasha blew at the hair that had fallen into her blue eyes. "He was fine with it."

"Kip was fine with trout on Turkey Day?"

She shrugged. "He agreed that trout and turkey both start with *T* and could therefore be substituted."

"Huh, really? Clever."

"Besides, he knew I had a turkey cooking in the roaster at home."

"Oh. What if your parents had served turkey?" I picked up the large bakery banner and handed Tasha one end while I unrolled the other.

"One thing I can always count on." Tasha walked down the side of the float until the plastic was completely unfurled. "My parents never do anything in the realm of normal."

I nailed the banner onto my side of the float. "That's why we make such great friends." I pounded the small nail into place with a couple of good strokes. "We both come from families who are a little . . . different."

"I prefer *creative*. Oh, speaking of families." Tasha nodded her head to the right.

I followed her line of sight. There was my Grandma Ruth driving her senior four-wheel scooter through the doorway of the county building. The red triangle flag my father had put on the back waved in the air current created by the automatic door.

Grandma was in her nineties and drove her scooter like it was a Formula One race car. Only she tended to drive it inside buildings as fast as she drove it outside on the road. Grandma had once told me she was an offensive driver.

"If everyone else is driving defensively then there's room for an offensive person," she'd reasoned as she sucked on the stub of a cigarette. "I go and everyone else gets out of the way." She chuckled then, low and deep, ending in a cough that rattled her bones. "It works for me."

Grandma drove down the aisle, her head moving side to side, looking for me, I assumed. She certainly wasn't looking where she was going. People dove to get out of her way before she ran them over. Maybe I needed to get her a horn.

"Grandma, over here!" I stood on the float and waved my hands over my head to get her attention. She plowed on through the crowd, nearly taking out the Chamber of Commerce's float. Red and blue streamers got caught in her wheels and trailed behind her like toilet paper on a shoe. "Grandma Ruth!" I jumped up and down and made a commotion.

Grandma was smart as a whip, but deaf in one ear. She hated her hearing aid, which meant she usually had it turned off. I watched in horror as she blew past Hank Blaylock. Hank was our local chief of police and not a big fan of mine.

I winced as she barely missed the far wall. Hank took off after Grandma. She didn't hear him either, but she did finally see me. The scooter sped up as she headed straight for our float. I jumped off and took my life in my hands by putting myself between Grandma's oncoming scooter and the float. I hadn't spent the last week with little to no sleep only to have my crazy grandma run it over, or worse, leave scooter marks across it.

"Stop!" I held my hands in front of me and closed my

eyes. I heard a screech and felt the wind rush up across my face. When I didn't feel an impact, I opened one eye to discover Grandma Ruth climbing off her vehicle and taking off the crash helmet her new beau, Bill Aimes, insisted she wear.

My heart pounded in my ears as I took note of the half-inch space between me and the edge of her bumper. I knew her scooter weighed more than I ever wanted running over my toes.

Grandma shook out her carrot-orange hair and grinned at Hank, who was storming up in anger. "Good afternoon, Chief. How's your float coming along?"

"Don't give me small talk, Ruth Nathers. You're dangerous on that scooter. I told you that the next time I saw you driving recklessly I was going to issue you a ticket." Hank's dark eyes flared. He looked like he wanted to reach for his gun. Instead he grabbed a ticket pad from his tool belt and proceeded to write on it.

"A ticket? For what? I have a right to drive my scooter in the building. It's indoor/outdoor mobility. Besides, I've got a handicap sticker." Grandma pulled the placard with the standard wheelchair symbol on it out of her red letter jacket. Grandma loved hand-me-downs. The red men's letter jacket had belonged to my brother Richard when he was in high school. Which meant the coat was twenty-three years old and smelled of cigarette smoke and Grandma's perfume.

The elbows had been patched several times. The current color of the patches was a lovely blue leather Grandma had cut off one of her old purses. "Reduce, reuse, and recycle" was Grandma Ruth's motto.

She also never saw a bargain she didn't have to have, and clothes from Goodwill were always a bargain. Today she wore a sparkly skirt that floated around her legs, black socks, Nike shoes, and a neon orange tee shirt that clashed with her hair. Grandma had told me once that the great thing about Goodwill clothes is that they were castoffs, which meant no one else would wear them. Therefore, she concluded, she had a 100 percent guarantee that her style remained forever on the "cutting edge" of fashion—a very difficult thing for a woman of Grandma's size.

Grandma was as big around as she was tall and was always trying a new diet plan. It was why she smoked. When she was young, a doctor had told her that smoking would help her lose weight. Grandma took to smoking like a duck to water. She often lamented that it didn't help her lose weight. It only helped her lose money.

But that didn't make her stop smoking.

"I'm giving you a ticket for disturbing the peace." Hank ripped a ticket out of the pad and handed it to Grandma. "You should be glad it isn't worse."

Grandma narrowed her eyes. "What do you mean worse?"

"You could have hurt someone. Then you'd be looking at jail time instead of a hundred-dollar fine." He stuffed his ticket book back into his tool belt and looked at me. "I'm holding you responsible, Toni. See that she doesn't hurt anyone on the way home."

I flinched. "I'll do my best."

Hank's right eye twitched. "You'd better." He turned and huffed off. I knew it was after duty hours for Hank, but he still wore his uniform. Come to think of it I couldn't remember ever seeing Hank wear anything else. The man was no-nonsense through and through.

Nothing like the members of my family—or Tasha's, for that matter.

"I hope he feels better now." Grandma tore the ticket into tiny pieces.

"What are you doing?" I winced at the horrified tone of my voice.

"Oh, please." Grandma stuffed the torn pieces into her coat pocket. Bits of the pink paper fluttered down around her blue-and-white athletic shoes. "You don't think that ticket was real, do you? He gives me those all the time."

"What?" I think my voice rose two octaves. "Grandma, how many tickets have you ripped up?"

She shrugged. "What are they going to do? Toss an old lady in jail?

"Grandma!"

"Let's take a look at your float." Grandma Ruth ignored me and made a beeline for Tasha.

All the spit in my mouth dried up in horror. I made a mental note to find out from Chief Blaylock how many tickets Grandma had and pay them before he decided to throw her in jail.

"Gluten-Freedom." Grandma laughed loud and husky. "That's brilliant."

"Thanks, Grandma." Tasha colored prettily. Tasha, like all the family friends, called Grandma Ruth *Grandma*. It had become Grandma's name more than a title. "It was my idea."

"See, Toni?" Grandma waved toward Tasha. "I told you the girl was smart."

"Yes, you did." I walked over and took Grandma by the hand. "Climb aboard and take your seat. I want to get the full effect."

"Here, put this on," Tasha handed Grandma a thick white satin sash with the words GLUTEN-FREE FUN ON HOMER EVERETT DAY.

"Nice," Grandma cooed as Tasha slung it over Grandma's head. "What goodies am I giving out?"

"We have small baggies with gluten-free cookies inside."

I helped Grandma up on the float and steered her to the oversized chair we had installed for her. "Kip and Lucy's Jeremy will give them away to people in the crowd."

"What kind of cookies?" Grandma Ruth settled into her chair with a sigh.

"Chocolate chunk and oatmeal raisin," Tasha answered. "We don't want to give away peanut butter in case anyone has allergies."

"That's fine. More peanut butter cookies for me." Grandma wiggled her orange eyebrows, then paused. "Unless you want me to ensure Hutch Everett gets the remainder. Or even better, give them to that oversized teenager of his. Get the kid to start eating at your bakery and you'll always have a job." Grandma cackled at the idea of Hutch's son, Harold, eating anything remotely good for him. Her freckled skin jiggled as she laughed.

"Grandma, don't be rude," I chided her.

"It's not rude when it's the truth. Everyone here knows Willy Wonka would have a field day with that teen." Her blue eyes sparkled with glee. "That's what you should do with next year's float."

"What?"

"A Willy Wonka theme. We can invite Hutch's kid to come drink out of the chocolate fountain. Or better yet, have him stomp around and say, 'I want it and I want it now!' " Grandma snickered. "That kid's mother is another one. If her boy wants it, it's his. If something bad happened, her kid didn't do it. If they weren't Hutch Everett's family, people wouldn't put up with their nonsense."

"Grandma!" I could feel my cheeks heating up as I glanced around. I was pretty sure everyone could hear her. Grandma Ruth had one of those voices that carried. When my mother was small, Grandma used to yodel when it was time for the kids to come home for supper. There wasn't a place in town where you couldn't hear her. She had a voice as big as her personality.

"It's true. Maybe we should put them both on the Willy Wonka float."

"I can't blame Mrs. Everett for defending her child. Family is family, Grandma. You know as well as I do that blood is thicker than water. There isn't a member of our family you wouldn't defend in a heartbeat—is there?"

"No." Grandma pouted. "But that doesn't mean I didn't deliver a good swat when it was needed. Speaking of family, doesn't Lucy have a float this year?"

Lucy was my oldest cousin. When you had fifty-two cousins on your mom's side alone it was sometimes hard to remember who was who, but Lucy and I were close. Lucy owned Grandma's Diner, two blocks from my bakery on Main Street. She bought out the original owner, "Grandma" Irene Nast, when Mrs. Nast retired to Phoenix to live with her children. Lucy was only two years older than me, but while I was still considering having children, Lucy'd had hers early enough that she was already a grandma. It was a thought that I didn't want to contemplate too closely.

The diner usually had a float in the parade, and Lucy's five kids would hand out treats.

"Simon has that band trip," I reminded Grandma Ruth. Simon was Lucy's second youngest. He played saxophone in the high school band.

"A band trip? Over Thanksgiving? Who does that?" Grandma groused. Her frown was huge. "He's going to miss my float debut."

"He's marching in the Macy's Thanksgiving Day Parade in New York City." I handed her a basket trimmed with paper flowers. "It's a big honor."

"He'll be on television," Tasha said. "You should be proud."

"Wait, my great-grandson is going to be on television and you're making me sit on a wooden trailer, hand out cookies, and miss his performance?"

"You won't miss it, Grandma." I straightened and put my hands on my hips. "I plan on recording the Macy's parade and playing it when everyone is over for dinner. You won't miss a thing. You'll be fine. Besides, you told me you always wanted to be in the Homer Everett Day parade."

"Is Grandma Ruth causing trouble again?" I turned around to see my brother Tim closing in on us. Tim was my favorite brother. While I loved my brother Richard, Tim and I had been partners in crime growing up. Now with all the new beginnings in my life, Tim had been there to keep me from falling too far into a funk.

"She thought she would miss Simon's opportunity to play in the Macy's parade."

"I may still miss it," Grandma said. "TV's on the fritz."

"Grandma, I said I would show it at my house when you're over for dinner."

"Now, you know I can't be watching television when my babies are around." She stuck her lip out in a pout.

"No worries, Grandma, we'll take care of it." Tim hopped up on the parade float and brushed a kiss on Grandma's cheek, then just as quickly hopped off.

My brother was tall and lanky. The kind of man who had a grace to his movements. He brushed his shock of blond hair out of his face. "We can buy you a television, and I'm sure Toni will get you a copy to watch."

"How about you get me one of those tablet thingies and I can stream the parade through Wi-Fi."

"What do you know about Wi-Fi streaming?" I asked.

"I'm a lifetime Mensa member." Grandma straightened in her seat. "There isn't much I don't know about."

"I heard Mrs. Martle got a tablet and has been showing it off at the senior center," Tasha said as she glued the last flower into place. "Roxanne Iger told me that the electronics department at Walmart can't keep enough in stock."

"Really?" It was hard for me to imagine senior citizens buying up tablet computers.

"We like to watch movies," Grandma pointed out. "And we like to ride on floats and hand out cookies."

"Wait, you said I was making you ride on the float—"

"Yes, but now that you're buying me a tablet, I don't mind so much. Tasha, did you know you can store hundreds of books on those things?"

I made a face and turned my back. Tim chuckled. Grandma had a way of getting what she wanted every time. I bet she planned that whole conversation. It wasn't like her to complain about her television—which, by the way, was a flat screen that I bought her this time last year. I stepped down off the trailer with a long sigh. I'd been had by a ninety-year-old woman. At least I could use the fact that she was a lifetime member of an organization for geniuses. It didn't make me look so stupid.

CHAPTER 2

"**N**ice float."

I turned to see Brad Ridgeway leaning on one of the metal poles that held up the roof. Why did the sight of him always make my heartbeat pick up? Was it his electric-blue eyes? The wide cut of his shoulders? The thick blond hair now sporting white at the temples? How was it that the man managed to still look like he was a teenage heartthrob?

"Thanks." I stepped toward him without thinking about it. Today he wore a tailored dress shirt tucked into nice-fitting Levi's. His shirt-sleeves were rolled up and there was a smudge of dirt on his cheek. "Are you working on a float?"

"Elks club." He pushed away from the beam. "What gave it away? My workman's tool belt or the cut on my thumb?"

His words had my gaze going to his belt. What was it about a man with a tool belt slashed across his hips? I forced myself to concentrate on the bandaged thumb he held out. "Neither," I admitted. "It was the smudge on your cheek."

"There's a smudge?" He rubbed at his face, smearing whatever the smudge was until he had a long dark streak.

"More than a smudge now." I pulled a handkerchief from my pocket. "May I?"

"As long as you don't wet it with spit."

I stepped in close and took a deep breath of warm male and starch. "Man, you take all the fun out of things." I reached up and wiped the dirt off. I really didn't want to step back. I really didn't, but we were in a very public place, he was my lawyer, and I had sworn off dating.

His blue eyes sparkled and the temperature in the building sizzled. I took two big steps back. "So which float is the Elks club's?" I congratulated myself for being nonchalant in the face of all his glory.

He reached over and put his hands on my forearms, turning me to the right. "It's the one with the giant bust of Homer Everett." He pointed unnecessarily and leaned forward far enough that I was enveloped in the heat from his body. "You can't see it with your eyes closed." His words were whispered near my ear.

I popped my eyes open and glanced around to see if anyone else had caught me nearly leaning back into him. Grandma Ruth, Tim, and Tasha were in a heated discussion about the merits of one brand of tablet over the next. No one else in the building seemed to notice how close we stood, so I pretended my skin didn't have prickles on it.

"Not the worst I've ever seen."

"What do you mean 'not the worst'? I have it on the best authority that ours is this year's winning float."

I turned to find him smirking. "Whose authority?" I placed my hands on my hips and widened my stance. I could feel my chin rising. "The floats aren't even finished yet." I waved my right hand about as if the state of incompleteness in the room wasn't obvious.

"That's for me to know and you to never find out." He leaned in to kiss me and I stopped him with a hand to his chest.

"I would never kiss a man who keeps secrets."

"Then it's a good thing we're not kissing." He laughed, straightened, and stuck his hands in the pockets of his perfect-fitting jeans as he walked away.

"Lawyers," I muttered. "Don't ever trust them."

"Don't trust who?" Grandma Ruth was back in her scooter of death.

"Lawyers." I tried real hard not to turn around and stare as Brad walked away. Instead I concentrated on Grandma's scooter with the tall red triangle flag waving in the air. My father had attached it to the scooter when Grandma's driver's license was first taken away. He thought it would give her some measure of safety. I, personally, thought that he should have installed wide bumpers all around, but he'd fallen ill and passed away before he could do it. The thought crossed my mind that he may have actually purchased bumpers. If that was the case they would be out in our old carriage house somewhere. I should go look.

"Oh, come now. Brad gave you good advice last month in that murder case you solved."

"You think his telling me to stop investigating was good advice? You're the one who pushed me into it in the first place."

Grandma looked away. "Oh, that reminds me. I think I've found another mystery we can solve."

"Grandma, I run a bakery. I don't solve mysteries."

"But you're so good at it. What about last month? I know you were successful figuring that out."

"I also promised everyone I'd give up crime solving, remember?"

"No worries." Grandma put her scooter in gear and pushed her fedora down hard over her short orange hair. "This is a mystery right now, not a crime. No one said you couldn't solve mysteries."

"Grandma—"

"Bill and I will be over for dinner tonight to discuss the mystery. See you at eight P.M." Grandma dodged through the float makers before I could comment.

I glanced at Brad. He waved at me from his professional-looking float. Seriously, it looked like it could have been a corporate float from the Rose Parade. I scowled. Maybe he stole it from the Rose Parade. I didn't want to think about how impractical it would be to get a float from Pasadena to Oiltop, Kansas. Maybe he brought in a float designer. Either way, he made my float look like a junior high project.

I blew out a long breath and knocked my frizzy bangs out of my eyes. There wasn't enough time to fix it. I would have to hope that the cookies would score me points.

Not that I expected to win. This was my first parade, but at the time I signed up I'd hoped for at least an honorable mention plaque. You know, something I could put up in the bakery window that would help me become more accepted in the community.

If my bakery was to be a success, I needed to try as hard as I could to fit in. No matter what Grandma Ruth said, I was a baker, not an amateur sleuth. My goal was for the community to think of tasty gluten-free baked goods first and murder last.

CHAPTER 3

My cell phone rang as I exited the fairgrounds four hours later. A quick look at the time and I knew it was Grandma Ruth. I was late to dinner, and since she expected me to cook, I would not be excused for being tardy.

"Hi, Grandma, there are chips in the pantry and spinach dip in the fridge." But then she should have known that. Grandma and Bill were never shy about helping themselves to food at my house. It had been her house first.

"Toni, honey, I'm not at the homestead." Grandma's tone was loud and excited. "I'm at the police station."

"I told you, you should have paid those overdue traffic tickets." I mentally sighed. Hard. "I'll be right there to bail you out. It better not be more than a few hundred dollars, because that's all I have in my checking account at the moment."

Grandma laughed low and throaty, ending in the cough of a lifetime smoker. "Oh, no, this isn't about my tickets."

I stopped in my tracks and scowled. "Did something happen to Bill?"

"No, silly." She switched to a stage whisper. "I'm a murder suspect."

There was a long pause as I swore to myself I had heard the wrong thing. "What?"

"Do you think they'll book me? I've always wanted to see how they do mug shots and fingerprints."

Okay, something was really, really wrong. "Don't say anything, Grandma!" I unlocked the bakery's white van and jumped up into the driver's seat. "I'll call Brad. Seriously, lawyer-up, Grandma, please . . . for me."

"Now you know I don't need a lawyer. I'm a lifetime Mensa member."

"Grandma, everybody needs a lawyer. That's why we have them."

"But, honey, it's so much fun. They ask me all sorts of interesting questions. I question them back, of course. That's why they had to take a break."

"Grandma . . ." I put the phone on speaker and backed out of my parking space. "Is this your one phone call?"

"Oh, I'm sure I'll get more phone calls. They're really nice young men. One brought me coffee. Another said he might even take me out back for a smoke if I cooperate."

"Grandma!"

"Don't worry, dear, I know better than to incriminate myself. Oh, here they come, I'd better hang up. Isn't this exciting? Do you think they'll try good cop/bad cop? I've always wondered how they did that."

The phone went dead. My heart beat in my throat as I gripped the steering wheel. I could barely see the road through the terror and rage at the fact that the police had my grandma in for an interview. For crying out loud, the woman wouldn't hurt a fly. The most she'd ever done had been accidentally running over a squirrel with her scooter, and even then she swore the squirrel was suicidal. Badly suicidal at that, since she simply knocked it out. By the time she'd gotten off her scooter to check its pulse, the squirrel had gotten up, shaken its head clear, and run away.

"Call Brad Ridgeway." My voice shook as I ordered my phone to dial while I drove. After Tasha's last boyfriend had attacked us I had gotten a new cell phone. One programmed with voice command.

"Hey, Toni, what's up?" Brad's voice was rich and deep.

"Grandma Ruth needs a lawyer . . . now."

"Calm down. What's going on?"

I hated it when people told me to calm down. It usually had the opposite effect on me. It made me want to strangle someone. "Grandma Ruth called me. She's at the police station in the interview room. Brad, I don't know what's going on, but she said she was a murder suspect."

"It'll be all right," he said. "I'm on my way."

"You don't know her, Brad." I turned a corner a tad too fast, and the tires squealed. "She'll confess to something only to see what happens next."

"I'll call Blaylock and tell him to stop until I get there."

"Thank you." I pushed hard on the gas pedal as I careened down Central Street. I didn't care if I got a ticket. In fact, getting a squad car to follow me to the station would be a good thing at this point.

It seems there's never a police car around when you want one, though. I made it to the station in record time, parking crookedly and hopping out before the van was completely stopped.

"Where's the fire?" Bill Aimes, Grandma Ruth's current love interest, strolled across the parking lot, cane in hand,

Fedora on his head. Five years younger than Grandma, Bill liked his food as much as she did, and it showed. Tonight he wore a corduroy suit coat over a tweed vest and white shirt. His dark pants clashed with his bright white athletic shoes.

"They've got Grandma." I took long strides and hit the door first. I opened it and waited as Bill took forever to make the short walk to the door.

"I know. I bet she's having a blast."

I rolled my eyes. "She needs a lawyer."

"HA!" Bill snorted. "More like the police need lawyers."

"Can I help you?" Stan Lomis sat behind the reception desk in full police blues.

"I understand you have my grandma, Ruth Nathers, in interview. I need to see her."

"Have a seat and someone will be out to speak to you." Stan pointed to the row of four plastic chairs that looked as if they had been purchased in the '80s from a thrift store.

I glared at the twentysomething gatekeeper. "I will not. I demand to see my grandmother right now."

"You can demand all you want." Stan went back to filling out paperwork. "Unless you're her lawyer, you can't see her."

"Have a seat, Toni." Bill shuffled over to the chair closest to the window. "This could take a while."

I leaned over the counter and put my face inches from Stan's. He didn't scare me. I changed his diapers when he was little. Since I was twelve at the time and I'm now forty, he had to be twenty-eight years old. "I want to see my grandma now!"

He raised a blond eyebrow and stared back. "Only lawyers are allowed in the back with suspects."

"I could be a lawyer."

He didn't even blink.

I let the staring match go on until it grew uncomfortable. Luckily Brad came through the door and broke the standoff.

"Hey, Stan, I'm here for Ruth Nathers." At six foot seven inches, Brad was far more intimidating than I was, even when he was dressed in jeans.

Stan hit a button, and the door to the back clicked open. I dashed over, but Brad must have anticipated my move.

He blocked the door with his arm. "I'd better handle this alone." His electric-blue gaze had me stopping in my tracks. Darn it. Why was I so susceptible to commands from good-looking men?

"But—"

"I don't want to have to represent you for unlawful conduct." His tone was firm, and he had the nerve to close the door in my face.

"I expect a full report!" I shouted through the bulletproof glass.

He didn't even bother to turn back; he simply waved me off. I might have cursed something dark and ugly. I might even have flung my arms around.

Bill laughed heartily.

I spun toward him. "What?!"

"You are so much like your grandma."

Oh my god, I am nothing like my grandmother. I stormed over to Stan but discovered he had conveniently disappeared. I pulled out my cell phone and called Brad.

He didn't even say hello when he answered the phone. "Sit down, Toni."

I narrowed my eyes and refused to budge. "What's going on? Is she okay? What are they doing to her?"

"Tell her it's more like 'The Ransom of Red Chief,' " I heard Grandma holler through Brad's phone.

"I told you not to say anything, Ruth," Brad's voice rumbled through the phone. "I mean it."

"Fine."

"Good. Now, Toni, hang tight. I don't have the facts yet."

I paced the reception area. "Then keep me on the phone." I was desperate to find out what was going on. "I'll be quiet and listen. I promise."

"Good-bye, Toni." Brad hung up.

I hit redial but it only rang once and he hung up on me—again. I wanted to fling the phone across the room. Impatience was a redhead trait. As the strawberry blonde version of my family's red, I always thought I should show more restraint. My shoulders slumped and I tucked my phone back into my purse.

Bill removed his hat and patted the bright orange chair next to him. "Have a seat. Ruth's in good hands."

"No." I could be stubborn simply to be stubborn. "What did she mean by 'The Ransom of Red Chief'?"

"It's a wonderful O. Henry short story." Bill shook his shaggy gray head. "Sometimes your lack of education is appalling."

"I've read O. Henry," I muttered, and sat down in spite of myself. "If Grandma is being uncooperative it will make things worse. That's what I was afraid of." I blew out a breath. "Do you have any idea what this is all about?"

"No clue." Bill intertwined his fingers and rested his hands on his portly belly. I had to say one thing for the man—he knew how to dress. I kept thinking he looked like a strange version of the Burl Ives snowman from *Rudolph the Red-Nosed Reindeer*.

Grandma Ruth loved characters, and Bill loved Grandma, so who was I to judge? I was hardly an expert at love. My marriage had been a disaster from the start.

I paced some more. "He's been in there a long time. Surely he knows something by now." I grabbed my phone and went to punch Brad's speed dial number when Police

Chief Blaylock walked into the building. He had a scowl on his face.

"Just the man I wanted to see." I practically leapt on him. "What do your men think they're doing holding my grandmother for questioning? She's in her nineties. Something like this could kill her."

Bill stood, his cane creaking. "Who'd she kill?"

"She didn't kill anyone." I scowled at Bill then turned to the chief. "What's going on?"

"I can't give out details of an ongoing investigation," Chief Blaylock stated. He took off his hat and scrubbed the top of his bristled crew cut with a heavy hand. "Does Ruth have a good lawyer?"

"Brad Ridgeway is in there with her." I didn't like the pit of sickness that had settled in my stomach.

"Good, she'll need him."

"I'm going to ask again, who did Ruth kill?"

I sent Bill an evil glare that should have withered him, if he'd been paying any attention.

"Lois Striker is dead."

"Good!" Bill said.

"What?" I asked.

Bill and I spoke at the same time. I scowled at him. "Wait, Lois Striker is dead? *The* Lois Striker, queen of the Chamber of Commerce?"

"Yes. She was found early this evening."

"And you think it may be murder?"

"We know it's murder," Chief Blaylock said.

"How?"

"I'm not at liberty to discuss that."

"At least tell me where she was found."

"Toni . . ." He shifted uncomfortably.

"Fine, you can't tell me any details, but you think

someone killed Lois Striker and Grandma Ruth is your suspect. Are you kidding me?"

"Everyone knows there was no love lost between Ruth and Lois," Bill piped up.

"You're not helping, Bill." I put my hand on his arm as if I could shut him up by touching him. "Can you tell me when Lois died? Grandma Ruth was with me today. I can be her alibi."

Chief Blaylock played with the brim of his hat. "I can't discuss anything with you, Toni. I won't jeopardize my case."

The door to the back of the building opened and Brad stepped out with Grandma clutching his arm.

"Grandma, are you okay?" I rushed to her and hugged her tight.

She gave a husky laugh. "Of course I'm okay." She patted my back. "Bill, did you bring my walker? They're keeping my scooter as evidence."

"Your scooter?"

"I've got the walker in the car," Bill said. "No sense in getting it out. I'll bring the car around." Bill popped his fedora on his head and ambled out.

"They're keeping your scooter?" I glanced from Brad to the chief and back. "Why?"

"Get this," Grandma said with excitement. "They found incriminating scooter marks near Lois's body."

"But half the people in assisted living use a scooter." I sent the chief a withering look.

"Yes, but mine has all-terrain tires on it," Grandma wheezed, then coughed and hacked so badly she had to cling to Brad to stay upright. Brad patted her awkwardly on the back and Grandma winked at me.

"There are at least six others with all-terrain tires," I pointed out as I stepped in and took Grandma's arms off Brad. She frowned at me.

"You take away all my fun," she stage whispered. The chief choked behind his hand in what sounded suspiciously like a laugh.

Brad's eyes twinkled. He all but winked at me.

"What's going on?" Tim rushed into the police station. "Someone at work said that Grandma Ruth was in trouble and I should get to the police station." He pushed me away from Grandma and put his arm around her slumped shoulders. "Are you okay?"

"I'm fine as a fiddle." Grandma waved a large, square, freckled hand. "Just having some fun with the detectives."

"What?" Tim looked at me.

"Someone killed Lois Striker and the cops requested your Grandmother come in for an interview." Brad crossed his arms.

"The questions they ask aren't nearly as sly as I always thought they would be," Grandma said. "It's a wonder anyone gets prosecuted in this county."

"Ruth came out willingly," Brad said, then turned his attention to the chief. "She and her family are cooperating fully."

Tim walked Grandma to the door and I shot the chief a serious look. "You do not have the family's permission to bring her in without her counsel. Do you understand? She's an old woman. She's not responsible for her words."

"Oh, please. I'm as sharp as a tack and everyone here knows it." Grandma gave Tim a slap on the arm. "I'm the one who suggested they bring me down. I wanted to see what it was like in the interview room."

"Grandma!"

"It's true, Toni," Chief Blaylock stated. "I sent Officer Bright to collect her scooter and she demanded that she be taken to the station with it."

"Don't worry," Brad said. "Ruth has promised me that she won't talk to another policeman without my being present."

Grandma grinned. "Always nice to have a handsome lad around. Don't you think, Toni?" She patted my cheek. "Have you eaten dinner yet, Bradley?"

"No, ma'am, I haven't."

Oh, no, here it comes. "Grandma . . ."

"Toni's cooking for Bill and me, and whatever other members of the family show up. I'm sure one more wouldn't be any extra work. Right, Toni? I mean, he did run to my rescue."

"I'm sure Brad has plans for the evening—"

"Actually, I'd love a home-cooked meal." He grinned. Darn him and his twinkly eyes.

"There is lasagna . . ." I knew a lost cause when I came across one. Besides, I did have the dish prepared. When my mom died last spring, she had left me the old Victorian painted lady house that was our homestead with the stipulation that any member of my family could use the house as if it were their own. Since Grandma Ruth had fifty-two grandkids, there was always one family member or another stopping by. I was used to having prepared dinners in the freezer. Of course, everything was gluten-free. Mom had not stipulated that I had to serve food I couldn't eat.

"Lasagna is my favorite," Brad said. "I'll bring the wine."

"The pasta is gluten-free," I warned.

"I wouldn't have it any other way." He winked.

"I'll have Bill stop and pick up one of those nice bagged salads on our way over. Tim, are you going to eat?"

"No, Grandma," Tim said. "I have to get back to work. Toni will save me leftovers. Won't you?"

"Sure." I nodded.

Tim walked Grandma out the door. Bill had pulled his white Lincoln up along the curb. Tim opened the door and helped Grandma inside. "Call me first next time, okay, Grandma? I don't like hearing about you on the gossip wire."

"Okay, Timmy." Grandma reached up and patted my brother's cheek. "You always were a good boy."

"What are you going to do without your scooter?" I asked as she buckled the seat belt over her bulky frame.

"Don't worry, dear, I have that all taken care of." She patted my hand. "See you at the house."

She shut her car door and Bill peeled out from in front of the station. I glanced at the door to ensure no one noticed. The last thing I needed was to cover yet another old person's ticket.

"Don't worry," Brad said. "I won't let anything happen to her." He ran a hand along my arm in an attempt to comfort me.

"Then maybe you should have driven her home." I tilted my head toward the blur of white that had just squealed out of the parking lot and down the street.

Brad laughed deep and rich. "I think everyone in town has their number."

"You mean they text each other to stay off the roads when they see Bill's car."

"Or your grandmother's scooter."

I sobered. "I used to joke all the time that the cops should confiscate her scooter, but this isn't funny."

"No," Tim agreed, his mouth suddenly grim. "It's not. Ridgeway, I expect you'll take care of her."

"I'll take care of her as if she were my own." Brad gave a quick nod of acknowledgment.

"Good." Tim opened the door of his pickup and hopped inside. "I'll be home late."

I turned to Brad. "Please help me with her. You know she's incorrigible."

"Don't worry. We'll talk more after dinner and come up with some sort of game plan." He waved his hand toward my van. "Billable hours—if you're worried I might think this is a date."

I cringed. I know I was the one keeping him at arm's length, but he didn't have to remind me.

"Minus the cost of dinner, of course," he teased.

"Right, like my lasagna is worth as much as your consultation." I did my best to keep things light.

"Oh, I think it is," he said, his expression sincere. I opened the van's door and climbed into the driver's seat. He waited until I started it up and pulled out before he unlocked his own door. Silly man. I was parked in front of the police station—what could possibly happen?

CHAPTER 4

"**D**on't scream."

"What!" I swerved into oncoming traffic, then righted the van with a wild careen.

"Gee, don't try to kill me either," muttered Phyllis Travers as she climbed from the back of the van into the passenger seat.

"You scared the devil out of me." I was hoarse because adrenaline had pumped like electricity through my body and my mouth was dry. "I swear, I've had twenty years taken off my life today."

"Which means you'll live to be one hundred, honey." Phyllis patted my knee. "Everyone knows your family lives forever . . . except for your mother, God rest her soul." She crossed herself. "Turn right here."

I did as I was told because my brain was fogged with remnants of terror. "What are you doing in my van?"

Phyllis was a slender, petite woman with big, deep blue

eyes and a sharp-angled bob of bright yellow hair. She, too, had been a redhead once, but woke up one day to find all the red had turned yellow. She was also one of Grandma Ruth's adopted daughters. It wasn't enough for Grandma to have eight children of her own. She tended to take in anyone who needed a good home. Heaven knew the house had been big enough.

I called her Aunt Phyllis even though she wasn't a true relative, as she was more a mother to me some days than my own mom had been.

"I had a feeling something was wrong so I hopped a train in."

"You don't mean that literally, do you?" I glanced at her. She watched out the window as if her life depended on it.

"Amtrak goes into Newton, dear. After that I hitchhiked into town. Got in and heard tell Ruth had been arrested."

"She was questioned, not arrested," I corrected. "And you know better than to hitch rides. A serial killer could have picked you up."

"Honey, at my age, it would have simply made things interesting." She was serious. I hated that. At only sixty, she was far from being old or ready for death.

"Not for me," I stated flatly.

She put her hand on mine and squeezed. "It's always nice to know someone cares where a body is."

Phyllis was one of the best women I knew. She had a heart bigger than the state of Texas and was always popping in and out of my life as I needed her. I had a feeling she did that with a lot of people. She simply didn't talk about it.

"Now, tell me what's going on," she said.

"I have no clue." I pulled into the parking lot next to the high school football stadium. It was Thursday and football season was over, which meant it was only me, Phyllis, and the scent of gravel. I parked and turned toward her.

She wore a fringed, brown, leather jacket, a white tee shirt, blue jeans, and a pair of expensive sneakers. While my hair was a wild, kinky mess, Phyllis looked perfectly polished, from her shiny, flat hair to the ironed crease in her jeans.

"Let me guess: Lois Striker died." She studied me. "The police think Ruth had something to do with it?"

"How do you do that?" I was stunned by her ability to know what was going on even when she lived in California.

"I have connections," she said, brushing my amazement aside. "Besides, Ruth always had a big aura. When something's going on I can feel it halfway across the world."

"How did you know about Lois?" If her aura reading was that good I was going to ask her for lottery numbers.

"Oh, Mary Hazleton called me the minute Lois missed their breakfast meeting. Not like Lois to not be there for free donuts."

"Amazing."

"Never underestimate the power of the senior grapevine, dear. Besides, Ruth and I were working on a top secret article together. Ruth was supposed to check in with me and didn't. I got worried and called."

I put the van in gear and started backing out of the parking lot, until I spotted an empty Volkswagen van with California plates in the lot. "I knew you wouldn't hitchhike." I stopped in front of the van.

Phyllis laughed and unbuckled her seat belt. "Had you going for a moment there, didn't I?" She winked at me. "I'll follow you home."

"You know where it is." I leaned out my window and watched her unlock and open the creaky old door.

"But that would have spoiled the surprise, now wouldn't it?" She hopped in and started the VW up. Its engines purred smoothly, even if the exterior looked as if it had gone through the ravishes of time. Phyllis had owned the van as long as I had known her, and it was an antique when she got it. But she had liked the look of it and the freedom of living inside its closet-like quarters.

I smiled as she followed me down the road. When I was a teen, spending a night in the van with Phyllis had been as cool as sipping pretend gin and tonics. She always made it all seem effortless—the easygoing lifestyle, the perfect clothes, the ability to come and go as she pleased. And always, always ensuring that everyone was okay before she left.

Having Phyllis around lifted my spirits. It made me think I could even battle my reemerging feelings for Brad. I simply had to make sure I didn't spend any nights in the van. These days I preferred the comfort of my oversized queen bed.

CHAPTER 5

"Homer Everett Day, what a hoot!" Phyllis put on sparkly reading glasses to study the pictures of my float on my computer. "Only in Oiltop."

"Homer wasn't the saint they make him out to be, you know." Grandma Ruth reached for a gluten-free cookie. She picked out a pecan and walnut scotchie. "I was working on an article that would have blown the doors off his untarnished reputation. That is, until Lois ended up dead."

"What do you mean by that?" I passed her a small plate to put her cookie on. She took a bite and held the plate under her cookie to catch the crumbs.

We were gathered in the den of my house. It was a small room off the front parlor of the old Victorian my family had lived in since the turn of the century. My mother had remodeled it in the late seventies. Her goal had been to restore the room to its turn-of-the-century glory. Instead it was an overly decorated red and black room with accents of hunter green. There was a chandelier dripping in beads and a floor lamp with red tassels. I think it was because the wing-backed chairs were so comfortable and there was one wall filled with books that it was the family's favorite room to gather. It certainly wasn't for the décor.

"Well, one of the rumors that I could neither deny nor confirm was that it was gambling debt, not a bum knee, that ruined Homer's football career." Cookie crumbs toppled from Grandma's lips, and she took a sip of coffee. "Couldn't prove it, though . . . until . . ."

Grandma stopped with a strategic pause until she was sure we were all waiting on her next words.

"Until what?" Okay I bit. I mean, being a good journalist, Grandma Ruth wasn't one to say something unless she had something, and even then she might not tell anyone until it was in the paper.

"I was going through old copies of newspapers and such." Grandma licked her index finger and dabbed the crumbs off her considerable chest. "Did you know that when Homer died, he left all his papers to the local historical society? I guess he thought some historian might want to write a research paper on him or something."

"Grandma . . ."

"What? I was thinking of archiving my memoirs. You know my parents were founding members of Haysville College. You should write yours as well, Toni. You never know who will want to research the area, and you have a story to tell, being a businesswoman and all . . ."

"Grandma Ruth!"

"I think she wants to know what all we were working on for our Homer Everett exposé." Phyllis sank into one of the overstuffed wing chairs.

"No, really, I want to know what this has to do with Lois's murder."

"She had secrets to spill. I knew she knew something, but someone got to her before she could spill them." Grandma reached for another cookie.

"Who knew about our investigation?" Phyllis asked. "It sounds as if whoever killed Lois knew about it and is framing you."

Grandma shrugged and grabbed another cookie. "Only people who knew are in this room."

"I didn't know," I muttered, and crossed my arms.

"That's because you would have spoiled our fun with insisting we go to the cops with stuff."

I was not surprised to see Bill and Phyllis nod in agreement. I turned to Brad. "Did you know about this?"

He held his hands up near his chest. "I'm hearing about it for the first time, too."

"As her lawyer"—I raised my right eyebrow—"what would you have advised her to do should you have known?"

"Not tell me," Brad quipped.

"What?"

"As long as she wasn't breaking any laws with her investigation, I don't need to know." He turned to Grandma and gave her a stern look. "If she were breaking laws, I would have advised her to stop."

"See—"

Grandma pooh-poohed us both with a wave of her hand. "A good journalist isn't afraid of breaking a few rules as long as they get the story."

"Unless someone dies," I said pointedly. "Grandma, if you're right in that this has to do with your story, then I'm glad Lois didn't tell you anything. Whoever hurt her would most likely not hesitate to hurt you, too."

"That's why I got Phyllis involved," Grandma said, cookie crumbs spraying about.

"If I knew what Ruth knew and Ruth came to harm I would go to the police with everything and the killer would be caught," Phyllis said.

"Oh, for crying out loud." I sat back, annoyed. Family—there's just no talking to them.

"Now I'm curious," Brad said. "What was it Lois knew, and was it truly the motive for her murder?"

"That's what I'm here to find out," Phyllis said. "Right, Ruth?"

"What makes you think you can find out anything now that Lois is dead?" Brad asked.

"We'll put the clues together, right, Phyllis?" Grandma said and winked.

"Right."

"What clues are you talking about?" I had to ask. I know I shouldn't have bought into their craziness, but I couldn't help myself.

"Lois worked for Homer back in the day."

"Really? I don't see Lois as the working-girl type." It was hard to imagine Lois as anything but the talkative old woman with connections to the Chamber of Commerce. I'd never asked how she got into the Chamber or why she had so much influence. As a kid growing up I'd simply known her as an enemy of Grandma Ruth. Maybe it was time to look at the two of them in a different light. "That explains why she was treated as the queen of the Chamber of Commerce."

"Yes, Homer was one of the founding fathers of the Chamber. Wherever Homer went, there went Lois. In fact, when I was a kid I thought they were married, because you rarely saw them apart." Phyllis picked up her coffee cup. "She was always right there taking dictation. We even pretended to be them sometimes, remember? 'Miss Striker, take a note . . .'"

"Exactly." Grandma nodded. "They were always together, until the night Champ Rogers disappeared."

Bill sat up straight. "I remember what a hullabaloo that was."

I looked from Bill to Grandma to Phyllis. "Disappeared? As in vanished? Never to be seen again by anyone?"

"Oh, he was seen again," Phyllis said. "Just not alive."

"It was quite a mystery." Grandma's eyes lit up. "I was on the case, of course."

"Of course," Brad and I said simultaneously.

Grandma Ruth was quite the investigative journalist. Even though she spent her life working on a small-town paper, she'd been noticed by the likes of William Allen White. Now retired, Grandma wrote a blog that had over a thousand followers.

"Long story short, Champ Rogers was a northern Oklahoma bootlegger," Grandma said. "He got himself caught in a crackdown in 1932 and went to Leavenworth for ten years. There he bragged he made more money bootlegging in jail than out." Grandma sat back with a twinkle in her eye. "It was a different time back then."

"By the time he got out of jail, we were into World War Two and Champ found himself in the army," Bill said, continuing the story. "He was assigned into the same battalion as Homer Everett. In fact, it was Champ who officially witnessed Homer's act of bravery and swore that Homer risked life and limb to save Champ and his squad from certain death."

"Really." I could not help but let my disbelief show in my tone. I mean, who today would believe an ex-convict?

"Oh, yes," Grandma said. "We were losing support for the war and they were desperate for propaganda heroes.

When Champ told the story of how Homer, a former football star, charged the enemy line, turning the battle, the army jumped on it."

"Interesting," Brad muttered, and crossed one long leg over the other so that his ankle rested on his knee.

"Indeed." Bill nodded. "After that Homer and Champ toured the States for a full two years, telling their story to raise war bonds."

"In fact I think the library archives have a recording of one of the live radio shows they did," Grandma said.

"Wait." I leaned forward. "So Champ's story got him and Homer out of the war?"

"Oh, yes," Phyllis said. "It was a very clever plan. Champ was a fantastically charismatic storyteller, and Homer was a clever, quiet man with the physique of an athlete. It was the perfect combination."

"So, how is this tied to Lois's death?" I asked again. Sometimes my family could go out on a tangent and never return.

Grandma brushed crumbs off her butterfly-patterned skirt. "Hold your horses, it's coming. You have to hear the whole story." She reached for another cookie and took a bite before she continued. "Once the war was over, Homer had his medal and his political connections. Champ favored booze and women. So Homer paid him to go away as quietly as a charismatic storyteller could go."

"They say Champ went out west to Las Vegas and lived off what his story could buy," Bill said. "Meanwhile, Homer was a local hero, a lifelong mayor with an eye on the governorship."

"Hearing that his war buddy was climbing the political ladder, Champ arrived back in Oiltop with his pockets empty and his hand out," Grandma said. "You see, Champ knew every one of Homer's secrets."

"And Lois?" I had to ask.

"Lois also knew Homer's secrets. Champ's arrival is when things got dicey. Right, Ruth?" Phyllis's eyes sparkled in the low light of the fake-Victorian porcelain lamps Mom had installed. The small fire in the green-tiled fireplace warmed the room, taking the edge off the cold wind that whistled through the old bay window.

"I heard *dicey* and *Ruth* in the same sentence. What did Grandma get mixed up into now?" Tasha walked in, pulling off her gloves and scarf. Kansas in November was the perfect combination of warm days and cold nights.

"Hi, Grandma," Kip, Tasha's ten-year-old son said as he slumped down on the rug intent on his handheld game. Tasha and Kip had moved into the homestead when her bed-and-breakfast went under. Now they lived in the suite on the fourth floor and Tasha worked as weekend manager at the Red Tile Inn.

"Kip, take your coat off and hang it up," Tasha scolded.

"Okay." The boy didn't move, his full focus on whatever game was in his hands.

"Kip, you know the rules—hang up your coat or I will take away the game."

"You can't take away my game," Kip said. "I'm on level eight. If you take it away I'll have to start all over."

"Kip." Tasha's tone was stern but soft. The thing about my best friend was that, unlike in my family, the softer her voice became the angrier she was.

"Better do it, boy." Bill leaned toward him. "She means it."

"Fine." Kip huffed and ripped off his coat. He was about to toss it into the corner when Tasha leaned down and lifted his game hand so his attention was level with her face. There was a long uncomfortable pause before Kip gave in. "I'll hang it up."

"Yes, you will." Tasha straightened and watched her son

go out into the hallway. I could hear the hall closet door open and then close.

"I'm going to my room," Kip said.

"Tell everyone good night." Tasha had her coat off and folded over her arm.

Kip popped his blond head into the room. "Good night, everyone."

"Good night, Kip."

"'Night, boy."

"Good night, dear."

"Don't forget to hang your coat up," Kip said to his mom right before he disappeared into the hall. Tasha rolled her eyes as the sound of her son charging up the stairs echoed through the hall.

She held up her hand. "Don't say another thing until I get back." Tasha was back before I could swallow the coffee I'd sipped. "Now, what did I miss? Besides the fact that Brad"—she sent me a look—"and Aunt Phyllis are here." She walked over and gave Phyllis a kiss on the cheek, then poured herself a cup of coffee, snagged a chocolate chip cookie, and sat down on the floor at Phyllis's feet. "Okay, speak. . . ."

"Ruth was interrogated at the police station this evening," Phyllis said.

"What?!" Tasha turned her blue gaze on me. "What happened?"

"I'm a murder suspect," Grandma Ruth said with a tad too much glee.

"Oh my god." Tasha nearly spilled her coffee. It sloshed around the cup rim. "Why? Who? When? What?"

"Now, see, Tasha knows all the right questions to ask." Grandma looked at me smugly. "She did not leap to the conclusion that I'd done anything wrong."

"Grandma—"

"She didn't," Grandma huffed.

Tasha sat up on her heels. "Someone had better tell me what happened right now."

"Lois Striker was murdered," Brad said.

"And the police think Grandma did it?" Tasha was smart enough to see the problem. "Why?"

"Apparently there were incriminating scooter marks at the scene," Bill added.

"But lots of people drive scooters," Tasha pointed out. "Right?"

"Not with my all-terrain tires on them." Grandma loved all the attention. "I could have done it, you know. I'm capable of a lot of things."

"Ruth!"

"Grandma!" Brad, Tasha, and I said all at once.

"What?"

"Don't say that," I said, horrified.

"You don't know who's listening," Brad said. "In the hands of the right prosecutor, it might be considered incriminating."

"Well, poop." Grandma pouted. "I didn't say I did it. I simply pointed out that I could have done it."

"Ruth." Phyllis's tone brooked no disobedience. "You were telling us about Lois's connection to Homer and why you think she was killed."

"Oiltop is a small town," I pointed out. "How many secrets can there be?" It certainly seemed like my life was constantly under scrutiny. Can you imagine if you were the town hero?

"Wait—Homer Everett was connected to Lois?" Tasha struggled to keep up with our conversation. "Wasn't that like sixty-some years ago? What secrets could Lois possibly know that would get her killed now?"

"She knew something," Grandma said thoughtfully. "I was this close to getting it out of her." Grandma held up her hand and put her index finger and thumb together. "It had to be good, too."

"What makes you say that?" I think my heart flopped over in my chest.

"Clearly someone didn't want her to tell me what it was that she knew about Homer."

"That's entirely supposition on your part, Ruth," Brad pointed out. "As of now we have no idea who wanted Lois dead, who killed her, or even how she was killed." He steepled his hands.

"You might not know, but I do," Grandma said with a certainty that made me nervous. "My investigation stirred up secrets. Secrets someone would kill to keep quiet."

"What could she possibly know about Homer?" Tasha asked. "Why would it matter after all these years?"

"It seems that will go to her grave with her." Grandma sighed and grabbed a lemon cookie. "I'd been working her for months trying to get her to spill her guts on Homer. When I gave her some details I'd dug up in old newspapers, she got nervous. Then today she suddenly called me and said she had made the decision to come clean.

"We were supposed to meet in front of the Statue of Homer near the courthouse. But she never showed."

"Where did they find her body?" I asked.

"They didn't say exactly." Grandma shrugged. "Somewhere in the courthouse square."

"They're keeping the details of the investigation closed," Brad said. He sent me a long look. "Chief Blaylock stressed that he did not want amateur investigators involved. He said, and I quote, 'Too many innocent people get hurt when non-professionals try to do a policeman's job.'"

I pinched my mouth in a partial frown. "I was not trying to do his job last time."

"No." Grandma Ruth nodded. "She was trying to do mine. I am an investigative journalist."

"No, no, I wasn't," I protested. "I was trying to do *my* job. I like baking. I love bringing a tiny bit of normal into gluten-free people's lives. I swear this time there will be no investigating."

"Hmmm." Brad swallowed the last of his coffee and stood. "As long as you're clear on that; because as your lawyer, I have to advise you against doing anything on your own here. That includes you, Ruth."

He gave Grandma a raised-eyebrow look.

She raised both hands in innocence. "I won't do the police chief's job."

"Good."

"Unless he doesn't do it, because someone has to. . . ."

"Ruth!"

Grandma laughed, a deep cackle that seemed to start at her toes.

"It's late. Thank you for the dinner and the conversation. It was . . . entertaining."

"Well that's one thing we always strive to be here in the Nathers household—entertaining."

I sent Grandma a stern look. She raised both hands in a gesture of innocence. Right, like anyone believed that Grandma Ruth was innocent. Wait—shoot—no wonder the police had her in the interview room. I sighed and walked Brad down the hall to the small foyer of the homestead.

"Thank you for coming to Grandma's rescue today. She really has no idea how much trouble she could be in with this investigation."

"You're welcome." Brad snagged his wool dress coat

from the stand near the door. "I'll try to find out what I can. You do your best to keep Ruth out of the way. Deal?"

"Deal." I opened the door.

He kissed my cheek as he stepped out. "Thanks for dinner."

"I'd say anytime, but you have to know I'm still not ready to date."

My divorce, just a few months prior, had been bitter.

I'd come home early one day to find my ex in my bed with his best friend's wife. It seemed so cliché, but at the same time hurt me more than I'd thought something like that would. I was scared. I'd watched too many of my divorced friends dive right back into a relationship. As far as I was concerned that was a big mistake. It took time to grieve the loss of your marriage and to figure out what happened. I didn't want to repeat my mistake in falling for the wrong guy. So I'd decided not to date until I felt ready to get back out there. It would give me time to put myself and my fledgling gluten-free bakery business first.

"I'm counting the days." Brad's electric-blue gaze grew serious. "And when you decide you're ready, I'm coming over for a real date."

"I'm not making any promises," I said, and hugged the door to my chest.

"Is that a 'No, thank you'?" he asked.

"Yes," I said. "It's the fairest thing I can do."

"One thing I know about you, Toni, is that you are honest about your feelings." He tucked a strand of hair behind my ear. "I'm going to keep asking. You keep being honest. Okay?"

"Okay."

He wasn't the only one waiting out my dating moratorium. Sam Greenbaum, rancher, handyman, and overall good guy, with the body to match, was also waiting. Sam and Brad knew about each other. I had made no promises to either, but eventually I was going to have to choose.

That was the worst part. Right now I didn't trust myself to choose. That was why I had told them both to date other people. If they could find love with someone else, then the decision would be out of my hands. It was the lazy way to go, I suppose, but right now it was the way that worked for me.

"Good night, Brad."

"Call me if you need anything." He stepped off the porch and out into the cold black November night.

Across the street, Mrs. Dorsky's curtains fell closed. It wouldn't be long before the entire community knew that Brad had had dinner at my house . . . and had kissed me good-bye. I touched the still-tingling skin on my cheek. Closing the door, I leaned against it and shut my eyes. If the man had slipped and kissed my mouth I might have thrown my arms around him and dived in.

Thank goodness that didn't happen. If it had, I would have disappointed myself, and worse, I would have let loneliness and fear decide for me.

"So, when do you want to get started on the investigation?" Grandma Ruth waddled down the hallway. She was a character with her tightly curled, carrot-orange hair and her square face covered in freckles. Her outfit, a combination of man's corduroy shirt and a butterfly-patterned skirt, matched in color theory only. You had to give her credit, though. The accent color on her knockoff Nikes matched one of the butterflies—a fanciful shade of fuchsia.

"Didn't you hear Brad?" I pushed off from the door. "Chief Blaylock said we are to stay out of the investigation."

"Pshaw." Grandma waved away the thought with her large square hand. "Damn the man. I am on to a good story, and nothing keeps an investigative journalist down."

I blew out a long breath. "You know I'm scheduled to make fifty piecrusts for the Thanksgiving weekend pie run. That means fifty pies in less than ten days."

"That's what you have Meghan for." Grandma took me by the arm and steered me back to the den. "Phyllis has this fabulous idea how to find out where Lois was found and how she died. . . ."

CHAPTER 6

Gluten-free piecrust is one of my favorite things to make. It takes a lot of shortening, but the rice-and-tapioca-flour mixes baked up lighter and flakier than wheat flour. The hardest part is rolling out the dough. Without the gluten, the dough doesn't stretch as easily, which means you have to be super careful when you roll it to ensure the proper amount of shortening dispersal and depth. I solve this problem by rolling the dough out between parchment paper. That way you can flip it over without tearing it.

Aunt Phyllis took Grandma Ruth to early Mass that morning, and afterwards they planned to stop by the bakery for coffee and leftover pastries. The idea was for us to come up with a plan for the investigation. I, as I'd already explained, wanted nothing to do with another investigation, but I agreed with their plot, mainly to keep an eye on them. If I had protested, they would only have investigated behind my back. Grandma Ruth could be a force of nature with a laugh to match.

I figured that the best I could do was pretend to go along. That way at the very least I would know what was going on. The last thing I wanted was to be surprised with another phone call telling me that Grandma was in jail, or worse . . . that she had gotten herself killed.

The back door to the bakery opened and Grandma Ruth came in in a wheelchair pushed by Aunt Phyllis.

"When my new scooter comes, I'm going to send the bill to Chief Blaylock," Grandma said, pouting. Her pouts were one part puppy-dog-adorable and two parts annoying because you knew you couldn't resist.

"And you should," Aunt Phyllis said. She wore a snappy ice-blue suit under a classic trench coat. A tiny pillbox hat sat at an angle on her bright hair. In contrast, Grandma Ruth wore a white men's dress shirt, a dark brown corduroy skirt, knee-high hose, and classic white Nikes. If Grandma ever had to run somewhere she was fully equipped . . . minus the fact that her knees and hips wouldn't let her.

"Grandma, where's your coat?" I waved the rolling pin at her. "It's November."

"Of course it's November, dearie. What does that have to do with my coat?"

"I think she's hinting that winter will soon be here." Phyllis pushed Grandma over the smooth black-and-white tiles on my floor. When they reached the small table next to the office, Phyllis took off her coat while Grandma adjusted herself to table height, tucking her chair neatly under the Formica top.

"Winter doesn't officially get here until the twenty-first of December," Grandma pointed out. "Coffee, dear, cream, and two packets of artificial sweetener."

"I know when winter gets here." I continued to frown at her. "I asked where your coat was."

"I took it to the dry cleaner last week." She ran her long

square fingers along the chrome edge in front of her. The table was a 1950s diner table with a bright red top and chrome legs. I'd found it rusty and a bit beaten up at a garage sale and rescued it. It took me a month to restore it, but I loved it and almost based the bakery theme on it—until I realized the red and chrome were more a match for a pharmacy's soda fountain than for Baker's Treat.

The "English library" theme for the bakery worked out better, considering my last name was Holmes.

"Grandma, a lie so soon after church is not good," I chided. "You did not take your coat to the cleaner. I saw you wearing it the day before yesterday."

"Huh, then I must have taken it to the cleaner yesterday." She gave me her best innocent look. "I'm old. I forget."

"You're a lifetime Mensa member. You never forget, and you remind me every day in case *I* might forget."

"Fine." Grandma flipped her hand. "I took it to the cleaner yesterday before I went to the police station."

"Why?"

"It was dirty."

"Grandma—"

"Coffee!" Phyllis came in with two oversized green cups with yellow daisies on them. She held one in each hand and set them on the table. "Pastries?"

I blew out a breath. It was clear I wasn't going to get any more information out of Grandma. Aunt Phyllis looked at me expectantly. "I'll get the platter."

Putting down the rolling pin, I went to the walk-in freezer, where I pulled out a platter of assorted pastries. Gluten-free donuts, muffins, and Danish did better if they were kept frozen. I popped the platter in the oversized microwave and hit forty-five seconds. In exactly forty-five seconds the once-frozen baked goods would be as warm and tasty as if they had come straight from the oven. It was how I kept all my gluten-free baked goods at home. Without preservatives and with a variety of flours, gluten-free was best eaten fresh and warm.

The microwave *ding*ed and I pulled out the platter and set it on the table. Aunt Phyllis had found yellow and green plates on the shelf in the kitchen to match the mugs. I let the piecrust rest and grabbed my own cup of coffee, sitting down with two of my favorite people.

The kitchen smelled of fresh apple and three-berry pies. The crust I was working on was meant for a series of classic pumpkin pies. Some were made with real milk and eggs and a couple were made with almond milk and an egg substitute for two vegan friends and one lactose-intolerant family.

"I love these cranberry muffins." Aunt Phyllis took one off the platter and unwrapped it slowly from the cupcake paper I had baked it in. "What do you put in them to give them that interesting taste?"

"I make them with almonds and walnuts and white chocolate chips for a sweetness to match the tart of the cranberry."

"They are good," Grandma Ruth said as she put two on her plate. "But I prefer the donuts."

The donuts were apple spice with maple glaze. All the best tastes of fall. There were apple-cinnamon fritters on the plate, and chocolate chip pumpkin muffins. I took one of the pumpkin muffins and unwrapped it. "Why don't you tell me what it was you wanted me to help you investigate before the police dragged you in for questioning?" It was my attempt at diverting Grandma Ruth from her need to discover who killed Lois and why.

"That's the most interesting part," Grandma said, and popped half a muffin into her mouth. Her blue eyes sparkled. "Good."

"Thank you."

"Ruth was working on her investigation into Homer Everett," Phyllis said, and used her fork to take a dainty bite of her muffin.

"Yes." Grandma pointed at Phyllis. "Right." She turned to me with the other half of her muffin in her hand. "As I was saying last night before we got interrupted by Tasha and her sweet kid, no one is as untarnished as Homer Everett appeared to be. There are secrets there, and I intend to uncover them."

"Grandma, you need to let sleeping dogs lie. Have you learned nothing from Lois's death?"

"Huh, what good investigative journalist lets secrets deadly enough to kill alone?" Grandma Ruth shook her carrot-top hair. "Nope. I fully intend to poke that dog with a stick."

I rolled my eyes. "Aunt Phyllis, talk to Grandma."

"Why?" she asked. "I'm all for uncovering the truth. Sometimes the only way to get rid of a boil is to lance it and let the bad stuff ooze out."

"Eww—stop with the nasty metaphors," I said. "I'm baking here."

"Fine, let's just say that it's clear whatever I stumbled on is worthy of murder, and as long as the bad guys made me a suspect then I have the right to investigate further." Grandma snagged another apple fritter.

"Let's make this simple." I put my hands on my hips. "Where were you when Lois was murdered? Please tell me you have an alibi. It's all you need, right?"

"My alibi or lack thereof does not matter." Grandma popped the apple fritter in her mouth and kept talking. "I believe that Lois was murdered because she knew things about the mysterious murder of Homer's best pal, Champ Rogers."

"Wait, I'm confused—I thought Champ disappeared."

I scooted in closer and put my elbows on the table, cradling my chin.

"Oh, yes. Well, he was reported missing, Homer organized a countywide search for his best friend. Eventually Champ was found dead in a picnic area near the lake. It was a big mystery. He was shot in the back of the head at close range, but the murder weapon was never found." Grandma reached for another apple fritter. "I investigated as best I could, but things weren't as easy back then as they are now."

"I remember how scared everyone was that a killer was on the loose." Phyllis cut another bite with her fork. "Mayor Everett demanded that the killer be found and brought to justice. It seemed that the more he stormed and fussed, the colder the investigation got. After a few months and no further murders, people went about their lives and forgot about it."

"Except for Paul Abernathy," Grandma Ruth said with her mouth full. "He was the doctor who did the autopsy. He spent the rest of his life going over the details of the case, but without a murder weapon or fingerprints there was little he could deduce."

"I remember." Phyllis took a sip of her coffee. "He would visit all the suspects once a year on the anniversary of the murder and ask questions."

"How long did he do that?" I asked.

"Nearly thirty years," Phyllis said. "I think he hoped someone would come clean on their death bed. But whoever did it took the deed to their grave with them."

"So they hoped," Grandma said, stopping long enough to wash down her fritters with the dregs of her coffee. She put down her empty cup and slid it toward me. "More, dear."

I got up and went to the large silver pot that I used for catering, but which mostly hung out in the bakery kitchen ready for any member of my oversized family to visit. I pushed the spigot down, and the rich dark liquid poured out, filling the room with the fragrance of organic coffee. "Let me guess, you found something no one else could find on Champ's murder."

"Of course I did." Grandma sat back, her eyes shining with pride. "I found the murder weapon."

I turned quickly, sloshing the coffee. "What do you mean you found the murder weapon?"

"We're pretty certain we found it. Right, Ruth?" Phyllis asked, leaning toward Grandma.

"There are too many coincidences if it isn't the right one," Grandma said, spitting crumbs.

"Okay, you two. Where is the mystery murder weapon and what does it have to do with Lois?"

"I'm getting to that part; hold your horses." Grandma took her refilled cup from me and fixed it up until it was unrecognizable as coffee. I shook my head as she sipped her cream and sugar with a little coffee. "Now . . . where to start? Ah, yes, I recently remembered that five years ago when they were renovating the county courthouse the original plans were to remove a wall from the old judge's chambers."

"Exactly," Phyllis said. "But there was some kind of structural issue that made them work around the wall. Right?"

"That's what we were told." Grandma raised one orange eyebrow. "When I researched Homer Everett, I found an old floor plan for the courthouse. They did a renovation in the late fifties."

"I didn't remember that until you brought it up last week." Phyllis sat back.

"That's because it was a small change to the judge's chamber. It turns out that Judge Jonas was a good friend of Homer Everett."

"And?" I sat and leaned toward her.

"And the renovation was a 'wall repair.'" Grandma made the quote marks in the air with her hands. "They said that there was water damage and they had to redo the wall."

"Okay . . ."

"Except it was on the first floor, and the redone wall was the same one that allegedly was used for support and unable to be torn down."

"Again, I say, and . . . ?"

"And the current support wall is eight inches thicker than the one in the original plans."

"How do you know?" I asked.

"We compared floor plans," Phyllis said.

"Yep." Grandma looked pleased with herself.

"How did you get the original plans?" I leaned back and chewed the inside of my cheek with worry. "Did you do something you shouldn't?"

"I would never. . . ." Grandma snorted and pretended to be insulted.

I crossed my arms over my chest and gave her a long look. Grandma grinned at me like a drunken sailor.

"The plans are a matter of public record," Phyllis said. "Every building in town has to have a permit to be built. Those permits and floor plans are all a matter of public record."

That thought sobered me. "Does that mean that someone can look at the floor plan to this bakery?"

"Yes."

"My house?"

"Yep." Grandma's grin widened. "So, you see, I compared the two courthouse floor plans. It was pretty clear to me that that so-called load bearing wall was a false front."

"When Ruth told me about it, I sent the plans to an architect friend of mine. He agreed with Ruth. It's not a load bearing wall—and the 1950s renovation added eight inches to it," Phyllis said.

I drew my eyebrows together. "How long have you two been working on this?"

"About three weeks," Phyllis said.

"Just a week or so," Grandma said.

Right, I thought. "Grandma when were you going to tell me?" I held up my hand to cut off her reply. "I know, right after you broke into the courthouse and cut a hole in that wall. Right?"

"Oh, no, we weren't going to cut a hole," Phyllis said.

"We rented a metal detector." Grandma looked so proud of herself. "I wanted one of those sound wave machines that bounce off metal objects and gives their shape, but we weren't able to get our hands on one."

"Besides the handheld metal detector will be easier to smuggle in." Phyllis sipped her coffee.

I shook my head. "What do you think you'll find in there?"

"The murder weapon, I hope," Grandma said. "At least I told Lois I'd found one. It's why she agreed to speak with me."

That made me sit back. "You told Lois you found a murder weapon, and she believed you?"

"Not *a* murder weapon; *the* murder weapon. The one that killed Champ."

"Over the years, Dr. Abernathy was able to figure out that Champ was killed by a military handgun. He thought maybe a Beretta."

"You think Homer killed Champ and Lois knew about it? Is that what you think is the motive for Lois's murder?" I don't know why my mind leapt to that conclusion, except that both men served in the war.

"Exactly," Grandma Ruth said, and slapped her hands

on the Formica table. "I was *this close* to getting Lois to spill the beans on the old story and *bam*! She winds up murdered. Anyone else here think that is more than mere coincidence?"

Phyllis raised her hand and I shook my head.

"So you think someone killed Lois before she could come clean about the murder?"

"The key word there is that I *think*. I have no proof. It's why I needed to know what Lois knew."

"It's also why we need to break into the courthouse and check that wall." Phyllis put down her coffee. "So, are you in or are you out?"

"Why don't you take your suspicions to Chief Blaylock?" I asked. I mean, it seemed like the obvious thing to do.

"Because he will think I'm an old woman with strange ideas." Grandma crossed her arms over her chest.

"You *are* an old woman with strange ideas." Phyllis laughed and patted Grandma's hand.

"Okay, my ideas may be strange, but that doesn't mean they aren't true."

"Here's a question: Why would Homer kill Champ?" I tugged on a wild curl and pulled it behind my ear. "Was Champ blackmailing Homer?"

"I'm still working on motive." Grandma rubbed her sandpaper-sounding chin. "Too bad you can't track money back then like you can now. We might be able to determine if Homer paid someone—say Lois—to kill Champ."

Phyllis's cup rattled as it hit the saucer. "Does Homer have any of his bank or office money ledgers in his archives?"

"Hard to tell." Grandma's blue eyes narrowed. "The historian in charge of his collection of papers is notoriously stingy with letting anyone read them. I even tried to bribe her with a twenty-dollar bill. All she did was look down her nose at me and ask me to put my request in writing to be considered by Homer Everett's family."

"Old ledgers might not be as easy to search as the Internet," I pointed out. "But that doesn't mean they aren't searchable."

"Too bad we can't bring those papers and journals home. We would have plenty of time to dig out clues," Grandma said.

"I have it." Phyllis laughed. "We can go to the courthouse and offer to scan in all Homer's documents to get them out on the Web for the entire world to see."

"I tried that." Grandma brushed off her hands. "It seems it was Homer's express wish that his papers and journals only be available for study *inside* the society. We don't have time to fiddle-fart around with historians—not with my life on the line. We need to get in there, make copies, and get the heck out."

"Wait, why can't we simply tell the cops what we suspect?" I stood and removed the nearly empty plate.

Grandma reached over and grabbed the last donut on the plate. "We can't go to the cops—old woman, strange ideas, remember?" She took a bite of the apple cinnamon donut. "I need evidence. It doesn't matter whether it is an accounting error or a scan of the weapon or both."

"Stop it, Grandma." I tossed the crumbs in the trash and the plate into the soapy dishwater in the sink. "I won't have you arrested for trespassing or, worse, breaking and entering."

"Oh, please, you know I'd be fine in jail."

"You might be fine," I retorted, "but I'd be a wreck. Phyllis, it's your job to see that she stays out of trouble. Is that clear?"

"Quite." Phyllis raised one blonde eyebrow and sipped her coffee.

"And neither of you are to go to the courthouse without

me." I pointed from one to the other and gave them my best stink eye. "I don't want to have to put my business or the house up as collateral to bail you out of jail. Am I clear?"

"Crystal." Grandma Ruth popped the last bit of donut into her mouth. She swallowed the dregs of her coffee. "Come on, Phyllis, I think we should let Toni get back to her work."

Phyllis got up and put on her coat, then pushed Grandma to the door. As she passed me, she leaned in to me and said, "It's Sunday and the courthouse is closed. Ruth plans a midnight escapade tonight. I expect you'll be there."

"I can't persuade you to go during business hours and perhaps tell the historian what you want to know?"

They looked at me, shaking their heads, their chins set in stubborn lines.

I blew out a deep breath. "I suppose someone ought to go and keep an eye on you two. Why midnight?"

"It's the witching hour, my dear," Grandma cackled as they pushed through the door and out into the parking lot.

CHAPTER 7

I had lost my mind. It was the only reason I could think of
that I would be hanging out in Phyllis's van in the middle
of the night, helping these two old women.

"Help me with my Camo makeup," Grandma demanded.
The green-brown makeup was supposed to hide her pale
freckled skin from detection in the moonlight, but it
wouldn't cover her bright orange hair.

"Where did you get the camos, Grandma?" I dutifully
rubbed more brown on her stubbled chin.

"I dug them out of your uncle Joe's closet," Phyllis said.
Uncle Joe was only ten years older than me and was
Grandma Ruth's happy accident. He'd spent time in the army
and liked to go hunting and fishing. Thus he had camouflage
clothing in his closet big enough to fit Grandma Ruth's
frame. Phyllis, on the other hand, wore a black catsuit that
made her look like a 1960s film star. Her bright yellow hair

was carefully tucked into a black stocking cap and her face and hands were painted green-brown.

I had come straight from the bakery. After making pies all day I'd taken the afternoon off to catch up on my reading. Then I'd gone back to the bakery to start the dough for the morning's pastries. So I wore a pair of black slacks covered in fine gluten-free flour, a black tee shirt with hand smears on it, and a stocking cap borrowed from Phyllis.

"You really should paint your face," Grandma Ruth warned.

"I think my face is fine." I ran the makeup sponge across her forehead, smearing the last bit of pale skin. "Tell me again why we are skulking around the courthouse in the dark?"

"Ruth told you, the historian won't let us take scans of any of the papers. For that matter she won't let you touch anything without gloves on. Heaven help you if you breathe on something. We just want to get in and get the journals we haven't read yet and get out.

"You agreed," Grandma pointed out and pushed my hand away. "Besides, this will give us a chance to take a good look at the courthouse square. Lois died somewhere in that square. Maybe we'll find something the police missed."

"How are we going to do that?" I asked, my arms akimbo.

"We're going to use flashlights, like all the crime shows," Grandma stated, and rocked herself up and out of the captain's chair that served as the passenger seat.

"That's television, Grandma, not real life." I didn't want to be negative, but Grandma was bordering on crazy here.

"That's right," Phyllis said. "In real life we use spotlights." She lifted up a small round super bright light that my brother used to spot deer out in fields at night.

"I hardly think we'll go unnoticed shining that thing around."

"That's the plan." Grandma grinned.

"What's the plan? To get arrested?"

"No, no," Phyllis said. "You are going to shine the spot-light around and see if we can figure out the crime scene, and if anyone notices, you can tell them that you are inves-tigating the crime."

"Why on earth would I do that?"

"Because they would believe you," Phyllis said, as if she had no reason not to think I'd be willing to shine a spotlight around near a patch of ground surrounded with crime-scene tape.

"No, they wouldn't." I tried to reason. "I've already been warned not to snoop."

"But you'll be providing a distraction so that Phyllis and I can see if that side entrance to the courthouse is unlocked."

"Why would the door be unlocked?" I asked.

"Because I was in there earlier and unlocked it," Phyllis said.

"Oh, no, no, I won't be party to breaking and entering."

"Good." Grandma stuffed the spotlight in my hand. "Because you won't be doing either. Now, go out there and look around. Who knows, you might actually find something the cops overlooked."

"Maybe I should call Brad."

"You do and we'll investigate on our own next time." Phyllis had her hands on her hips. She knew she had me. Neither one of us wanted Grandma Ruth arrested. She might be wicked smart, but she would not last long in prison. I was stuck between a rock and a hard place. The very least I could do was ensure I was around to explain the madness when these two got caught.

"Fine." I gave in and took the spotlight. I opened the van door and stepped out into the quiet of the cold November night. Phyllis had parked in the courthouse parking lot on the left side. It was the only car in the lot and stood out like a sore thumb even when parked as far from the streetlight as possible.

I tugged my jacket around me and glanced about. The courthouse was made of red rock and limestone. It was over one hundred years old and had been built for a time when there was reverence for the law. I wondered if Grandma Ruth's missionary grandmother was turning over in her grave. I stepped out onto the cold, dew-damp grass. The trees were bare against the moonless night. Stars twinkled above the dim streetlight. The air was crisp with newfound cold and the scent of dead leaves. The wind whispered there was snow on the way even though the sky was crystal clear.

The air was filled with that deafening quiet that comes after the first frost when the insects were either hibernating or dead and the birds long gone to warmer climes.

My tennis shoes squeaked on the grass as I made my way around the courthouse to the area that had been taped off. I could hear Grandma Ruth and Phyllis whispering back and forth to each other as they stumbled around in the dark. Their tiny flashlights were not as revealing as they had hoped. I wanted to go over there and hand them the spotlight, but thought better of it. Phyllis wasn't kidding. Grandma would keep me out of their investigation if I didn't follow along.

And having Grandma investigate on her own was a nightmare I didn't want to ever know about. I turned on the spotlight and dutifully ran it along the ground on my side of the taped-off section.

I had no idea what I was supposed to be looking for, and I was a little weirded out by the idea of walking around alone, possibly steps from where a woman was murdered not twenty-four hours ago. I reached into my pocket and wrapped my free hand around my cell phone. If worse came to worst I could speed dial my way out of trouble—at least I wanted to believe it could happen.

I ran the spotlight along the ground and to the foot of the statue of Homer Everett. As a kid I'd been half-frightened and half-fascinated by the bronze likeness so clearly profiled against the night sky. Homer was balding with a bad comb-over that the sculptor had captured in all its creepy good-ness. The man would forever be wearing a 1970s leisure suit and a heavy chain around his neck. The only thing missing was the John Travolta pointed finger in the air. The crime-scene tape ran from the back of the statue to the side of the courthouse. The taped-off area was about ten feet deep and thirty feet long. It encompassed a line of thick bushes with entangled empty branches and piles of leaves at their feet.

I ran the spotlight across the grass, wondering where exactly Lois had been found. It wasn't like the police had left a chalk outline or anything. Could she have fallen from a window? I ran the light up the side of the courthouse. There was a small window three stories up. From where I stood I couldn't see if it was big enough for someone to push Lois out. I made a mental note to stop by the courthouse in the morning and see if I could figure out what room that window belonged to and if the frame showed any signs of a struggle.

Although I supposed if it did the police would have already known it and have it taped off. I ran the light across the grass again looking for the incriminating scooter tracks that made Chief Blaylock bring Grandma Ruth in for questioning.

There were indeed dark twin tracks that looked as if they might be the same width as Grandma's scooter. I stepped as close to the crime-scene tape as I could, but it was difficult to gauge the width. What I needed to do was go under the tape and measure the distance myself. It would give me a better idea of what kind of vehicle made the marks.

A quick glance around, and I saw I was alone. Heart pounding, I decided to go for it, and ducked under the tape. I was careful to walk in a single line so as not to tamper too badly with the scene. Unlike in crime shows on television, real-life police work was pretty much done and the scene released the first day. I reasoned it was simply out of respect for Lois that the tape was still up.

My athletic shoes made a squishy sound on the damp ground as I crossed to the tracks. The ground certainly had a bit of a bounce to it. If Lois was pushed or fell from the window she might not have died immediately. That thought gave me the shivers. I hunkered down and examined the scooter tracks, if that was indeed what they were. They were about a half inch deep, and the tread did look like Grandma Ruth's all-terrain tires. Something was not quite right about them. They appeared to start and stop on either side of the bushes. I shined my light under the bushes, and something sparkled through the leaves. Reaching my hand into the pile, I hoped whatever I grabbed wouldn't be a critter with sparkly eyes.

A snapped twig made me let out a slight squeal as adrenaline flooded my system. I stood and whirled quickly, the spotlight landing on the outstretched hands of a man of about five foot ten and a body that would make the oldest woman drool. "Turn it off, Toni, you're blinding me!"

I blew out a breath at the familiar voice and pointed the spotlight toward the ground. "Sam, you scared me silly." My heart pounded in my throat as I ducked quickly under the crime-scene tape before he got his vision back enough to figure out I wasn't where I should be.

"I didn't mean to." Sam lifted his cowboy hat and ran his hand through his gray-tipped, dark brown hair. "What are you doing out here this late at night?"

"I could ask you the same thing." I stepped closer,

keeping my back to the crime-scene tape in hopes of distracting him from where I'd been.

"I finished up a job at the Murphys' place across the park." He pointed toward a big old house made of limestone block from the turn of the last century. "The Dumpster is parked in front of the house, so I parked in the courthouse parking lot."

"Oh, right, Grandma said the Murphy house was being remodeled," I said, and slipped my arm through his and pulled him along the sidewalk. "Did you design the remodel?"

"No, I'm putting in the bathroom and patching up the living room." He walked with me under the stars. I was careful to turn my spotlight off and keep it away from him in case he remembered I had it.

"Really? Are they going with a modern bathroom, or one that matches the era of the house?"

"There were no bath fixtures contemporary to that structure. It was one of the first buildings built in town. So we picked something close."

"Oh, did you choose one of those flush toilets with the tank way up high on the wall?"

"Yes, and small tile and a pedestal sink. Now tell me what you were doing behind crime-scene tape with a spotlight."

I swallowed. It was easier to distract Sam than to lie to him. He lifted a dark eyebrow, and I noticed that his eyes glittered in the streetlight.

"I wanted to see the tread marks where Lois Striker's body was found," I said. "Chief Blaylock brought Grandma Ruth in for questioning because he said the tread matched Grandma's scooter."

"It's after midnight, Toni."

"I had to wait until this late to keep Grandma from finding out I was here." I said it with as much conviction as I could. "She would have wanted to come with me, and the last thing I want is for the police to think Grandma was out here tampering with a crime scene."

"But it's okay if you tamper with a crime scene. . . ."

"I wasn't tampering." I began to feel a little too desperate.

"Methinks thou doth protest too much." He crossed his arms over his magnificent chest. Tonight he wore a jean jacket opened to reveal a white tee shirt tucked into tight cowboy jeans. His big shiny buckle was a testament to his rodeo days.

"Really . . . you're quoting Hamlet?"

"What, a rancher can't be educated?" He sounded seriously offended.

"No, I wasn't saying you weren't educated." I stumbled for the right words. "I was merely saying, really, you would quote Shakespeare at a time like this?"

"You mean after I caught you snooping around a crime scene where you don't belong?"

I opened my mouth to say something, then caught the twinkle in his dark eyes. Thank goodness the parking lot had streetlights or I wouldn't have known he was kidding.

"Gotcha."

I could feel the heat of embarrassment rush over my cheeks. To cover it, I gave him a small shove in the arm. Sam was a thoroughly well-built man, and my shove did more to my muscles than to his. It crossed my mind more than once that seeing him shirtless in jeans and his tool belt might be fun.

We reached his truck. "Where are you parked?" he asked.

"Oh, I borrowed my Aunt Phyllis's van." I pointed to the vehicle with the hippie peace signs painted on it. "She's visiting from California."

"I don't remember your mom having a sister named Phyllis."

"That's because she's not my mom's sister. She's one of Grandma Ruth's adopted kids. She's a bit of a free spirit."

"I see." He opened the driver's door to his black truck. "Sounds like someone I need to meet . . . have dinner with . . . at your place."

I could feel the heat rising again. It was pretty clear he'd heard about Brad being over at my house. Oiltop was a small town. Not much happened that didn't get around in a matter of hours. "Sheesh, if only murderers were noticed as quickly as my house guests," I muttered.

"Wait—you had house guests?"

I winced. Maybe he hadn't known and I just gave myself away. I shoved my hands in my back pockets, the spotlight hanging from my wrist like a bad purse. "Grandma invited Brad over to dinner to pay him back for getting her out of jail."

"Ruth was in jail?"

I tilted my head. "Now you're messing with me."

He grinned and climbed into the driver's seat. "Last I heard, you swore off dating. Is that still the case?"

"Still the case," I said. "I promised myself I'd wait until I got my feet under me."

"I can respect that." He closed his truck door and rolled down the window. "As long as I get a fair chance at taking you out. If I remember correctly, I did ask first."

"You asked first." I took a step toward the truck.

"So what does a guy have to do to get your grandmother to ask him over for dinner?"

I shrugged. "Give Grandma your get-out-of-jail-free card?"

"Oh, right." He started up his engine. "I don't have one of those."

"I'm sure you'll think of something."

"Let me drive you over to your van." He pointed toward the empty passenger seat.

I knew better than to get into a truck with him. That much lovely maleness in a tiny enclosed space and I might end up throwing myself at him. "No, thanks, I can walk."

"Go ahead, then." He jerked his chin toward the van. "I can't leave until I know you're safe."

"Men," I muttered. "I'm a big girl. I'll be fine."

"I'm sure you will," he agreed. "But that doesn't mean I'm going to leave you alone in a dark parking lot near a murder scene."

He did sort of have a point. The place had been creeping me out before he got there. Trouble was, I wanted to go back and find out what the shiny thing in the leaves was. I blew out a breath. It appeared I was going to have to pretend to head home "Fine."

"Good. Have a good night, Toni."

"Bye, Sam."

I waggled my fingers and strode with firm purpose toward the van. I had every intention of getting in and waving him on, then popping out to look at the crime scene. Then someone tripped the courthouse alarm.

Lights flashed and bells rang at eardrum-piercing decibels. It was so loud, in fact, that it was deafening—and I was at least half a block away. Sam was out of his truck and beside me before my brain could register the movement. "Someone else is here," he said, pushing me behind him.

I rolled my eyes as sirens wailed and Grandma Ruth and Aunt Phyllis popped out of the bushes. The two older women were moving faster than I would have imagined they could. I mean, all Grandma had was her walking cane, and still she was puffing right along.

"What the—"

"Get in the van," Grandma ordered as she and Phyllis rushed by us. They opened the van's side door and hopped in. "Quick, before the cops show up."

I didn't even glance at Sam. Grandma's loud voice was so stern it had me leaping into the van's driver's seat and turning the key in the ignition. I squealed the wheels and peeled out of the parking lot, leaving Sam in the dust.

"Who was the handsome guy?" Phyllis asked as we turned a corner out of sight of the courthouse.

"Sam Greenbaum." I looked into the rearview mirror to see Grandma settling into her captain's chair next to Phyllis.

"Don't worry," Grandma said. "Sam won't tell the chief it was us."

Phyllis's eyebrows drew together, confused. "Why not?"

"Because I'll invite him to have dinner with us at Toni's house." Grandma's wide grin sparkled against her paint-darkened face.

I rolled my eyes.

"What exactly did you two do to set off the alarm?"

"We established beyond a doubt that that wall contains Champ's murder weapon," Grandma said with pride.

"You what?"

"No worries," Aunt Phyllis added. "We didn't dig it out of the wall. That would be tampering with evidence."

"And you wouldn't do that, would you?"

"Who us?" Grandma grinned. "Of course not."

Why then did I worry that they did?

CHAPTER 8

Thank goodness for my new bakery assistant. Without Meghan, I would be in deep trouble. I hadn't slept but an hour before my alarm went off and I had to go to work. Pie on an hour's sleep tended to be a bit crisp around the edges.

Today Meghan wore her black hair in a fauxhawk. One side was shaved close. The hair at her crown stood up stiffly, and the rest reached halfway down her back and was twisted up in a 1940s-style hairnet. Her beautiful blue eyes were rimmed with liner with a small kitten flick. The rest of her makeup was pale, except for her lips, which were bright red. She wore a puffed-sleeved blouse in a green stripe, a green plaid skirt, ripped fishnet stockings, and heavy combat boots. The girl certainly had her own style.

"We have fourteen pumpkin custard and seven pecan." Meghan pointed at the trays of pies on the roller cart. "How many of the chocolate silk are we making?"

"Ten," I said, and hid a yawn behind my hand. "I left

them for last because you have to stand and whisk the pudding until it thickens."

"Do you want me to do that part?"

I waited for her to push the rack into the big walk-in freezer. "I'll do half while you observe, then we'll have you do half."

She took long strides as she came over to see me mix the sugar, cocoa, cornstarch, and milk.

"It looks so runny."

"I know. The thing about this kind of filling is that you have to stir until it thickens, then stir another minute. Then add it to the egg gently and cook it another minute. Once it's done, you add the butter and vanilla and combine. Then pour it into the prebaked shells."

"I will never go back to instant pudding after your chocolate silk." She pulled up a stool and sat down beside me. It was a rule in the kitchen that if you were cooking you had better be standing, but if you were watching you could sit.

"I use the same recipe for banana cream and coconut cream; I simply substitute bananas and coconut for the cocoa."

"Like I said, yum!" She chewed on her lower lip for a moment, coloring her teeth with her red lipstick.

"What?" I asked.

"I heard about your grandma killing Lois Striker."

I frowned. "She did not kill Lois."

She shrugged and intertwined her fingers. "I heard the cops have proof she did it."

"No," I stated firmly. "They only asked her some questions then sent her home. Trust me, if Grandma had been the killer they would have arrested her right away." I pulled the pot of thickened, bubbling cocoa from the heat and added a small portion to the beaten egg and whisked. Slowly adding pudding to the egg and combining it without cooking it was an art. It had taken me a while to perfect it. Finally, when the egg was brought up to a temperature close to the pudding I added the entire thing back into the saucepan and stirred for another minute. Then I removed it from the heat and added butter and vanilla, then whisked it all together.

"If she didn't do it, who did?" Meghan asked. "Do you know?"

"Why would I know?" I had to wait five minutes before I poured the chocolate into the prebaked pie shells lined up on the table.

"You were seen going into the police station. We figured you were investigating the crime." She shrugged and stood.

"I went to collect Grandma before she drove the police crazy. We both know the cops in this town couldn't keep up with Grandma's mind."

Meghan giggled. "She is one sharp lady."

"Isn't she?" I scraped out the filling into the last crust and washed the pan in the deep sink full of hot soapy water. "Do you have a clue who did it?"

"No." I rinsed the pan and grabbed a towel to wipe it dry so she could make the next batch. "

"Poor Lois." Meghan shook her head. "I heard they bashed her head in with a rock, then left her lifeless body near Homer Everett's statue."

"Where'd you hear that?"

"My friend Emily's mom works at the morgue. She said that Lois's head was a mess. Then John Ellsworth—his dad owns the funeral home—said that it took his dad an hour to clean her up and make her appear presentable for the visitation."

"Huh, are they certain it was a head-bashing?"

"What do you mean?" Megan took the pot from me and measured in the corn starch and sugar.

I sat down on the stool and watched her work. "There's a third-floor window above the area where Lois's body was found. There was some speculation that she might have been pushed from that window."

"Oh, no, that window is in the ladies' restroom and has been painted shut my whole life."

I wanted to know how she knew which window I was talking about, but then thought better of it.

She paused and waved a wooden spoon in the air. "Come to think of it, there was a break-in at the courthouse last night."

"I saw that on the police blotter this morning. They think it was a raccoon or something."

"I highly doubt it."

"Why?" I tried not to sound too obvious. "Don't they get critters opening windows and such? Especially in the fall when they're looking for places to hibernate for the winter."

"No, Mrs. Thacker told Chief Blaylock she spotted a VW van racing away from the courthouse. Rumor has it she even got the license plate number."

My stomach flipped a little. "Huh, did she see who was driving?"

"No, it was too dark." Meghan stirred the thickening pudding. "But I have no doubt Chief Blaylock will be able to figure out who was in the van."

"Right." I paused. "Stir that harder or it will scorch on the bottom and you'll have to toss the entire batch."

"Anyway, Mrs. Spader told my mom that she's seen a VW van around town the last day or two. There aren't too many of those in Oiltop." Meghan stirred slowly as the pudding boiled with soft thick plops. The scent of cocoa filled the air. The little volcanoes in the pot always reminded me of the trip I made to see the geysers in Yellowstone National Park. I'd been eighteen and a girlfriend and I had taken a last-minute road trip to the area. Funny, but it didn't seem to bother either of us that we had no reservations and no tent should we have to camp at the busy national park.

I let out a sigh. It had been a lot of years since I'd taken a carefree, spur-of-the-moment trip. There's a certain freedom in the innocence of youth. Since I'd been married and divorced and was now in the countdown to turn forty-one I felt past such moments of spontaneity.

Meghan chatted away about how awesome it would have been to own a VW van. "We could totally make a party bus out of it. You know, in a *Scooby Doo* sort of way. Hey!" She smiled big as the inevitable came to mind.

"Don't say it."

"What? That a VW van would make a great Mystery Machine?" She giggled. "Too bad you didn't buy a VW van for the bakery deliveries. It would have been super cool. We could paint MYSTERY MACHINE on the side."

"I am not solving any more mysteries," I insisted—not that anyone ever listened.

"Oh, come on, everyone knows it was you out in the VW van." She pointed the whisk at me. Chocolate dripped off the end.

"Don't stop stirring!" I jumped up as she stuck the whisk back into the pot and continued to stir.

"Got ya!"

"Got me? How did you get me?" I asked as I grabbed a paper towel, wet it, and cleaned up the floor.

"You totally were in that van last night, weren't you?" She wiggled her apron-covered behind. "Whose van is it? Can I see it? Did you find out anything about Lois's murder?"

"I have no idea what you are talking about." I rinsed the towel out and did a second once-over of the floor, then tossed it away. I glanced at the pot and held out my hand. "Let me test the thickness."

She handed me the whisk and I ran the implement around the pot once. The perfect little plops of chocolate mocked me.

"Oh, come on, Toni, you can tell me. Who owns the van?"

She wore a striped apron around her outrageous outfit. Since there were no customers today, she had her nose ring in, along with the rings in her eyebrow. Her blue eyes glistened in the sunlight that came in through the door between the front and the kitchen.

"This pudding is done. Here." I handed her back the whisk. "Stir it once and concentrate on the feel. When it gets this thick then it's ready for the egg."

Meghan stirred the pudding. "Cool." I monitored her while she added the pudding to the egg.

"Careful with the egg. If you go too fast you'll cook it and have pieces of cooked egg floating in your pudding."

She slowed down her stirring. "Do you have to add egg? I mean, you don't add egg to cooked packaged pudding. Why would you need it here?"

"It makes the pudding richer," I said, and kept an eagle eye on her. "Okay, that's good. Now add the egg back into the entire pot and cook it another full minute."

One more minute of cooking and she turned off the flame and pulled the pot across the metal racks of the stovetop.

"Now, add the butter and the vanilla." I watched as she added the premeasured ingredients. Most people have no idea that most vanilla has gluten in it. It really depended on what solution the vanilla was distilled in. The thing about gluten sensitivity was the sheer variety of foods most people took for granted that held secret gluten, like vanilla or soy sauce or even ketchup. "Stir until the butter is melted and both ingredients are incorporated."

"Got it. Do we pour it straight into the pie shells?"

"No, let it cool five minutes." I twisted the timer to five and left it ticking on the counter. "Once it dings, stir it with the whisk, or the top will form a skin."

"Got it." She studied the surface of the cooling pot. "How's it working out with you and Tasha? Is she, like, going to live with you for a long time?"

"I don't mind having Tasha and Kip around. It helps fill the house."

"How come you live in such a big house anyway?" Meghan poured hot water into the sink and added dish soap. The resulting bubbles smelled of lemons.

"You mean, why don't I live in a VW van?" I sat on the stool and teased her.

"Oh, come on, you have to admit the Mystery Machine is pretty awesome."

"Yes, yes it is." I nodded. "Too bad that last month's bad guys weren't as easy to detect as someone from *Scooby Doo*."

"So, how come you, like, came back here instead of staying in Chicago? I mean, it's, like, Chicago . . . and Oiltop is . . . well . . ."

"Oiltop," I said, finishing the sentence for her. "You know, when my mom died last year, she left me the family homestead."

"I know, but your family is huge. You could have given it to someone else, right?"

I worried my bottom lip with my teeth. "Yes, I suppose that's true."

"Instead you moved in and opened your bakery here. You have to admit, it wasn't easy."

"Opening a gluten-free bakery in the middle of wheat country?"

"Yeah."

"My family has a long history in this town."

"Lots of people's families have long histories in Oiltop," she said as she washed up the utensils from the pudding. "And they got out."

I shrugged. "Grandma Ruth isn't as young as she thinks she is."

"Okay?" She shook her head to emphasize that she didn't follow my train of thought.

"I wasn't here for my mom's last couple of years on this earth. I want to at least be here for Grandma's. I might have lost my mom, but she lost a daughter." I stood and checked on the timer.

"I hadn't thought of it that way," Meghan said. "So, it's like your mom can't be here for her mom, so you are."

"Something like that."

The buzzer chimed and I turned it off. "Stir it really well."

Meghan attacked the pudding with a whisk until it was smooth and even. Then she poured it into the prepared gluten-free crusts. The recipe made five pies. When you had twenty pies to create filling for, only five pies at a time felt like it took forever, but I was proud of the small batches and home-cooked taste of the bakery.

Gluten-free food can be hit or miss. In fact, the best advice I ever got after my celiac diagnosis was to eat only whole or fresh foods. That way you knew for certain what was in them. Sometimes even naturally gluten-free items held enough gluten to really make a super sensitive person sick.

Which was precisely why I prepared small batches with only certified gluten-free ingredients. When you only got baked goods once in a while, it was really important to ensure that they didn't make you sick . . . ever.

"Done." She rinsed the pudding out and dumped the pan in the hot water.

"So, now that you know how to do that, I'm going to leave the next batch for you," I said. My cell phone vibrated in my apron pocket. I pulled it out and stepped through the door from the kitchen to the front of the bakery. "Hi, Grandma."

"Toni, did you get a chance to get out to the courthouse and see if you can't figure out what you saw in the mulch?"

"Not yet." I bit my tongue to stop myself from trying to explain that I had a business to run. With my luck, Grandma would use that as an excuse to go out and look for herself. "I had to show Meghan how to make pudding."

"Do you need me to—"

"No, I'm headed out that way right now." I tried my best to sound firm. "You stay away from the courthouse. People already suspect that I'm the one who tripped that alarm last night."

"Who suspects that?" Grandma demanded.

"Meghan said that Mrs. Thacker told Chief Blaylock that she saw a VW van speeding away from the scene last night. And Mrs. Spader remembers seeing a VW van around town yesterday. It won't take them long to put two and two together."

"Those two old hens," Grandma muttered. "I'll tell Phyllis to stash her van in your carriage house for a few days. Meanwhile, I'll handle the rumor control. You get yourself out to the courthouse and see if you can't find that clue."

CHAPTER 9

Have you ever noticed how things look completely different in daylight than they do at night?

I tried walking casually through the town square, passing the crime scene as I went so that people wouldn't notice me looking into the bushes. On my third pass I gave up the ruse and stood in front of the tape and studied the scene. My shoe imprints were right there bold as life in the mud next to the incriminating scooter marks. I shrugged deeper into my black trench, raising the collar up to protect my neck from the chilled November wind.

"Looking for something?" Chief Blaylock stopped beside me.

"I wanted a good view of the crime scene," I said. "I had to see for myself what it was that made you bring Grandma Ruth in for questioning."

"Those scooter marks are pretty damning."

I rolled my eyes at him. "Seriously?"

"That and Ruth was the last person to see Lois alive."

"Neither one of those things points to murder." I turned back to studying the ground at the bottom of the bushes. What was it that had caught my spotlight the night before?

"Perhaps I should bring her in for breaking and entering," he said.

"She's in her nineties!"

"So we aren't going to argue that she was the one who broke into the courthouse last night."

I didn't answer him. I knew better. I was tired from only an hour's sleep and spending all morning making pies for next week's holiday weekend. "Don't you have family things to do? Or a parade float to work on?"

"We don't have a float. We're marching in dress blues. Less work that way," he said. "Which, it turns out, is a good thing, especially when there's a killer on the loose."

"How do you know Lois didn't simply trip and fall?"

"She had evidence in her hand."

That made me turn and look into his flat gaze. "Evidence? What evidence?"

"That's for me to know." His eye twitched.

"And me to find out, right?"

He answered with a silently raised eyebrow. "Go back to your bakery, Toni. There's nothing here for you to see. Don't make me have to charge you with interfering with an investigation."

"Did Grandma Ruth tell you her theory?"

"That Lois was killed to protect some sixty-year-old mystery? Yes. Do I believe her? No."

I crossed my arms. "Why not?"

He lifted his hat, scratched his head, and plopped his hat back on his head. The action gave him enough time to think about his answer. "A good suspect has motive, means, and opportunity. What the hell was the motive? Lois was a talker. There wasn't anything in her head that hadn't already come out."

"Grandma thinks Lois knew where the bodies were buried." I touched the Chief's khaki jacket–covered arm. "Metaphorically, of course."

Chief Blaylock snorted in derision.

"I know, it sounds crazy, but Grandma thinks she discovered a hiding place for the murder weapon that was used to kill—"

"Champ Rogers? That's a myth. Trust me, Chief McMillan searched his entire life for that thing. If there was a murder weapon to be found, that man would have found it."

"Did he read Homer Everett's papers?"

Chief Blaylock shoved his hands into his pockets. "I believe that he did. I know he spent hours at the historical society."

"Maybe he wasn't looking in the right place." I bounced on my toes as a chill wind blew up out of the north and rustled brown leaves across the sidewalk.

"Like the courthouse?"

I shrugged. "Grandma claims she found a hidden cache in the wall of the judge's chambers."

"Oh . . . kay." Chief rocked back on his heels.

"What can it hurt to look? I mean, there was a reason for the renovation in the fifties that we can only speculate about, but it may have created a hidden compartment, right? Maybe that reason is holed up in the wall."

"I would need a warrant to bust a hole in the wall, and for that I need just cause. Does Ruth have just cause?"

"Could you use a metal detector?" I asked. "Grandma claims she verified her find with a metal detector."

He shook his head. "A metal detector is useless with the amount of wiring in the wall."

"Well, what about—"

"Those sonogram things cost hundreds of thousands of dollars and aren't built for a vertical wall."

I grimaced. "I'd been hoping to not mention this, but what if there was a hole in the wall that needed to be patched? I mean, if there's a hole, then there's nothing to keep you from looking inside before they patch it, right?"

"Now, I'm not saying I would look in such a hole should there be one, but I'm pretty certain any evidence in the wall would be compromised by a hole. I mean, what would prevent someone from planting evidence in a hole and trying to convince me or one of my deputies that they found the evidence in the wall?"

"What if there isn't already a hole?"

"You would need probable cause."

"What would you or a judge consider as probable cause? I mean to get a warrant to open up a wall?"

"Now, if I were to tell you that and then such a cause should suddenly appear, it would be questioned." His eyes narrowed. "And questionable evidence is evidence thrown out of court. Do you understand me?"

"Yes, sir." I nodded and paused. "Can I offer you some coffee?" I tucked my arm through his and pointed him toward my bakery, two blocks down on Main Street.

"Are you bribing me?"

"Gosh, no." I batted my lashes at him. "I'm giving you an excuse to ensure I stay out of your crime scene."

He sniffed.

"And I'm hoping you'll buy a dozen or so pastries. I know your wife's a fan."

We walked along the sidewalk away from the courthouse and Homer Everett's statue. Across the street from the square was a squat brick building with several law offices. Beside that on the corner was the men's apparel shop. The shops were all open, and I waved at Todd Woles, manager of the men's shop and one of my new friends in Oiltop. Todd waved back, then raised his eyebrow at the police chief walking beside me. I silently let him know I'd tell him later.

"How come you're out and about, anyway? Didn't I hear you were swamped with dessert orders for next week?" he asked me as we crossed Main and passed the office supply shop, the quilt store, and the movie theater.

"I was taking a few minutes to clear my head. Sometimes walking a bit outside helps clear the mind and bring on more creativity. Besides, we're not horribly busy this time of day."

In the afternoon, Oiltop was a Western ghost town populated by the bronze sculptures that had been placed along Main to draw tourists. There was a bronze horse trough and tie post in front of my bakery. It had been the scene of an extremely unfortunate incident—a murder—earlier in the fall. Watching while the police fished a body out of the trough had been my worst memory to date.

And now there had been another murder in Oiltop. I opened the front door to the bakery. Inside it was warm and smelled of chocolate, coconut, and piecrusts.

"I've got fresh coffee in the pot." I pulled off my gloves and poured two paper cups full of coffee. "You like yours black, right?"

"Hmm, cream and two sugars," he corrected me. Chief Blaylock was a believer in a man taking his hat off inside. It was a reflex, I supposed, that his police hat was now in his hands. I stirred the condiments in the coffee.

"Why don't you come on back?" I offered. "You can sit at the table in the kitchen and warm your hands."

"No, thanks. Just the coffee, then I best be going." He took the cup from me. I'd finished it with a sipper top and a paper sleeve to insulate the heat from his hand. "I really wanted to ask you to keep an eye on your grandma. Murder isn't anything to play at." He eyed my face. "You should know that after last time."

"I'm as concerned as you are, Chief," I reassured him. "But you know how stubborn Grandma is. She thinks she's still an award-winning journalist on a story."

"Right." He blew into his cup and took a sip. "Coffee's good. Thanks."

"You're welcome."

"Seriously, keep Ruth off this case, and if you get any threats or any concrete evidence, I expect you to bring it to my attention. Okay?"

"Okay."

"Good. Have a nice day." He stepped to the door and paused long enough to put on his hat before he opened it. He stopped in the doorjamb. "Oh, and whatever you were looking for under the bushes is most likely gone. I had the crime scene guy comb over the area after the alarm was sounded. If there was anything there, they would have found it."

"Wait, how did you—Sam?"

"He caught you looking under that bush. Just like I did. What are you looking for?" He tilted his head and studied me.

"I saw something shiny." I shrugged. "I was reaching for it and got caught—er—interrupted."

"Greenbaum is a good guy. You're lucky he's looking out for you."

"Yeah," I agreed. "I know."

"Have a good afternoon. Be safe."

"I will." I watched as he swung through the door and stepped out. He walked across the street, patted the bronze cowboy in front of the pharmacy, and headed down the street.

I dug my ringing cell phone out of my pocket. "This is Toni."

"Toni?"

"Yes."

"Get home as soon as you can. Kip is missing."

CHAPTER 10

"What happened?" My heart raced as I hurried into the house.

Officer Bright stood in the foyer taking notes in his book. At six feet tall and two hundred or so pounds, he was one of the more substantial members of the Oiltop police force. There was something about him that reassured you things were going to be all right. He had his hat tucked neatly under his arm. His shoulder walkie squawked and he reached up and turned down the dispatcher.

Grandma Ruth and Phyllis flanked Tasha. The older ladies wore sober expressions as Tasha sat in one of the two foyer chairs with dark cherry wood backs and pink-and-white striped cushions. Tears ran down Tasha's cheeks as she twisted a damp handkerchief in her hands.

"Oh, Toni, thank goodness you're here." Tasha jumped up and reached for me. I hugged her close and noted by the way she trembled that she was working very hard to keep herself together.

"Tasha, what happened?" I asked.

"We were at the park on Third Street. Kip likes to go for walks, so we walked down. He played on the playground equipment and I sat on that bench nearby." She paused and took huge gulps of air.

"Okay, so you were at the park. . . ."

"I was texting." She shuddered. "It's not like Kip's a toddler. He and I have gone to the park lots of times. He knows the rules. He would not wander off."

Tasha was right. Kip was a stickler for rules. It made it easy to watch him, in a way. He was more likely to catch you not following the rules then he was to disobey them himself.

"Were there any other kids at the park?" Officer Bright asked, his tone reassuring.

"No." Tasha shook her head as I led her back to the chair. The girl needed to sit before she crumpled to the floor.

"What is all the noise about?" Tim tumbled down the stairs wearing jeans and a black tee shirt, his hair standing on end.

"Kip's missing," I said.

"I've looked all over," Tasha said. "Please, help."

"Well, crap," Tim said and ran his hand through his hair, making it even wilder. He turned to Officer Bright. "What's the plan?"

"Plan is to get more details before we send out a search team. Proper action is better than simple action."

"Right." Tim shoved his hands in his jeans pockets, his bare feet evidence that he had been sleeping. Since Tim worked nights, he often crashed at the house during the day.

"Here, sip this." Phyllis walked back into the foyer with

a brandy snifter in her hand. There was an amber liquid in the bottom.

"No." Tasha held up her hand. "I want to stay sober."

"A sip will help with the shock," Grandma said flatly and nodded as Phyllis offered it again.

This time Tasha took it and took a small sip. You could tell she decided that she needed help calming down, because she took a second, longer drink.

"You were in the park with Kip. What time was it?" Officer Bright pressed.

"It was three P.M. I know because my phone recorded my last text."

"Who were you texting?"

"My coworker Emily Porter. She was having an issue with a maid and asking for my advice." Tasha's blue eyes filled with tears and her nose turned red. Her mouth was a thin line, her distress clear in her features.

"Would you say Kip's father was in the area or not?"

"No." Tasha shook her head vehemently. "Definitely not."

Tim and Officer Bright exchanged glances.

I patted Tasha's shoulder. "It's okay. Officer Bright has to ask the question, right?"

"Right." He gave a short nod. "Many of our cases of missing children can be traced to an estranged parent."

"Not this one," Tasha said. Her blue eyes turned dark and glittered. "Andrew hasn't been in the picture since Kip was diagnosed with Asperger's five years ago."

"I see. Do you know if he lives in the area?"

"No, last I heard he went out to Las Vegas."

"Have you had any recent tiffs with his family or friends?"

"Whose? Andrew's?" She let out an inelegant snort. "As far as they're concerned, Kip is mine and mine alone. No one in their family has ever had Asperger's, so he can't be Andrew's."

"Would there be any reason for them to take Kip from the park?"

"No, no reason." Tasha twirled the cup in her fingers. The remaining sip of brandy sloshed perilously close to the surface. Tasha wore a gray sweaterdress over black leggings. Ankle boots finished her chic outfit. Her fingernails were painted a soft shell-pink. Her fingers were bereft of rings.

I was the ring person, not Tasha. She loved nail art and usually wore some outlandish pattern on her fingers. She once told me that after Andrew left, she vowed never to wear a ring again. It was then she learned how much she liked nail art. It was unusual for her nails to be bare of pattern.

"Why are we sitting here? Shouldn't we be out there looking for Kip? I feel like we're wasting time. The sun is going down soon, and it will get cold fast."

"Yes, ma'am, please be assured Officer Emry and Officer Remington are combing the neighborhood for your son."

"Did you issue an Amber Alert?" Tim asked. "We are very close to the turnpike."

In fact, Oiltop was one of the exits off of Interstate 35, the Kansas State toll road. We had truck stops near the exit. Any bad guys had easy access to a quick getaway unless an Amber Alert was issued. Then the toll gate operators were issued a warning and a picture of the missing child in hopes that they could stop an abduction at the gate.

"Oh my god! The turnpike!" Tasha nearly leapt out of her seat.

I put my hand on her shoulder and pressed her back into the chair. "I'm sure they issued an Amber Alert the moment you called 911."

"Yes, ma'am, they did." The officer's brown gaze was warm with concern, and it seemed to calm Tasha. "Please, finish your story. You were texting a coworker around three P.M., and when you looked up your son was gone?"

"Yes." Tears welled in her eyes again. "I looked up and he was gone. Just . . . gone."

"Please try to remember exactly what you did."

"I jumped up and called his name." She took in a ragged breath and blew it back out as if to collect her thoughts. "I looked around. I thought he might have been distracted by a bug or a small creature. You know how big the park is, and there aren't many trees."

The Third Street Park was a full city block of meadow. There were soccer goals at one end of the field and a small playground set with swings, slide, and jungle gym at the other. My brothers and sisters and I had played in that park all the time when we were young. It was only half a mile away—far enough to create the illusion we were away from parental influence and yet close enough that when my brother Richard fell and broke his arm, Tim was able to run and tell Mom within five minutes.

A wide open field, it wasn't likely a boy Kip's size and age could hide from his mom. Not that Kip would hide. His Asperger's meant he hated surprises and therefore hated to play hide-and-seek. I used to feel sad that Kip never played the classic childhood game. But right now I was thankful we could rule out that he was simply hiding from his mother.

"Have you had a fight lately?" Officer Bright asked.

"Only the usual mother-son things," Tasha answered, her fingers cupping the bowl of the brandy, warming it and throwing the scent into the air.

"Such as?"

"We always struggle with his transition times."

"Transition times?"

"When Kip focuses on something it is difficult to make him put it away when it's bath time or dinnertime or time for church . . . transitions." Tasha's voice broke.

"I see. And did you fight before you went to the park?"

"Are you implying that Kip ran away?" Her voice rose two octaves. "Because he would not. He's ten and he has an autism spectrum disorder. For crying out loud—I've had the same car for nine years because he throws a fit if anything changes. The last thing he'd do is run away."

"Okay, all right, my job is to explore all possible avenues." Officer Bright's tone was deep and mellow and seemed to dampen Tasha's anxiety whenever he spoke.

The man was good. I'd have to give him that.

"Did you check the house?" he asked. "Kip may have come home."

"Oh my god, no!" Tasha jumped up, shoved the brandy glass in my hands, and rushed up the stairs calling Kip's name. We all held our collective breath, as if the sound of our breathing would mask a response. We could hear her opening and closing doors.

"Kip? Kip!"

"I doubt he's here, Bright," Tim said, his jaw tight. "But I'll get my shoes on and start looking."

When Tim put on his shoes, I went into action, handing Grandma Ruth the brandy glass. "I'll check the basement."

"I'll check the carriage house." Phyllis jumped up to help.

"I'll stay here near the phone," Grandma Ruth said and tossed down the last of the brandy.

I rushed into the kitchen and yanked the basement door open. "Kip? Kip, are you down here?" I hurried down the stairs into the cold darkness. The fact that the basement light was not on was not a good sign. Kip was not a fan of the dark.

I reached for the dimmer switch and rotated it, illuminating the finished basement. Basements were rather rare in Kansas, as the bedrock was close to the surface, making cellars expensive. Some of the older homes were set on raised foundations, while the modern homes were simply built on slabs.

Slabs were fine as long as the weather behaved. The neighbors who had torn down old homes and replaced them with McMansions were dependent on the kindness of their neighbors when tornadoes came through. Trust me, you would rather be underground than in a closet—or worse, a mobile home—when those storms hit.

"Kip?" The only sounds I heard were the frantic footsteps on the floor above me. I did a quick turn around the paneled room to ensure that there were no ten-year-old boys playing hide-and-seek, then headed back up the wooden steps.

"Kip! This isn't funny. If you are here, come out now." Tasha's voice held the edge of panic. I closed the basement door and stepped into the kitchen at the same time Tim and Kip came in the back door.

Relief washed through me. "Tim has him!" I shouted and went straight over to throw my arms around the little boy, who was quick to squirm away from me.

"I don't like hugs!" he stated.

"Kip, thank goodness!!" Tasha rushed to him and got down on her knees, face-to-face with her son. I noted that her hands fluttered around him without touching him, and my heart ached. We all wanted to grab him and hold him close, but with Kip's autism spectrum disorder, hugs were painful to him. "Where have you been? You frightened me so much."

"I found Aubrey," Kip said, and held up a squirming brown-and-white puppy. "Can I keep him?"

"Aubrey?" I tilted my head to the side.

"Aubrey is Kip's imaginary friend," Tasha said.

"Aubrey is not imaginary." Kip lifted the puppy in the air. "He's right here."

"I'd say he certainly is right here," Tim said from the doorway. "Young man, you need to apologize to your mother. You wandered off and scared her very badly."

"I did not wander off," Kip told him matter-of-factly. "I rescued Aubrey and came straight home."

"I see that you did indeed rescue Aubrey," said a male voice from behind me. "That was very nice of you, but your uncle Tim is right. You should apologize to your mother. You frightened her very badly." Officer Bright was so calm and so sincere I wanted to hug him.

"Why?" Kip nuzzled the puppy that wiggled in his arms.

"Honey, I couldn't find you. I have two police cars, Aunt Toni's family, and Officer Bright all looking for you. I thought something bad had happened to you." Tasha brushed the hair out of her son's eyes. I don't know how she had the discipline not to hug the stuffing out of Kip.

"But I was rescuing Aubrey. How could anything bad happen to me?" He raised one blond eyebrow.

"Remember that we have a rule where you have to tell Mommy before you can leave the park?" Tasha put her hands on her bent knees. It was then that I noticed how white her knuckles were. She wasn't as calm or cool as she let on.

"I didn't leave the park."

"Kip," I warned him. "This is very serious. You scared your mom and she called the police. Lying—even a white lie—is not acceptable here."

"What's a white lie?"

"A white lie is when you only tell part of the truth. For instance, you rescued Aubrey—but maybe you had to leave the play equipment to do that. Maybe Aubrey was in distress and you hurried to save him and in your haste you forgot to tell your mommy that you were leaving."

"I didn't forget, 'cause I didn't leave the park."

For the first time I noticed the streaks of dirt on his shirt and knees.

"Okay, son, why don't you tell us how you rescued Aubrey." Officer Bright pulled out a kitchen chair, turned it around, and sat down. He draped his arms across the top in the most casual manner. His attention was fully on Kip. Right then my admiration for the young gun surged. I highly doubted anyone else would have been so patient.

"Are you going to put that in your notebook?" Kip asked and rubbed his dirty cheek across Aubrey's back, revealing a white streak. Maybe the puppy wasn't brown-and-white after all.

"Why, yes, in fact, I will." The young officer pulled his notebook back out of his pocket. He flipped it open, withdrew a small pencil, licked the tip, and poised it over the paper. "Go on then."

"Will you tell the news?" Kip asked, his blue eyes alight with expectation. "I read once that they give awards to heroes."

"And you are clearly Aubrey's hero," the officer said. "Of course, I'll tell the news. But first you have to tell your story."

Kip sat cross-legged on the black-and-white tiled kitchen floor. "I was playing in the tunnel under the slide when I heard a noise."

"What kind of noise?" Tasha got into the spirit of things, matching her son's posture on the floor.

"It was like this—*hmm, hmm*." He made a high-pitched whining noise. The puppy stopped squirming and licked his face. Kip giggled, and my heart warmed.

I sat down on a kitchen chair and put my chin in my hands. Tim had his arms crossed and was leaning against the doorjamb.

"Then what happened?" Officer Bright asked. He wrote in his notebook as if our very lives depended on it.

"I followed the noise."

"Where did it lead?" Tim asked.

"It went through the tunnel and out across the sand pit. I crept up on it like this." He let go of the dog long enough to do an army crawl of elbows and knees a few feet into the kitchen. The puppy barked at him and pounced on his head. "No, Aubrey!" Kip pushed the puppy off.

"Then what?" I asked, wondering when Kip'd left the park and where he'd found Aubrey.

"I went into the grass and I kept sneaking up on the noise."

"Why did you sneak?" Tasha asked.

"'Cause I wasn't sure if it was a bad noise or a good noise and I didn't want to rush toward it if it was a bad noise."

"Good thinking." Officer Bright nodded and wrote a note.

"Mommy taught me," Kip said proudly. "I sneaked up until I saw this hole in the ground."

"How big of a hole?" Tim narrowed his eyes.

"About this big." Kip made a circle with his arms the size of a pie pan.

Tasha and I made a noise at the same time. I glanced at Officer Bright, who leaned toward Kip, his expression rock-hard. "Was it very deep?"

Kip pursed his lips and sat up straight. "I had to put my arms and head in to reach Aubrey." He lifted his arms over his head in a diving manner.

I took a deep breath and let it out slowly. We always heard

of little kids falling into old wells and getting stuck. This sounded like a well in a park in the middle of town. Why hadn't anyone noticed it before?

I tried not to think about what would have happened had a small child fallen in that well, or worse, if Kip'd gotten stuck. I glanced at Tasha. She had turned two shades of pale. I patted her back. "Breathe," I said under my breath, hoping Kip wouldn't notice. Officer Bright was a step ahead of us.

"If I asked you to show me this hole, could you do that?" he asked. It wasn't the first time I noted how careful he was not to react and upset or overexcite Kip.

"Oh, sure." The boy stood. The puppy at his feet jumped on him and licked his hand. "Can we go now?"

"How about we ask your mom first?" Officer Bright stood and looked expectantly from Kip to Tasha and back.

"Mom, can I show Officer Bright where the hole is?" He turned to Tasha, who clearly wanted to hug her child against her chest and never let him go. "It'll be okay, 'cause he's a police officer that I know. Can I?"

"How about I go with you?" Tasha stood. She gave Officer Bright an expectant look.

"Of course, your mommy should come," he said.

"And me," Tim said.

"And Uncle Tim," Kip said. "But who's going to watch Aubrey?"

Everyone turned to me expectantly. I held out my hands. "Okay, you all go. I'll give Aubrey a bath and see if we have something for him to eat."

"You need dog food," Kip said.

"That's true." I held the dirty, wiggly creature at arm's length. "But since I don't have a dog, I don't have any dog food in the house."

"Oh." Kip glanced around. "Officer Bright, do you have a dog?"

"No, son, I don't. I work too much to leave a dog home alone."

"Oh."

Tasha took Kip's hand. "We'll go to the store after you show Officer Bright where the hole is, okay?"

"Okay." He skipped along beside his mom as they headed out the back door. "Can I get a new sticker book?"

"Don't you think we ought to come straight home from the store? Aubrey might be very hungry from his time in the hole and all."

Kip's expression fell a little. "Oh. Okay."

Tasha looked over his head at me and mouthed, "Thank you."

I smiled. "You're fine. Go." I raised the puppy up and waved its paw. "We'll be here waiting."

"So, buddy," Tim said as he held the door open for everyone. "When did you leave the park? Did you head straight home? Because, dude, you were gone a long time."

The door closed behind them before I could hear Kip's reply. Aubry and I stood at the back window and watched the police officer open the squad car door and let Kip into the backseat. Next he held the front passenger side door open and talked Tasha into taking the shotgun seat. I noticed the accidental hand touch and the look that passed between the two. Maybe, just maybe, there was hope for my best friend. I continued to wave the puppy's paw until the car cleared the driveway.

"Huh." I lifted Aubrey into the air. "So much for the old-fashioned 'Mom, can I keep him?'" It seemed, at least for Kip, that rescuing Aubrey made having a puppy a done deal.

It was after I had that thought that Aubrey decided to piddle on me. "Oh, no, no, no!" I rushed out the back door and set the puppy down on the small patch of grass between the house and the carriage house. Aubrey sniffed around the peonies, then waddled through the grass a moment doing figure eights until he or she—I hadn't looked yet—squatted and peed. Then the puppy bounded toward me on playful legs.

I knew then I was sunk. Its big brown eyes gave me this knowing look while it stretched its front paws up and stretched against my leg. I reached down and picked up the puppy. A big smear of brown colored my arm. "I don't know if Kip rescued you or you rescued Kip." The puppy licked my cheek.

It was hard not to giggle like a schoolgirl. I tucked the wagging tail under my arm and went back inside to give the dog a bath and mop the kitchen floor. It seemed everyone wanted to live at my house.

The phone rang as I walked inside. I let the door slam, put the puppy into a cardboard box I used for recycling, and grabbed the phone with one hand and the mop with the other. "Hello?"

"Toni?"

"Hi, Rosa, what's up?" Rosa was my oldest younger sister. She lived in Wichita with her professional rodeo cowboy husband, Brand. Rosa, Eleanor, and Joan were closer to each other than I was to any of my sisters. You see, I was the oldest sister, born between the two boys—Richard, who was the oldest, and Tim, who was only eighteen months younger than me. Mom and Dad took a few years off and then had Rosa, Joan, and Eleanor. Which meant that the boys were close and the sisters were close and I sort of hung out on my own.

"Did I hear correctly? Did the police arrest Grandma Ruth for breaking and entering?"

"Excuse me?" I ran the mop under the faucet, turned off the water, and squeezed the mop head to wring out the excess water.

"Is Grandma Ruth in jail for breaking and entering the courthouse?" Rosa's voice sounded tight and full of blame.

"No," I reassured her. "Grandma Ruth and Aunt Phyllis are here. They were helping calm down Tasha. She thought Kip had gotten lost and called the cops."

"Don't lie to me, Toni." Rosa sounded breathless. "I saw Georgina Christenson at the club this afternoon. She kept going on and on about how sorry she was to hear that my poor Grandma Ruth was being held against her will . . . accused of breaking into the courthouse last night and of murdering Lois Striker. I wouldn't put it past Grandma to break into the courthouse if she was looking for a story. But I told Georgina that surely my sister, who was right there in town, would tell me if such a thing happened."

"She's fine, Rosa, really. Chief Blaylock had her in for questioning yesterday, but I called Brad Ridgeway and he got her out." I tilted my head and tucked the phone between my ear and my shoulder as I mopped up the piddle spots.

"Then you'd better call him again," Rosa said. "Because I checked with Sarah Hogginboom and Grandma is in lockup as we speak."

"What? No." I rinsed the mop head again and squeezed it dry. "That's not possible. She's here in the house. Besides, I talked to Chief Blaylock less than two hours ago. I promised him I'd ask Grandma to lay low and let the professionals investigate Lois's death."

"If I were you, I'd be calling Brad, because I believe Grandma used up her one phone call on you yesterday. And Toni . . ."

"Yes?"

"Don't make me have to come home to straighten this out. It's embarrassing enough without having to explain why my older sister can't keep my grandma in line."

She hung up and the line buzzed in my ear. I rolled my eyes and turned to see that the puppy had escaped from the box. He rolled on the clean but wet floor, smearing mud everywhere. "No!" I raised my voice a tad too loud and he piddled on my floor . . . again. "Darn it," I muttered and went to grab him when he escaped from me and took off down the hallway.

It took me five minutes to corner the puppy in the formal living room. He growled at me but I picked him up and scolded him with my finger. He reacted by biting me.

There was a knock at the front door. I'd forgotten that I'd left the screen door open when I'd come in. "Toni?" Brad opened the door.

"Here." I must have been a sight. The puppy was like a greased pig, slick from mud. I could see it streaked on my blue shirt and black pants. I tried to wipe it off my face, but that only seemed to make it worse. I'm certain my hair stuck out all over. "I'm in the living room."

I stepped out and nearly ran into Brad as he stepped in from the foyer. "Whoa," he said and grabbed me by the forearms to steady me. "What happened to you?"

"Meet Aubrey." I lifted the puppy into the air. "Kip rescued him."

"Oh. Hello." He stepped back from both me and the dog.

"I promised to give him a bath. Want to help?"

"You, soapy water in the bathroom . . . nice image. I'd love to but I'm headed to the police station."

I tilted my head. "Then why'd you stop here? Oh, no, don't tell me. . . ."

"Yeah, sorry." He frowned, drawing his thick blond eyebrows together. "I'm afraid Chief Blaylock caught Grandma Ruth and Phyllis at the courthouse."

"But they were just here."

"Not anymore."

CHAPTER 11

"Mama said there'll be days like this. There'll be days like this, my mama said." The song played on the radio as I paced the front porch. The sun set early in November, and the black of night hung thick over the street lamps. The wind whipped up a nice icy cold and carried the scent of snow. The big oak trees in front of the house had lost all their leaves last month, and their thick outstretched arms stood firm and sleeping.

Brad had called from the police station to let me know that he'd extracted Aunt Phyllis from the police for the price of a small fine. Grandma Ruth, on the other hand, was playing hardball. I could not wait to get my hands on her. What was she thinking going back to the courthouse in Aunt Phyllis's van? Even worse, they'd crossed the taped-off section and opened the side door and walked in as if they owned the place.

"Technically, we do own the place," Grandma had said over the phone. "It's the county courthouse, and I pay my taxes."

"That doesn't give you the right to walk in whenever you want." I rested my tired head against the wall of the bathroom. Grandma called while I was bathing the puppy. It turns out it was a very large, very fluffy white puppy. From the size of its paws, we might be in big trouble in a few months.

The puppy decided that it needed to shake from nose to tail, flinging soap and water all over the tiny pink rosebud wallpaper I'd put in the second-floor bathroom. It was pretty and I'd been reassured it was the same period as the house. My goal was to slowly decorate the house to my taste, starting with the floor with my bedroom and adjacent bath. It'd been three months before I'd settled on a small but tasteful amount of period wallpaper on this floor in pale creams with pastel flowers and stripes.

I grabbed a thick green towel and covered the puppy. It growled and grabbed the towel until I scooped it up and wrapped the squirming wet creature.

"What is that noise?" Grandma asked on the phone. The woman was hard of hearing until it was something you hoped she didn't hear.

"Kip brought home a puppy."

"Really? What kind?"

"White. Now, don't try to change the subject on me. Rosa heard you were in jail before I found out," I scolded. "You know how that makes me look."

"Like a busy career woman?"

"Grandma, don't you think I've had enough excitement in the last forty-eight hours, between you being arrested once and Kip going missing?" I fluffed up the puppy and let it go. It circled the floor and proceeded to lift its leg and piddle against my pedestal sink. "Aubrey, no!" My shouting only made the puppy run, piddling as it went.

"Aubrey?" Grandma asked.

"Kip named the puppy." I grabbed up the pup and took it in one hand and my cell phone in the other as I headed down the wood steps to the foyer. "When will you be home?"

"When I convince the chief to look in the wall for Champ Rogers's murder weapon."

"Grandma! Do you know what a long shot it is that there is anything in the wall, let alone a long-lost murder weapon?"

"As long a shot as the idea that I killed Lois." Grandma said that last part very loud. "I have to go."

"Wait!" I froze at the bottom of the steps, but it was too late. Grandma had hung up. "Darn." The puppy licked my hand. I blew out a slow breath and lifted the little guy up until we were face-to-face. I studied his broad forehead and square nose. "If your coloring matched the breed, I'd think you were a Saint Bernard."

"Heaven help us." Tasha walked in from the kitchen and crossed herself. "There's no way I can rent an apartment if I've got a Saint Bernard."

"Aubrey!" Kip raced around his mom and took the fluffy puppy from me. The dog's tail wagged fiercely as Kip gathered it up in his arms and buried his face in the white fur. "Come on, Aubrey. We bought you puppy food. Uncle Tim says that you have to eat special food until you're one year old so that you'll have strong bones and teeth." Kip disappeared back into the kitchen.

"You're stuck with Aubrey now. Let's hope no one comes forward to claim him." I leaned against the staircase and studied my friend. Her cheeks were pink and her eyes sparkled. Her blonde hair escaped from her headband, but in such a way that she looked like a Hollywood starlet stepping out of a convertible after an exciting ride with—what was the name of that movie star? Ryan something . . . Ryan Goose? Ryan Goss? Anyway, it starts with a *G*.

Okay, so I wasn't up on my Hollywood stars. I had a business to run, and that meant that my movie viewing was limited to the three and four A.M. old movies that played on cable channels. I liked to have movies playing in the background while I baked. Ever since the murder outside my bakery door in the wee hours of the morning, I'd decided I'd rather have a movie plot than simply music. A movie plot kept my mind engaged and my thoughts from wandering off in scary directions.

I straightened from the staircase. "Are you okay?"

Tasha sat down hard on one of the chairs that rested against the wall in the square foyer. "I'm not sure." She looked nearly as afraid as she had been when I'd first gotten home.

"Kip seems all right," I pointed out. "Was the hole scary deep?"

She closed her eyes and tilted her head back against the wall. "It was about four to five feet deep. I have no idea how Kip got that dog out of there." She opened her eyes and her expression grew sober. "He could have fallen in and it might have been hours or even days before we found him."

"He's fine."

"I know. I kept saying that as I watched him show Calvin the hole."

"Calvin?" I raised my right eyebrow and waited for her to blush in five . . . four . . . three . . . two . . .

"Don't you think he did a good job with Kip?"

I noticed she didn't tell me who Calvin was and left it up to me to assume it was Officer Bright. "He seems like a nice guy."

"I swear, Toni, I thought I was going to fall apart until

he got here. There was something calm and confident about him." She paused, her gaze softening.

"I noticed." I shoved my hands in my pants pockets.

She shook off the mood that had struck her. "He said he was going to see that Kip got a hero award for not only rescuing the puppy but saving the neighbor kids from certain harm."

I tilted my head, a little confused. "So, what was it? An old well?" It seemed odd that no one would have noticed an old well in a park that had been there since before I was born.

"Calvin thought perhaps it was a sink hole. It's been so dry this fall, and then we had that rain last week."

"I remember. The downtown would have flooded if not for the new lake and dam project."

"We're lucky it all worked out," Tim said as he walked in. "Bright called in an emergency crew to cover the hole before anyone else fell inside."

"Thanks for your help, Tim," Tasha said with a sigh, the tension leaving her shoulders.

"No problem," Tim said and shoved his hands in his pockets. "Any other emergencies before I go up and try to get a little more shut-eye?"

I noted that the sunlight was fading in the living room windows. It was the time of year where it grew dark at five P.M. From the look of the light it was nearing twilight. "While you were gone, Grandma Ruth and Aunt Phyllis were picked up by the police."

"Not again!" Tim muttered something dark under his breath.

Tasha sat up straight. "When, where, how? Aren't they here?"

"That's what I said." I shrugged. "It seems Grandma

heard Kip come in and decided it was time she and Phyllis go down and continue their search of the courthouse building."

"What would make them do that? Didn't you tell them to lay low?"

I rolled my eyes and tucked my frizzy hair behind my ears. "When have we ever known Grandma Ruth to listen?"

"You should have asked her how she thinks she's going to investigate Lois's murder from inside the jail," Tim said.

"You are brilliant!" I rushed over and hugged my brother— then pulled out my phone and dialed Brad's number.

"Ridgeway."

"Hi, Brad, it's Toni."

"It's okay, Toni, I'm calling in some favors to get your grandma out of jail."

"Maybe you shouldn't." There, I said it. I went out on the front porch and sat in the porch swing.

"What? Why?"

"As long as she's in jail she can't investigate any further." I pushed off on the swing and watched the sun go down.

"Hmm. Do you think she'll be all right in lockup?"

"Knowing Grandma, she'll be fine. It's the guards I worry about." I laughed short and tight, then sobered. "Wait, seriously, you'd better check in with Chief Blaylock first. I don't want to leave her there only to have her get into worse trouble than if she were home where I can keep an eye on her."

"Toni, she sneaked out of your house and willfully broke into the courthouse. How much more trouble can she get in?"

"Seriously, Brad, do you know my grandma? She's a Mensa member. If there's a way to get around a problem, she'll find it."

"Point taken."

I pushed off the swing and hung on to the silence our

phone conversation had fallen into. Clearly we were both thinking through the fine points of being between a rock and a hard place where Grandma was concerned.

If I didn't get her out she'd have to sleep on the cot in a jail cell. And worse, I'd have to hear from Joan, Rosa, and Eleanor about how irresponsible I was for not keeping a better eye on the old lady.

It was a risk I would take if it kept Grandma safe. We must have reached our decision at the same time.

"I'll talk to the chief," Brad said.

"Thanks," I said, my heart pumping as I crossed my fingers and toes that Grandma wouldn't find more trouble in a jail cell than she did running around in Aunt Phyllis's VW van.

CHAPTER 12

The week before Thanksgiving was almost as busy for the bakery as Christmas. People were planning their huge family celebration meals. If they weren't gluten-free but had GF family, they often came in to pick up their pies, breads, stuffing, etc. It was too much to cook a feast for their regular guests, let alone the special eaters.

I didn't mind. It meant I worked long hours, but the extra money I made from the holidays could help sustain me through the leaner times early in the next year. Now that I had the actual bakery separate from my kitchen I was able to bake all night without interrupting the others in my household.

Pushing racks of pies into the freezer, I closed the door to the little room tight and marked the time on the sheet taped to the front door. Each group had to freeze for a specific number of hours before I could box them and package them for shipment the next day. It was hard when everyone wanted their pies Thanksgiving day or, at the very earliest, the day before.

The first year I'd run my online bakery I'd been able to spend the entire night before Thanksgiving Thursday baking and packaging. Come Thursday morning I'd hand-delivered my boxed creations. From those fifty desserts my business had grown to five hundred and then this year, a record eleven hundred desserts. Most of them were pies, but there were a few cakes, and even some cupcake requests.

Luckily most of my new clients were local enough that they had scheduled to come in and pick up their desserts. And still many more paid the extra ten dollars to have theirs delivered. Meghan would spend the first three days of the week distributing pies over the three closest counties. It was my hope that people would tip her well; if they didn't, then I would give her a bonus. It took a lot of effort to ensure the desserts arrived on time and in fresh-from-the-oven condition.

It was all good practice for Meghan. She was saving her extra cash to enroll in culinary school next year with the goal of opening her own bakery someday. But for now it was my pleasure to teach her my business from the ground up.

For now, I was as caught up with work as I could be and so it was that I was the one who stepped out of the kitchen to answer the ring of the door bells when Candy Cole came in.

"I understand Ruth was investigating Homer Everett when she murdered Lois Striker," Candy said as she stirred sugar into her tea. "What was Ruth's connection to Lois? Was it truly all about Homer Everett, or was it something even more sinister?"

"Candy, I'm not speaking on the record," I said as I wiped down the coffee bar in my bakery. "Why don't you write a piece on Thanksgiving?"

"Thanksgiving has been celebrated since the pilgrims;

officially celebrated by the federal government since 1863. And modern Thanksgiving has been celebrated since 1941. That's a lot of years to cover the same story, Toni. I need something fresh, something local, like Homer Everett Day and the murder of a cornerstone of the Oiltop community."

"Find another story, Candy. My family is off limits. Now, do you want apple or pumpkin pie for your holiday order?"

"It wasn't pumpkin," she said absently. "If you don't tell me what Ruth was researching I'll have to go to Ruth myself . . . and I can't promise I'll be all that nice to her in my exposé. I can see the headline now . . . 'Local grandma guilty as charged for the murder of Chamber of Commerce icon.'" She spread her hand through the air as if setting out each word in the headline.

I tried not to flinch. When it came to Candy, our resident newspaper reporter, you had to watch every body movement. She had a tendency to jump on any perceived weakness. "I'll have Meghan deliver your pies on Wednesday. Will that work for you?"

"Yes, of course."

"How many people will you need to serve?" I asked. It was a good question and also a way of discovering what her plans were for the holiday. If she had a lot of relatives coming, then it was a safe bet she already had her article written. If she only had a few relatives, then she would still be out looking into who killed Lois Striker.

"I'm serving ten," she said, and sipped her tea. "You know twelve is too many and eight is too few."

"I wouldn't know." I shrugged. "I'm serving twenty-four and that is only my closest relatives." I stopped from writing down her order and looked her in the eye. "Would you be interested in trying the chocolate-chip pecan pie? I'm making it with dark chocolate chips."

"Oh, sounds wonderful, yes, throw one of those in my order. What's a few extra pieces, right?"

"Right."

"Besides, isn't gluten-free better for you anyway?"

"Only if you're gluten-sensitive," I answered honestly. "It can be too full of fats for a normal diet."

"That's okay." She shrugged. "It's not like pie is diet food, right?"

"Right." I added a chocolate-chip pecan pie to her order and ripped off the top sheet, handing her the pink bottom sheet. "Keep this for your records. I don't plan on any mistakes in the order, but I'm cooking a lot of pies and there's no telling."

"Great," she said. "How's Meghan doing? I hear she might be quitting—is that true?"

"No, it's not true." I tried not to bristle. Investigating and asking questions was what Candy did for a living. It was my fault if I felt it was rude or off-putting. Candy and I'd been in the same class in high school. She had been on the school newspaper and the yearbook staff. Meanwhile, I'd been in debate. It was a bit of popular girl versus nerd. It was hard to believe we would grow up to be friends, but college had brought us together.

My divorce and last month's murder investigation had split our friendship apart, though. I didn't forget too quickly that she had tried to pin the murder of a wheat farmer on me. She was so happy to investigate that she forgot the cardinal rule: first do no harm—no, wait, that was the Hippocratic oath. So what was it? Do unto others what you would have others do unto you? Or is it . . . don't suffer any fools?

Either way, she tended to go with public opinion and not the facts. It only made her look worse when the truth came out.

"Oh, come on, when are you going to forgive me for last

month?" she asked and put on her best sad puppy dog look. I wasn't buying it.

"I forgave you last month."

"Oh." She straightened. "Then why the disconnect?" She pointed her fingers back and forth between herself and me.

"I didn't say I'd forgotten that you all but hung me out to dry in your exposé."

"Come on now, it was business, not personal."

"That's the trouble, Candy," I said. "I can't tell with you when business stops and personal begins and vice versa."

"I'm no different than your grandmother Ruth." She sipped her tea. "We are very much alike, she and I. I'm sure she had a very good reason for murdering Lois."

"Now, there, see, that was ridiculous. You just took a personal conversation and twisted it to see if I would reveal something about my grandma."

"Oh, come on." She flung her arms wide. "I'm a reporter."

"I suppose that means you have to try."

"Yes," she said most sincerely, "I have to try."

"Look, Grandma Ruth didn't kill Lois. She wasn't even there until later."

"You're absolutely certain?"

"I'm certain," I said and crossed my heart. "You need to go looking for new leads . . . ones not found in my bakery."

Candy pouted prettily. "I don't have any other leads."

"Then why not write a story on the parade floats?"

"Can't," she said and finished her tea. "Rocky Rhode has that covered. He's doing a photo story. He met with Hutch Everett last night to get some candid shots around the floats. Rocky was in the office when I left this morning. I swear it isn't right when a silly parade makes the front page, especially with a murder in town."

I leaned on the counter, dishrag in hand. "I hate to break it to you, Candy, but no one reads newspapers anymore. They're slower than the Internet, and people don't want to wait. Even blogs have been abandoned for short things like Tumblr and Twitter."

"How do you know so much about the Internet?" she asked. "I thought you spent every waking hour in your bakery."

"I do. Grandma Ruth keeps me up to date. It's amazing what the senior set is up to these days."

She opened her mouth and I raised my hand in a "stop" sign. "Don't say murder."

"I won't say it," she agreed. "But that doesn't mean I won't suspect it."

Early the next morning, I sat in my office and studied the computer screen. The bakery office used to be a utility closet. It still held the faint scent of pine cleaner and damp mop. I had all the lights on in the back of the bakery. In the background, *The Wizard of Oz* played on my small television. The movie was a Thanksgiving classic. I'd learned long ago to stop questioning why they showed it on this particular holiday and simply enjoyed the familiar sound of Judy Garland trying to figure out how to go home.

"Stay in Oz!" I advised the television. No one listened. Couldn't they see the appeal of colorful munchkins and glittery ball gown–wearing witches? Seriously, why would you leave all that to come back to Kansas?

I sat down at my tiny desk, which held my computer monitor, keyboard, and stacks of receipts . The computer tower sat on the floor. A small printer perched on the thick window casing above my desk. Why the builder had thought to put a window, even a window as small as this one, in a closet had always perplexed me. But for now the sill made a nice place to put my printer.

I entered a handful of receipts into my accounting software before checking on the list of supplies and orders for the week. The sharp scent of dark roasted coffee mixed with pine. Besides the holiday dessert orders, I still had the daily pastries, cookies, cupcakes, breads, and other goods that were sold in the shop itself. Not to mention the sub rolls that I had convinced the deli owner to purchase. His gluten-free customers increased his profits by ten percent that first month. He repaid me by ordering more rolls, along with the occasional dessert.

When it came to the holiday season, I'd planned a careful, yet diverse, menu for the bakery. People needed to be able to run in and order take-home boxes to please last-minute guests. So I concentrated on donuts, muffins, and pastries in the morning. Yeast breads, quick breads, and desserts came out in the afternoon. Then there was the notice that had gone up last week letting people know that limited varieties would be offered between Thanksgiving and New Year's to accommodate all the holidays. And, hopefully, start traditions that included my gluten-free bakery.

A pounding at the back door startled me, sending a pile of receipts flying. "Darn it." I jumped up and grabbed the baseball bat I kept in the corner of my office. After last month's vandalisms and attacks, I'd thought it wise to have something on hand that I'd actually think to use.

My brother Rich had painted KILLER on the handle of the bat in red, while Tim had painted a bull's-eye around the new peephole in the back door, along with the words LOOK HERE FIRST!

Whoever was out there pounded again. I bit my lower lip to keep from yelping at the startling sound.

"I know you're in there!"

The voice was definitely female. I looked through the peephole to see Aunt Phyllis glaring back at me.

"Toni, open the door!"

I unlocked the two deadbolts and opened the door. "Aunt Phyllis, what time is it?"

"It's four A.M.," she said as she strode in and made a beeline for the coffeepot. "It's also cold outside. The cops took my van and the tent is freezing this time of year."

"The tent? What tent?" I closed and double-locked the door.

"My tent, of course. Where else was I going to sleep with the van in lockup?"

"Good Lord, Aunt Phyllis, I have four empty bedrooms, plus the apartment over the carriage house. There is no need for anyone I know to ever sleep in a tent, let alone in a tent in the winter." I ran my hands up and down the length of the bat and wondered if I needed to knock some sense into her.

She grabbed a white mug from the mug tree next to the coffeepot, poured thick black coffee into it, and added creamer and sugar. Her blue eyes sparkled as she blew on the steaming liquid. "How could I sleep in a comfy bedroom knowing Ruth was spending the night on a cot in a chilly jail cell?"

"Aunt Phyllis . . . you didn't."

"I most certainly did."

"No, you didn't."

"Yes, I did. When they told me I was free to go but Ruth was going to remain in jail overnight, I pitched my tent on the front lawn of the police station."

"Aunt Phyllis!"

"I also informed that Sergeant What's-his-face that I was a taxpayer and the police station is funded by taxpayer dollars, therefore I own the land it's sitting on and pitching my tent is not trespassing."

"Sergeant What's-his-face?" I collapsed on the stool next to the counter.

"You know . . . the one who looks like Barney Fife."

"Oh."

"Yes. Oh. The man is a nincompoop."

Officer Joe Emry was one of five police officers who worked the city of Oiltop beat. He was a thin, nervous sort and reminded me of the character from the old Andy Griffith television show that I watched on the classic TV channel.

It didn't help that Officer Emry was not my favorite member of the Oiltop police force. But I wasn't going to tell Aunt Phyllis that. She got to leave Oiltop when this was over. I, on the other hand, was trying to fit in here.

"Aunt Phyllis, you can't camp out outside the police station."

"I wouldn't have had to if you had bailed your grandmother out like I expected."

I winced at the accusing look in her eyes. "Hey, I warned you both to lay low. I told you that they had witnesses who could identify your van as driving from the scene last night."

"Technically it was the night before last." Phyllis sipped her coffee and climbed up on the other stool in the work area.

"Not to mention that you both snuck out on me while I was busy helping Tasha figure out where Kip was."

"The boy was home safe and sound. We made sure before we left." She wrapped her small, thin hands around the mug.

"How would I know? You didn't tell me you were leaving or where you were going." It was my turn to practice my accusing glare.

She shrugged and grabbed a donut off the cooling rack. She bit off a hunk of cinnamon apple and chewed thoughtfully before she washed it down with more coffee. "We didn't tell you because you were busy."

"Not that busy."

"You would have kept us from going."

I wanted to say, *Duh*, but I refrained. She knew it as much as I did. Maybe when Grandma finally got home I'd sing the "I Was Right" song.

"I know, I know," she said without my having to answer. Phyllis took another sip of coffee and settled into her suede jacket. The fringe swayed with her movement as she nibbled on the donut. "Ruth thought she remembered another question from her investigation and thought Homer Everett's papers might hold the answer." She sipped again. "If it helps any, we were simply going to go and dig through the collection one time."

"The courthouse is closed after five P.M. on weekdays." I hated to point out the obvious, but someone had to do it. Besides, she needed to know I was smart enough to shoot holes in whatever tall tale she and Grandma had come up with on their way to being arrested.

She waved my objection off like a silly gnat. "We made a key impression the other night. The key we had cut should have worked."

"Aunt Phyllis!"

"How were we to know they had rekeyed the thing? I mean, the government is supposed to be slow. We broke in over the weekend and by Monday evening they had it rekeyed? First of all, how did they know we made a key? Second, where'd they find anyone to fix it anyway?"

I got up and put the bat back in its corner behind the office door. "I'm sure with it being the county courthouse and next to a crime scene, they called someone to rekey the entire building."

She followed me into my office when I sat down in my chair and wiggled my computer mouse to bring up what I was working on earlier.

"Speaking of new locks, did you know that they don't have to cut a new key when they replace a lock? All they did was put a new center in the lock and then used a master key to rotate the pins to match."

"Oh, no . . ."

"Yes." Phyllis grinned and held up a key. "I have a friend on the inside with a master key. Of course, if that doesn't work then there's always my ability to pick a lock."

"No!"

" 'No' as in 'Yes, let's go make copies of all the files'?"

I put my elbow on the table and dropped my forehead in my hand. "No. 'No' as in 'No, I'm not going anywhere near the courthouse at this hour of the night..' "

"Technically, 4:30 A.M is morning."

I shot her a dirty look.

"No problem." She raised her hands in surrender, went out and came back into my office pulling one of the stools. "I can wait."

I turned back to my paperwork. "You'll be waiting a long time."

"Will I? Ruth will be out by three P.M."

I sat back in my seat.

Phyllis had both eyebrows raised and her arms crossed over her chest.

"Really?" I said. "You're going to blackmail me now?"

"Oh, it's not blackmail when it's the truth."

CHAPTER 13

"**B**rad is going to be so mad when he has to bail me out of jail," I muttered. "We could have waited until the courthouse opens at nine A.M."

"Shush and hold the light up a little higher." Phyllis had a hairpin and a lock pick in her hands and was doing an impressive job of unlocking doors in the courthouse. There was a double *click* sound and the door opened.

"How did you learn to do that?" I asked as we stepped into the darkened records room. A chilled breeze snaked around my legs. I refused to think of all the ghosts that ran the halls of this old building. Even worse was the thought that Lois might be one of them. "Why not use the copy of the key you made?"

"I dated an escape artist in my twenties." Phyllis grabbed a flashlight from me and walked by the shadowed research table, around the librarian's desk and straight back to the glass-covered shelves in the back. "I like to keep up on the skill. If you don't use it, you lose it."

"You dated an escape artist?" I shook my head. "Is there such a thing? I mean, didn't Houdini die in the nineteen thirties or something?"

"Houdini died in 1926 and that's beside the point. Ferdinand worked the carnival circuit." Phyllis counted three shelves over and found the display with Homer Everett's pro uniform and Purple Heart medal. "He was quite handsome. I remember paying a quarter to see his act and falling in love on the spot."

"You fell in love with a carny?"

"It was one of the best summers of my life. We traveled with a little circus to all the county fairs and church festivals from Illinois to California."

"What year was that?"

"The year before I met your grandma." She deftly unlocked the case and stuck her flashlight under her chin so she had both hands free. "I was . . ."

"Sixteen," we both said at the same time.

"You ran away and joined the circus when you were sixteen?" I asked.

"Of course not." She pushed aside the presentation boxes and yanked out the archive boxes at the back of the shelf. "I had an affair with an escape artist when I was sixteen. Just because he was with the circus doesn't mean I was. The fact that I wasn't a true carny was a bone of contention that finally split us apart. The circus stopped in Oiltop. When it left, Ferdinand went with it and I stayed here."

"The traveling circus must have been pretty bad for you to ask to be left in Oiltop." I took the box she handed me. It was heavier than I imagined.

She took hold of her flashlight and replaced the presentations. When she was done I doubted anyone would know the things had been moved. Locking the glass case behind her, she waved me forward. I took the box and placed it on the research table.

"Not here," she said and grabbed the box off the table. "This is coming home with us."

"Oh, no." I stood firm. "It is one thing to break and enter, and another thing completely to be a thief. I draw the line when it comes to taking something."

"We're not taking it," she said and scooted out the door. "We're borrowing it. I promise to bring it right back."

I hurried after her. The door slammed shut with a dreadful echo. I froze at the sound, but Phyllis kept going. She might be small and as old as my mother, but that woman could book it when she wanted to.

I heard a soft voice whisper, "Don't stand there. Run!"

So I did. The chilled breeze wrapped itself around my shoulders as I pounded down the stairs and out the side door. I learned a few things on this adventure. One: Aunt Phyllis had an affair with a carny when she was only sixteen. Two: the courthouse is definitely haunted. And three: borrowing was not stealing if you intended to give it right back.

"You stole a box from the courthouse archives and brought it back here? Way to be a rebel." Meghan raised her thumb in a sign of approval. Her fauxhawk had pink tips today. She still had on torn fishnet stockings and combat boots with heavy heels. This time she also wore a pencil skirt, a blue-and-white striped boatneck tee, and a leather jacket with metal spikes. Her lips were painted with a blue tint and the corner of her right eye was decorated with thin, black, stylish whirls and loops.

"It's not stealing. It's borrowing," I said as I packed pies in a large box for her to put in the delivery van. "Besides, I couldn't take it home. Not with Tasha and Kip staying with me. I wouldn't put them in that kind of danger."

"Oh, so there's danger attached to that box? Cool, what's in it?" She took the pies from me. Her hands were covered in black gloves with the fingers cut out to display navy blue painted fingernails with white swirls drawn on them.

"I'm not sure. Phyllis left to go see to Grandma Ruth as soon as we got back." I put three apple pies and two mince-meat pies in a second box. Each big box was marked with an invoice number and a copy of the order. I then numbered each pie according to its invoice order. It was the only way I could keep things clear and simple when I had two hundred orders a day going out for the next week.

"You went through all that, broke the law, and still haven't even looked in the box yet? You stink at being a bad guy."

"I have a business to run." I couldn't tell if that sounded whiney or full of disdain.

"Face it—you can't stand to break the law, can you?"

I straightened and put my hands on my apron-covered hips. "I've been known to bend the rules in my day."

"Really? And here I thought you were a good girl," a male voice said behind me.

I gave a little startled sound and whirled to see Sam Greenbaum standing in the kitchen door. "Sam! You scared me." My heart pounded in my ears. Why did I feel so guilty? Had I admitted to a crime within earshot of him? "What did you hear?"

He lifted one corner of his lovely mouth and gave me a sideways smile. "Enough to know that dating you will be an interesting adventure."

"She's not dating anyone, Uncle Sam." Meghan took the box and went out the back door.

"Yet," he answered and came over to buzz a kiss on my cheek. "Hey, lovely lady, I'm here for my mom's pie order."

"Right." I couldn't stop the tiny shiver that went through me every time he touched me. The man was a walking dream in his snap-front Western shirt and tight-fitting jeans. He had his brown cowboy hat in his tanned hand. His black boots shone, not from lack of use but from careful polishing.

"Are you happy to see me?" he asked, his dark eyes sparkling in the midmorning light.

"I'm always happy to see you." And I was, just not when I was admitting to possible larceny. "I still need to box up your pie order."

"That's fine. How's your grandma?"

"She spent the night in jail."

"What? No. I'll go speak to Blaylock. That's outrageous—"

I put my hand on his chest and tried to ignore the fact that it was solid as a wall, yet warm to the touch. "I made the decision not to bail her out."

"Why?"

I was very aware of his heartbeat under my fingers and dragged my hand away. Maybe if I made myself busy packing his pies I could stop feeling conflicted by my attraction to him and my guilt over making Grandma spend the night in jail. I mean, when was tough love too tough? I pulled out a big box and placed it over on the prepping station. "I told her that Chief Blaylock was getting suspicious of her behavior the other night and that she should knock off her investigation and lay low."

"And?"

I liked the fact that he didn't leap to any conclusions. He simply waited for me to fill in the blanks. "And Grandma went back anyway and got caught breaking into the courthouse."

"I see."

I picked up a boxed pecan pie. "Do you? Because I haven't slept and I've been feeling so guilty about it."

"Your grandma is a grown woman. A brilliant, stubborn, grown woman." He studied me as he spoke. "Like you, she needs a firm hand, and to be reined in on occasion."

"Like me?"

"You are related."

"I see." I turned and put the pie into the bigger box and was reaching for another when he touched my forearm.

"I meant that in a good way," he whispered near my ear, causing the hairs on the back of my neck to stand up and take notice. "I like a gal with spunk."

"Okay, there's room for one more box in the van and it's ready for delivery." Meghan walked into the kitchen, breaking whatever spell Sam was attempting to weave on me. It was working, which meant I was glad she'd interrupted. I mean, for a moment there I thought he was going to say something corny, like he wanted nothing better than to spend his life handling a spunky filly like me.

"Good, grab that final delivery box and staple the top invoice to it," I instructed as I finished packing Sam's mother's pie box.

"Hey, Meghan, how's the CI fund coming along?" Sam asked as he casually let the space between us grow.

"I've got a good thousand dollars in it so far," Meghan said with pride as she stapled the invoice to the box.

"That's a lot considering you only started working here a month ago." He frowned.

"She gets good tips," I said and slid two pecan pies into the carrying box. Each pie was in its own box. Two boxes were easily managed. Sam's mom had ordered two pies for the Sunday before the holiday. It's when his family celebrates. Unlike Sam's grandmother's order of ten pies for her Thanksgiving day gathering. My guess was she planned to strike up another lengthy card game. It was his grandmother's card games that had brought Sam into my bakery in the first place. After that he had come in every day for one thing or another.

I was never sure if that was his idea or his grandmother's. Not that it mattered. I enjoyed a lovely, well-built cowboy as much as the next girl. Just because I wasn't dating didn't mean I couldn't look.

CHAPTER 14

'd lied to Meghan. I had opened the box we'd "borrowed" from the Homer Everett display. My curiosity had gotten the best of me. I wanted to know what was so important that Aunt Phyllis had risked going to jail for it. Inside were a series of journals from the 1950s. They were carefully written in a flowing feminine script.

Feminine, not masculine, slants and curls on pages that were carefully dated. Who kept Homer's journals? Lois, perhaps? It was a log of all of Homer Everett's activities. The first journal held a tone of admiration and love, but by the third journal the tone had turned to one of anger. Interestingly enough, whoever took dictation for Homer's journal added her own side notes. What was that note? *He always puts Champ's needs before mine.*

Who was the woman behind the man? Was it his wife? Wait . . . Grandma Ruth and Aunt Phyllis never mentioned

Homer Everett's wife. How strange. Why would his wife have allowed this? He had to be married. . . . Interesting . . . I knew Homer had a son. Hutch Everett and his wife, Aimee, were a force to be reckoned with in Oiltop. Hutch was on the Chamber of Commerce board of directors. He was the marshal of the Homer Everett parade every year. And Aimee ruled the country club as if she were Princess Diana. Their son, Harold, seemed to be following in his parents' footsteps.

"I'm back." Meghan popped her head into my office, startling me out of my thoughts. "It's getting kind of warm out. We might want to figure out a way to keep the pies cool—"

I turned in my seat and placed my arm across the stack of journals.

"What are you doing?" She stepped in and took in the open box. "Is that the stuff you stole from the courthouse?

"I didn't steal it. I borrowed it." Yeah, I know, it sounded lame even to my own ears. "It's not like I'm reading the words off of it."

She pushed my arm aside and snagged one of the open journals. "Wow, neat handwriting. 'June 2, 1958. Homer has a meeting tonight. I hope he comes home in a good mood because I plan on telling him the news. The doctor confirmed that the rabbit has died.'" She paused and looked at me, her well-groomed eyebrows drawing into a *V*. "What does that mean, 'the rabbit has died'? Is it some kind of wacko stalker? Did they have those in the fifties?"

I snagged the journal out of her hands and added it to the pile. "I think it means—"

"She was pregnant," Aunt Phyllis said as she walked into my office. "Used to be they tested a lady's pee by injecting it in a rabbit. So if they turned up pregnant, they would say the rabbit died."

"Ew—animal testing, really?" Meghan said.

I sent Meghan a look that said I cared less about animal testing than I did the fact that she picked up Aunt Phyllis.

She shrugged. "Yeah, I was about to tell you that I saw your aunt hitchhiking so I picked her up."

Phyllis went through the books in the box. "So, 1940 to 19 . . ." She pushed my hands aside and counted the journals. "Looks like 1960."

"What's so important about a bunch of journals?" Meghan asked.

"We're trying to prove that Homer Everett killed a man back in 1959," Aunt Phyllis said.

"Whoa, you mean *the* Homer Everett? The guy whose statue is in the town square? The one with the parade every year?"

"The very one." Aunt Phyllis opened the 1958 journal, licked her thumb and turned the pages too quickly to read them.

"Awesome." Meghan grabbed one of the kitchen stools, rolled it into my little closet of an office, and sat down. "Who'd he kill and why? Is it in the journal? Can I read one of those?"

"No, you cannot read those." I got up and rolled Meghan out into the kitchen and closed the door, shutting Phyllis and the confiscated journals in my office. "As far as the world is concerned you know nothing about that box or those journals. Do you understand?"

"Sure. You're worried I might get in trouble." Her grin was the biggest I'd ever seen on her lovely face. "You care about me."

"That's right," I said, and my heart squeezed a little. "I don't want to see anything get between you and your goal of culinary school, especially not my family."

Meghan whirled the stool in a circle. "Sweet. You care." She stopped the stool with her hand to the stainless steel counter. "Seriously, though, I am eighteen. I can vote. That makes me an adult, and as an adult, I am fully capable of making my own choices."

"No one is capable of making their own choices around my family," I muttered as I put on a fresh apron. "Now, you were saying something about keeping the pies cool?"

"Yeah, I know it's November and all, but have you been outside? It's like eighty and especially the cream pies are all, like, wilting toward the end of the delivery."

I frowned. "Did you have the air conditioner in the van turned up?"

"All the way," she said with a shrug, "but it kind of spit out this funny vapor and died on me."

"Great," I muttered and chewed on the side of my cheek. "Fine. I'll make a call to get the van into the shop . . . after the holiday. In the meantime, let's pray for cold weather and deliver the cream pies first thing in the morning and last thing at night when it's cooler out."

"Okay, I'll go reorder the pies in the cooler," she said and put on a fresh apron. "What about the orders that have both cream and other pies? Should I do the same thing? Wait for the cooler hours?"

"Yes, we'll do the same. When you get done in the freezer, run down to Safeway and get a couple of the biggest coolers you can find and some bags of ice in case it remains warm the rest of the week."

"Will do, boss." She opened the walk-in freezer and closed it behind her. I glanced at my office. I was tempted to go in and ask Aunt Phyllis some questions, like *What happened to Homer Everett's wife? Why would she let his affair with Lois go unchecked?*

Fortunately the front bell to the bakery rang. I turned my back on the office and went out to attend to my customers.

After the morning rush, I usually gathered the breakfast pastries onto one tray then put out more cookies, cupcakes, and mini pies. People who came into the shop after noon usually were here for the coffee and tea and wanted afternoon snack foods, or they popped in to grab something tasty for after-dinner dessert.

I kept a schedule posted on the white board in the café of what goods were featured on which days. That way people knew what would be here when. Of course they could special-order anything for any day of the week, but for walk-ins the schedule was set.

On Fridays, I featured chocolate. It was my slowest day and I figured it was the universal favorite to draw in clients. I had a group of three or four regulars who came to take advantage of the free refills on coffee or tea. Today was the monthly meeting of the knitting club.

Mary Stewart, Tasha's mom, was the first to come in and help herself to coffee. She took a seat in the corner nearest the windows.

"Hi, Mary, I wasn't sure if you all were meeting today," I said as I came out. "It's so close to the holiday."

"I know," Mary said. "I'll be surprised if Francy and Julie show up. But I had to get out of the house. I've been cleaning up a storm in preparation for the holiday, and I needed to take a break."

I picked up the coffeepot and refreshed her mug. "Do you want anything?"

"I'll take some of those wonderful chocolate chip cookies," she said. "I might be baking, but I'm not eating." She winked. "I need to ensure I don't run out before the guests leave on Sunday."

"If you do run out, give us a call." I returned the coffeepot to the coffee bar. "I've made a few extra pies for emergencies."

"You are so thoughtful." Mary pulled her knitting out of the blue-and-white tote at her feet.

I slipped three chocolate chip cookies on a white plate and added a tiny garnish of curled chocolate and white chocolate dots. I straightened and took in the warm expression on Mary's face.

Like Tasha, Mary Stewart was a beautiful blonde. Her hair more of a champagne color, but still perfectly coiffed. I swear neither Mary nor Tasha's hair dared to stray out of place—unlike my own curly mass. But then again I never had the time it took to curl, straighten, and spray my hair into submission. I'd learned long ago that my hair had a mind of its own. We sort of had an agreement. It wouldn't look too bad and I wouldn't do too much to it.

Currently it was pulled back into a low ponytail, with bits and pieces allowed to escape in a flyaway manner.

Mary wore dark jeans in a flattering cut and a simple tee shirt and cardigan of pale blue. Her gold hoop earrings and diamond tennis bracelet gave her a look of understated wealth. Mary and Tasha were members of the country club set, something my quirky family scoffed at—yet I secretly wondered what it was like to have that easygoing elegance old money could buy.

I wiped my hands on my yellow-and-white striped apron. My uniform of black slacks and white button-down shirt was clean, my black tennis shoes meant to be comfortable after ten hours on my feet.

I slipped the plated cookies on the table next to her cup. "What are you working on?" I asked, admiring the fine, even stitches of blue and white.

"I'm making a baby sweater and bootie set."

I must have looked startled, because she laughed. It was a crystal clear, bell-like sound.

"No, it's not for Tasha," she reassured me. "We are putting together bassinet sets for Mercy Medical Center. In this economy there are quite a few young mothers struggling to make ends meet. Poor babies are going home wearing only little white onesies. We thought we'd donate as many sweaters and booties as we could this year."

"That is so nice," I said. The woman had a heart of gold, even if she did serve trout on Thanksgiving. "Maybe we can do a box for donations here in the bakery. I could ask Mrs. Becher next door. I'm sure she knows quilters who come into her fabric shop who would be happy to make quilts or blankets for newborns."

"Oh, there's Francy," Mary said as she looked out the window and gave a little wave.

"I'll bring more coffee and cookies." By the time I had Francy settled in, Julie McGee had shown up. I made two fresh pots of coffee and put out plates of cookies, then left the ladies to their knitting. Francy knitted a pale green blanket. Julie knitted a lemon-yellow sweater. They sat in companionable silence and I went to the back to give them room to chat a bit. Besides, I'd heard the back door open and close twice. Either Meghan and Phyllis had left, or Grandma Ruth was out of jail.

The sound of the copy machine whirring came through the open door of my closet office. I went back to see who was busy copying. Grandma Ruth's walker rested beside my office door. Inside my office, Grandma sat in my chair, taking up all the extra space as she used my printer/copier to make copies of the journals.

"Grandma, where's Phyllis?"

"She went to go get bail money." Grandma didn't even look up from her copying.

"Bail money? But I bailed you out."

Grandma shot me a look. "After you left me to rot in jail all night."

"We both know you loved the experience. You'll probably do an exposé on your blog: 'How the county jail wastes tax-payer money.' " I used my hand to draw a headline in the air.

"That's beside the point," Grandma said. "I know you were trying to teach this old dog a lesson. I get it. That's why I sent Phyllis to get bail money."

I shook my head, confused. "I still don't understand."

She stopped what she was doing and turned to me, her blue eyes serious. "We have to return the box tonight. If we get caught, I want to be able to post my own bail."

CHAPTER 15

"Don't ask and I won't tell," I said as I set the stolen box of journals down on Brad's desk. His office was richly appointed and spoke of his family's oil background. There was dark cherry paneling halfway up the wall. The rest of the wall was cream-colored with hunter green and deep red accents. One wall was covered completely by a cherry wood piece of furniture with shelves and cupboards accented with proper lighting. He had pieces of aeronautics memorabilia and photos of his granddad and the Ridgeway family's first oil well.

Then there were the framed diplomas; the tiny replicas of the personal jets he loved to fly. A basketball signed by the KU championship team from the year he played.

I tried not to be intimidated by it all, or by the Armani suit he wore. I know I was a bit ragtag, my hair coming out of its confines and my clothes still smelling of frosting.

"Toni, I'm happy to see you." He got up in one long, fluid motion, unfolding his six-foot-five-inch, Nordic-god frame from the leather desk chair. His cherry wood desk had a marble top and stood three feet from the shelves on the back wall. There wasn't a paper in sight except for a neatly stacked brief in the leather folder open on his desk. He worked on an ergonomic keyboard wirelessly connected to the thin LCD monitor hanging at eye level on the wall to his left.

"I should come see you at work more often," I said as he kissed me on the cheek. "If nothing else, it reminds me how very different our worlds are."

"What are you talking about?" He pulled his thick blond brows together, rested his lovely backside on the top of his desk, and crossed his arms over his chest.

"This." I waved around at everything in his office, including him and his Italian loafers. "It doesn't really work with this." My hand waved in front of my wrinkled baker's uniform with the food stains and scents of my bakery.

"Oh, come on, now, you know this is all for show. It's how I get the bigwigs to give me their money. It has nothing to do with who I really am."

I winced, because my outfit was every bit of who I was. "Right."

"Now, don't take that as anything but the compliment it was meant to be. One of the things I love about you is how real you are. Your warm heart, your inquisitive mind, your dedication to improving lives . . ."

I lifted the left corner of my mouth in a half smile of denial. "You make me sound like Florence Nightingale."

"You are, in a way." He reached up and tucked a stray lock behind my ear, making all my nerves twitch. "You care about people getting to have memories of good food even though they have special needs."

I let out a nervous laugh. "Here I thought I was running a bakery."

"What's in the box?" he asked.

"I said, don't ask so I don't have to tell," I replied, my cheeks warming. "But this box might have gone missing from the Homer Everett display in the courthouse historian records."

He glanced up, freezing me with his electric-blue gaze. Suddenly he was all lawyer. "This is stolen material?"

"I heard it was borrowed."

"Without permission, if this belongs to the records department in the courthouse."

"I brought it back to you. They were going to break in agai—" I snapped my mouth closed.

"Again." He finished the word and gave me a long hard look. "What's in the box?"

I kept my mouth shut. Don't ask. Don't tell. Don't ask. Don't tell. Don't tell. Seriously, don't tell.

"Fine." He blew out a long perturbed breath. "I'll see that it gets returned. But this better be the last time you bring me something stolen—"

"Borrowed," I interrupted.

"Maybe we don't come from the same world." He raised an eyebrow.

"That's what I said." I shifted from one foot to the other. "If it helps any at all, it was done out of good intentions."

"Stealing is stealing."

"Yeah, that's what I thought you were going to say." I brushed my hands off on my pants. "Thanks for your help."

"You're welcome." He stood, and I took off toward his door. "What, no invitation to dinner?"

"I didn't want this to feel like a bribe." I waved my hand in the general direction of him and the box. "You're a good guy, Brad. I'll try to keep you out of my family's mischief from now on." I had my hand on the doorknob, this close from escape.

"Oh, no, you don't."

"What?" I asked, looking over my shoulder. "Do I need to give you a retainer or something for your time? Because I can. Have Amy bill me. You have my address."

"Billing isn't an issue, and you know it," he said. "I don't want you to leave me out of whatever your family is up to, do you understand? If you need a lawyer, you come to me, day or night. I mean it, Toni. Even if we never date, I'm here, and I want to help you."

"Why?" I was a bit taken aback. I was used to men like my ex, who were there for my help, not the other way around.

"Because you need someone to be," he said, "and I happen to be good at taking care of people."

"Oh, okay." I opened the door and shot out of there like a bat out of hell. I'd think about what he said later. After a few hours' sleep and a long hot shower. Right now, I was trying to keep Grandma out of jail.

That's what I told myself, anyway.

Doing a little investigating on my own couldn't hurt, right? I mean, if I was going to stay one step ahead of Grandma, then I needed to find out a few things about Homer Everett and how he had been connected to the poor murdered Lois Striker.

The smells of fall and Thanksgiving—you know, that particular scent of cold rain that always come with football and turkey—wafted into my home office. It was early evening and Aubrey was playing with a chew toy at my feet. Kip had relinquished his new best friend while he took a bath.

I had my computer up and was going through some old news pieces on Homer Everett. Since Oiltop celebrated him every year, there were plenty of stories about the man's greatness and achievements. I can understand why Grandma Ruth wanted to dig deeper and discover what flaws he may have had.

Instead of concentrating on Homer, I decided to do some research on the people around him. The first was Champ Rogers. Who was he? Why did his parents name him Champ? Who would have wanted the man dead in 1959? And why? Finally, was there a connection between Champ and Lois Striker? Grandma seemed to think so. But that didn't make it a fact.

I typed Champ's name into my search engine. I discovered a few small news articles. Born William "Champ" Rogers, he had been raised on a ranch in northern Oklahoma until the dust bowl had him and his family moving east to live with relatives in Pennsylvania.

Champ had gotten into trouble bootlegging and spent ten years in Leavenworth prison. Once he got out he was drafted and by 1944 was on his way to Europe. It was while he was in the army that he became friends with Homer Everett. One article asserted that he'd run interference for Homer, taking on his duties at KP or latrine. Champ made himself Homer's best friend and confidante.

Then came the infamous day when Homer had climbed out of his foxhole and run headfirst into enemy lines. He'd looked like a madman and scared the Germans so bad they'd run the other way. This cleared a path for American soldiers to stream into a small French town and save its people. And an American hero was born.

Champ and Homer went on a USO tour afterward, never seeing battle again.

"Brilliant," I muttered.

Aubrey paused from chewing one of his many chew toys.

"It all sounds so convenient, doesn't it, Aubrey? Do you think this is the secret that got Lois killed?"

The pup tilted his head as if to think over what I said. I chuckled and picked up a toy and tossed it. Aubrey chased after it and sat down to chew on the caught prize.

I turned back to my computer. Who was the force behind the war story? Homer? Champ? Was it just a story, or did it really happen? I had to learn more. I scrolled through the search engine looking for anything that might help me.

"Hey, sis." Tim stuck his head into the office. "What're you doing? Aren't you usually in bed by now?"

"What?" I glanced at the time on the computer screen. It was nearly nine P.M. "Oh, huh, I got caught up in research. What about you? Aren't you late for work?"

Tim leaned against the doorframe and crossed his arms. "It's Friday, my night off, remember?"

"Oh, right." I went back to my screen. Tim, acting like an older brother, walked in and started reading the monitor.

"'Homer Everett, famous football player and war hero, married Susan Fisher of Kansas City in 1949,'" Tim read out loud. "Why are you researching this? I thought you weren't helping Grandma Ruth and Phyllis with their little adventure."

"I'm not." I sat back and crossed my arms.

Tim hitched his hip onto the edge of my desk and gave me the look that said I couldn't deny the obvious.

"All right, fine, someone has to keep an eye on them," I said, and it sounded silly even to my own ears. "Don't you have a date or something?"

"I'm meeting Tom Thomas to work on the American Legion's float," he said. "Shouldn't you be working on your float?"

I glanced around to make sure I wasn't in earshot of Tasha or Kip. The look had me realizing that Aubrey was gone. Kip must have come in while I was deep into research. "If I never see another tissue-paper flower, it would be too soon."

Tim chuckled. "So no tissue daisies for the Prairie Port Festival?"

"No!" I made a face.

"After looking at your float, I have to agree."

"Thanks," I grumbled.

"Tell me what you're researching." He crossed his arms.

"I'm trying to figure out what it is that Grandma Ruth thinks she knows about Homer—besides her supposition that Homer murdered Champ and hid the murder weapon in the county courthouse. I thought I might find a clue to how Champ died or a motive behind whoever killed him."

"Do you really think it was Grandma's investigation that got Lois killed?" He tilted his head in thought. "It doesn't seem plausible that Champ's death had anything to do with Lois. It happened a long time ago. I mean, Hutch is what . . . nearly sixty?"

"I was getting to that part. Grandma's thinking the war hero story is not quite what they made it out to be. Champ could have been blackmailing Homer over the truth."

"Interesting—blackmail is good motive for murder."

"Right? Anyway, Grandma and Aunt Phyllis are combing through Homer's journals looking to see if he spilled the beans about lies, blackmail, and murder. What we've noticed is that he didn't write his journals—some woman did. We all know that he dictated regularly to Lois. Maybe he told her the truth and she's spent the rest of her life hiding it."

"So why come clean now?"

"Grandma told her she knew where the murder weapon was. Maybe Lois was hoping to stay ahead of the scandal. Hutch could have found out and killed Lois. After all, his father had gotten away with murder. There's no reason why Hutch couldn't."

"Would it be that easy?"

I shrugged. "I don't know. Think about it, though—the way Hutch and Aimee act, it would be the height of embarrassment if the war hero story were untrue."

"Embarrassment, yes, but is that enough to kill over?"

I shrugged. "People will kill over a carton of cigarettes. Can you imagine what would happen if it was discovered Homer was a fake war hero and a murderer? Why, Aimee wouldn't be able to show her face around town—people would not treat her nicely after the way she's treated them over the years. Her kid, Harold, would be ostracized—what mother would let that happen to her child?"

"How are you going to go about proving that theory?" Tim straightened.

"I have no idea. It's not like you can put 'murderous war hero' in a search engine and have Homer's name pop up."

CHAPTER 16

Friday morning, there was a knock at the back door of the bakery. I peeked out the peephole, my right hand ready to grab the bat. Aunt Phyllis stood outside. I unlocked the two locks on the door.

"Auntie, it's four in the morning. What are you doing here, again?"

"The same thing you're doing here," she said and stepped inside. The tip of her nose was blue and she had frost on her eyelashes. She wore her fringed leather jacket and a pair of blue pajama pants with white fluffy sheep scrawled on them in a random pattern. Her feet were covered in long, white, fluffy fur slippers with bunny ears on them.

"I'm making pies," I said, and went to close the door while she rushed over to the coffeepot.

"Open the door." Grandma Ruth's grizzled voice barreled through the cold night air. Her big, square hand slapped on the door, pushing me and it aside. The woman was strong, considering she was in her nineties. I tried not to squeal as she brushed me aside like yesterday's news.

"I told you she'd have coffee. Two pots, from the looks of it." Grandma rolled her walker forward as if it were a battering ram. Today she wore a black stocking cap and a black hoodie with the word HOODLUM painted across the chest in yellow. Under that was a pair of men's corduroy slacks in a dark green. Grandma wore Elmo slippers. Her hands and fingers were tipped with blue as well.

A quick glance at my indoor/outdoor thermometer told me it was a chilly thirty-two degrees outside. "How did you two get down here from the house?"

"Shank's mare," Grandma called over her shoulder, and took the thick mug of coffee Phyllis offered her.

"What?"

"We walked," Aunt Phyllis said as she blew on her mug and took a sip of the thick brew.

"It's too cold to be walking out there. With the wind chill it must be—"

"Freezing," Grandma interrupted. "We know. Just like Kansas weather to sucker you in with eighty-degree weather one day and slam you with frost advisories the next morning."

"It is the end of November," Phyllis pointed out. "If you wanted better weather you'd have gotten out of the Midwest."

"You walked?" I was shocked by the idea. "That had to have taken you—"

"Almost an hour with the walker." Grandma grabbed a chair and lowered herself into it. "When we planned this excursion yesterday it was still seventy degrees out. I would have gotten Bill to bring us if I'd have known it was going to be this cold."

I checked out the peephole for any lagging relatives before I locked the deadbolts. "Why did you plan this excursion?" I asked. "I know you like my gluten-free donuts, but there has to be a better reason."

"We want to know what you found out when you dropped the box off at Brad's office," Phyllis said, and sipped some more. "A few pastries wouldn't hurt now that we're here and half frozen."

I tried really hard not to roll my eyes. Leave it to my relatives to turn a grown woman into a teenager again. "I'll get you some breakfast."

They waited as I placed two white plates in front of them, added spoons and forks, then set a platter of pastries down on the table. Everything from donuts to sweet rolls to gluten-free Danish filled the platter. Half of them were day-old, but I knew Grandma wasn't picky. She loved it all.

"Do you have any butter?"

"Hold on." I went over to the small refrigerator and pulled out a stick of butter. As far as I knew, only my family put butter on sweet rolls and sticky buns. I'd never seen anyone else do it.

"I didn't find out anything returning those journals—except that taking them in the first place was a very bad idea. Now, you two tell me what you're plotting while I roll out pie dough. Please tell me you aren't thinking of doing anything else illegal. Brad was not happy when I returned the box. I don't want to lose him for a family lawyer."

I pulled a new marble rolling surface out of the freezer and put the old one inside. Marble was a great surface for pastry. Soft dough didn't stick to marble, and when the surface was cold it kept the butter from melting.

Before I could afford the marble, I had used parchment paper. Gluten-free dough tends to be a bit stickier than dough with gluten protein. Rolling it between pieces of parchment or wax paper is a good way to keep the work surface clean and not add extra "flour" to the dough.

The best part about gluten-free dough is there is no such thing as over-working it. So whenever I made a mistake, I'd simply put it all back in the bowl, remix it and start again.

I pulled a round blob of dough out of the refrigerator, placed it on the marble slab, and rolled it with my rolling pin. I turned it every few strokes to get a nice evenly round pie.

"We knew Brad wouldn't be happy. We figured you'd read the journals and we wanted your take on them," Grandma Ruth said with her mouth full of cinnamon roll.

"What do you mean?" I learned early on not to make assumptions with Grandma. She had a way of helping you feel stupid. It was always better to let her lead you through a conversation. Answer Grandma's questions with a question and you learned a lot.

"What did you think of the handwriting?" Phyllis asked. "Meghan said you thought it was female."

"You know, men our age had to have good handwriting, too, to get through school. It wasn't like kids nowadays who learn to type before they can print."

"Grandma, Kip has to learn to write as well as the next kid." I placed a pie pan on top of the dough and nodded when it fit with two inches around the sides for edging. Setting the pie pan aside, I folded the dough in half, slipped the dough off the marble and into the pie pan, then trimmed and fluted the edges.

"They don't teach cursive in schools anymore," Phyllis said.

"What?" I shook my head. "Of course they do. Everyone has to learn to write their name."

"Not on computers. All they need is a pin number." Phyllis's tone was one of disgrace. "The fine art of handwriting analysis is going to go away. Pretty soon we'll all be into numerology."

"No, I'm pretty sure they still learn cursive," I contradicted her.

"Ask Tasha, she'll tell you. If you want your kids to know cursive you'd better be prepared to teach it yourself."

"My kids will know cursive," I said. "And they'll be able to tell feminine handwriting from masculine, too. Like you taught us, Grandma."

"So you agree it was a woman who wrote those journals." Grandma laughed at how she'd tricked me. I rolled my eyes and took out another round of dough.

"Who do you think wrote the journals?" Phyllis asked. She bit into one of my apple spice donuts and closed her eyes at the taste. "These taste like real donuts."

"They are real," I said. "They're just gluten-free. And I have no idea who the author of the journals was. Whoever it was, was not only in love with Champ, but was pregnant at the beginning of 1959 about the same time Homer's wife Susan was pregnant with Hutch. Which leads me to conclude that it was Susan who wrote Homer's journals."

"Not necessarily," Grandma said as she forked up a piece of cinnamon roll and slathered it with butter. "We think Homer had a mistress and a wife."

"Really?" I couldn't let grandma know she was confirming my own suspicions so I played along.

"Yes," Grandma said with her mouth full of roll. "We went to the nursing home and talked to Mrs. Henderson, Homer's housekeeper at the time."

"Seriously? How old is she?"

"Ninety-two, but her mind is still sharp as a tack—like me." Grandma licked her fingers and picked up crumbs off the table and popped them into her mouth. "She said that Susan and Homer were married for nearly ten years before she got pregnant with Hutch. A lot of things happened that year—Champ was murdered, Susan had her first and only child, and Lois quit her job and became a friend of the family."

"What does any of that have to do with Lois's murder?" I turned and looked at Grandma, whose blue eyes twinkled. "What?"

"Everyone was surprised when Hutch came along. Susan never looked pregnant until *poof*, one day she was driving home from a Wichita hospital with a baby in her arms. Homer was deliriously happy, and back then no one was going to say anything bad about him or his wife."

"You think his mistress had Hutch and Homer took him home as his own? What about Susan? Why would she stand for such a thing?"

"Maybe Susan couldn't have kids of her own. You know how crazy some women get when it comes to wanting a baby. . . ."

I stabbed the air with my rolling pin. "You think Homer took up with a mistress to get her pregnant and to make Susan happy?"

"I think a lot of things," Grandma answered cryptically.

"Another one of Homer's secrets," Phyllis said. "Not so secret if you read between the lines in the journals. Whoever wrote them was in love with Homer, chronicling his every movement and how wonderful he was."

"She wrote about their love," I added thoughtfully. "Until something happened to make her angry. There was about six weeks of anger in the 1959 journal. Then the tone grew . . ."

"Scared," Grandma added. "That's what we thought, too."

"You think the mistress wrote the journals. That she was in love until she gave Homer her child and he abandoned her."

"Then something happened that scared her." Aunt Phyllis

turned toward me, her tone rising in excitement. "We think when Champ was murdered, the mistress saw it as a sign that even close friends couldn't cross Homer."

"She kept her head down and her secrets close after that." Grandma reached for a muffin. "Until this week, when she was going to tell me the truth."

"You think Homer's mistress was Lois?" My eyes grew wide. "Hutch is really Lois Striker's love child?" I had to work hard to contain the shiver that ran down my back.

"Have you taken a good look at Hutch's kid? Harold looks every bit of Lois in her youth. I'm surprised more people haven't put two and two together." Grandma Ruth took a bite out of a chocolate chip pumpkin muffin.

"Lois always seemed so old to me," I said and went back to rolling out pie dough. "No one my age or younger would even suspect she was anything but a strange old woman with a habit of spitting when she talked."

"Whoever killed her, killed her in the heat of passion," Grandma Ruth said. "I heard from my friends at the morgue that she had seven blows to the head. That, my darling grand-daughter, is passion."

"And Chief Blaylock knew it. He had no excuse to hold Ruth like he did. We think he wanted her to tell him what she saw when she was in the park that day. Tell him why her scooter marks were at the crime scene."

"Now, why does that make sense to me?" I muttered, and pushed another crust-filled pie plate along the stainless steel counter. I stopped, straightened and turned to face the two ladies at my table. "Grandma, did you witness a murder and keep it to yourself?"

CHAPTER 17

"Maybe I did and maybe I didn't." Grandma's chin grew stubborn and she closed her mouth tight.

"Grandma, if you saw something, you have an obligation to the police and Lois's family to tell them what you saw."

"I have an obligation to my investigation first." She crossed her arms over her ample chest. "Stumbling upon Lois's body doesn't necessarily mean I saw anything."

I grabbed the countertop to keep from beaning Grandma over the head with my rolling pin. Or maybe it was to keep my legs from buckling. Was it possible to do both?

"I saw the picture Ruth snagged on her phone," Aunt Phyllis piped in. "It was pretty awesome as far as news goes."

"Grandma took pictures?" My eyes grew wide and I turned on Phyllis. "You knew and kept this from me? Out. Out!" I waved my hands, pulled Phyllis's chair out, and practically tore the muffin from her hands. "You can't keep me in the dark and feed me nonsense, then come in here and eat my baked goods. I won't have it."

Grandma got up in a huff. Phyllis flew out of her chair as I railed at them with my rolling pin in hand. "Get out!" I pointed at the door. Aunt Phyllis unlocked the door while Grandma grabbed her walker and pushed herself through the open door as if the dogs of hell were at her feet.

I was so mad I didn't care. "Stay away from me today," I shouted. "And I'd better not hear a peep about you from the police or Brad, do you hear me?"

Grandma's mumbling was overtaken by the slamming of the back door. I twisted the locks in place and leaned against it, shaking. I slid down to the floor and hugged my knees as anger turned to laughter and then to despair.

Those two old women were going to be the death of me yet. Here I was working close to seventy hours a week between the bakery and the float. Then to be pulling them from jail—and for goodness' sake, I broke into the court-house and stole files!

All because I thought Grandma was being wrongfully accused. When it turns out she was rightfully accused. She had taken it upon herself to write about murder and madness and the end of a hero. In doing so, she had led me astray. This after I thought I was smarter than that.

No more. No more indeed. Grandma and her little inves-tigation had gone far enough. From now on I was out of it. As far as I was concerned I was strictly a baker with a busy bakery to run. Heck, I might even do something crazy and start dating again before the year of divorce was up. That was the kind of thing normal forty-year-old women did. Right?

Let's face it, no normal forty-year-old would start up a gluten-free bakery in the middle of wheat country. Or deal with an endless array of her family's wild antics. I took a deep breath, stood, and peered out the peephole. Grandma was outside the door nonchalantly smoking a cigarette. Phyllis paced beside her, puffing out her breath and beating her arms against the cold.

I rolled my eyes and opened the door. "Why didn't you two leave?"

"Where are we going to go?" Grandma asked. "It's five A.M."

Phyllis came up to the door and tried to look contrite. "Can we come back in? I was so enjoying my coffee."

"Oh, for Pete's sake." I opened the door wide and waved them through. "Don't think that you are forgiven. You are going to take those photos to the *police* this morning. Is that clear?"

"As a bell, sweetie, as a bell." Grandma rolled out her ashes, stuck the remaining bit of cigarette in her pocket, and patted me on the cheek as she came inside. Her hands were cold as ice and dry to the touch.

"Where are your gloves?" I locked the door behind them.

"I left them in my other coat." Grandma shrugged.

"You need to make sure she has a pair of gloves for every coat." Phyllis sat down and hugged her cooled coffee mug as if it would warm her.

I grabbed the pot of fresh coffee and poured them both cups full of the hot brew. "I can't believe you witnessed Lois's murder—took pictures—and didn't tell anyone!"

"Technically, I took pictures of her dead body. I have no idea who killed her—yet," Grandma said. "That's where you come in. What are your thoughts on the journals?" Grandma asked. "We know you looked through them."

"I thought you copied them." I put the coffee back on the hot plate, washed my hands, tightened my apron, and returned to rolling piecrusts.

"We did copy them," Grandma Ruth said as she slowly sat

her body down on the chair. It creaked under her and I made a mental note to make sure all the screws were tightened. "But they don't tell us what you think of them, now do they?"

"Fine, I agree with you. It does sound as if they were written by a scorned lover. I would need a copy of Lois's handwriting before I could verify if she was the mistress or if it was someone else altogether." I trimmed another pie shell and set it down on the counter. A quick count told me I had five pies ready to be filled. My recipe called for six. I planned on making pecan and chocolate chip sour cream pie.

When I first started baking I was terrible at piecrusts, until I learned that the secret to creating tender piecrust is to add a small amount of acid, such as vinegar, sour cream, or lemon juice. I varied the ingredient depending on which type of pie I made—lemon for fruit piecrusts, sour cream for cream piecrusts, and vinegar for chocolate piecrusts.

"I happen to have a sample of her handwriting in my purse." Grandma reached over and pulled her quilted bag off her walker. She dug around in it for a few minutes, then gave up and pulled out the contents one by one. "Got it!" she said, waving a scrap of paper in the air.

"Let me see." Phyllis grabbed the paper out of Grandma's hand and studied it through her glasses. "Hmmm."

"What does that mean?" Grandma bellowed.

"Did you get a recent sample or an old sample?"

"I got a recent sample, of course. What else could I get?"

"This is no good." Phyllis gave the paper back to Grandma with a sigh. "It looks like an old person wrote this."

"An old person did write this." Grandma pouted and put on her glasses to look at the writing. "Huh, you're right. You can't tell anything from this."

"Maybe if we could get ahold of some old documents from the time when she worked with Homer . . . like her property deeds," I said. "Or even something she must have signed when she was Homer's secretary.

"Public records!" Grandma and Phyllis said at the same time.

"Exactly." I couldn't help but feel a bit smug until I realized that the county records were stored in the courthouse. "Oh, no, you two are not going back inside that courthouse."

"Why not?" Grandma asked. "We're taxpayers."

"Because Chief Blaylock will throw you back in jail, that's why." I trimmed my last pie, then washed my hands again. The room was silent for a few long moments until I turned back to the women. "What?"

"You can go into the courthouse," Grandma said.

"Yes, no one knows you helped me steal that box in the first place. You didn't tell Brad, did you?"

"No."

"Then they won't suspect you at all." Aunt Phyllis nodded her head, her bright yellow bob swishing around her jawline.

"And who will watch the shop while I'm at the courthouse investigating?" I dried my hands on a towel and put them on my hips, hating where the conversation was going. "I told you, I will have nothing more to do with this investigation. As soon as the police chief gets into his office, you two are going down there, giving him those pictures on your phone, and telling him everything you know."

"He won't believe us," Grandma said, her mouth turning down into a pout.

"It's true, Toni, he won't."

"He'll believe you when you give him those pictures."

"It's only two pictures, and he'll charge me with hampering an investigation."

"Then you deserve to be charged. Trust me, it will go far easier if you turn yourself in."

"He never investigated the remodeled wall like you told him to. How could you expect him to understand this?" Grandma shrugged.

"He didn't investigate the wall because he had no reason to investigate. The man follows the law, and the law says you have to have a warrant before you can bust down walls in judge's chambers. In order to have a warrant you have to have just cause. Where is your just cause?"

"In the wall, of course." Grandma crossed her arms over her chest.

I shook my head. The woman was as stubborn as she was smart. "It will take another remodel before they can open that wall."

"That's why we've started a petition to update the courthouse next year," Aunt Phyllis said. "It's clear they need better security."

"And updated wiring," Grandma said. "They have a lot of new gadgets that need to be plugged in, you know. We can't have computers getting killed by spikes in the electricity, now can we? It is so much more energy efficient to replace the wiring and update the floor plan."

"That's thinking." I had to give them props. It wasn't like Grandma to hatch a plan and wait for it to happen. She said once you hit the age of seventy, delayed gratification went out the window. She wanted it all and she wanted it now. She could be dead tomorrow, you know.

"We thought you'd be pleased," Aunt Phyllis said. "Now, the courthouse opens at nine A.M., about the time your morning rush dies down. We'll stay here and watch the shop while you go there and . . . oh, I don't know, pay your property taxes or something?"

"My property taxes aren't due." I tilted my head. "And you can't turn yourself in and watch my bakery."

"Then you'd better hurry and make sure your divorce decree was finalized by a judge." Grandma took a sip of her coffee. "You never know when things like that could come back to haunt you."

"I signed my decree and I saw Eric sign his," I said, trying my best not to let her rattle me.

"That doesn't mean the judge signed them," Grandma pointed out. "Why, last year MariJo Johnson had to postpone her second wedding moments before it started all because there had been a mix-up in her divorce paperwork."

"There wasn't any mix-up in my divorce." I played with the edge of the terry cloth towel I had in my hands.

"Go down to the courthouse, dear," Aunt Phyllis said and picked out another donut. "You'll feel much better after you've checked that little fact out."

"We promise we'll turn ourselves in after you get a copy of Lois's handwriting—preferably from 1959," Grandma said. "Cross our hearts and hope to die."

They both crossed their hearts and held up their hands to show they weren't lying.

I blew out a deep breath. I hated that she was right. I hated that Grandma had put a little niggle of doubt in my head that would not be ignored. If I didn't go down to the courthouse myself and get a copy of Lois's signature, I wouldn't sleep another wink.

"Fine. I'll go—by myself," I clarified. "You two have to promise to never keep anything from me ever again."

"Not even a surprise party?" Grandma asked.

"Not even a surprise party," I replied.

"Not even if it's a surprise engagement party?" Aunt Phyllis asked.

"Even then," I said firmly. As far as I was concerned I was never getting married again, so the last thing I needed to worry about was spoiling some surprise party for an engagement that would never happen.

"Fine," Grandma said.

"Fine," Aunt Phyllis agreed.

"Good." I filled a new platter with pastries and set them on the table. "I'll go down to the courthouse." After all, how much trouble could I get into all by myself?

CHAPTER 18

"I heard Ruth Nathers had been spit on one time too many and ran her over with her scooter. And we all know that Ruth isn't a small thing. A woman that size in a scooter can do a lot of damage." Helen Bishop had her back to the door when I walked into the public records office. "I can't believe that Chief Blaylock let her go without so much as a slap on the wrist."

Sharon Sutton straightened at the sight of me. She nodded and pointed her finger as if I wouldn't see her telling Helen I was there. "Hi, Toni," Sharon said, a bit overly loud. "What brings you here?"

"I'm doing some research for my grandma," I replied, trying to sound like I hadn't caught her and Helen gossiping about my family. "Hi, Helen. What brings you to records?"

"Oh, Sharon and I take our breaks together every day, isn't that right, Sharon?" Helen shot me an innocent smile. "Look at that, ten thirty already. I must get back to work. Busy, you know, I'm terribly busy. Sharon, I'll see you at lunchtime?"

"Yes, I'll be ready at noon, as long as no one stays too long in records." Sharon gave me the same look her mother had when she was the head librarian at the high school. I simply smiled. The records department was supposed to be open from nine A.M. to five thirty P.M., and if it took me eight hours to find what I needed then Sharon would simply have to eat her lunch at her desk.

"Bye, Toni." Helen scooted by me. "Best of luck on your float this weekend."

"You've got a float in the Homer Everett Parade?" Sharon leaned on the counter.

"Yes, I thought it would be good to show my community support," I said. "After all, my family is one of the founding families in Oiltop."

"Huh, what an odd little fact." Sharon batted her lashes at me. "Weren't they missionaries or some such?"

"They started the college here."

"Oh, yes, of course." She straightened. "Why is it that the overeducated always end up poor as church mice? Anyway, rhetorical question." She giggled. "What brings you into the courthouse today? Here to pay your taxes?"

"My taxes aren't due yet." I sent her a small smile. "I'm here to do some research."

"My, whatever for? I thought you had your hands full with that odd little bakery of yours. What's the matter? No customers over the holiday? I can certainly understand people wanting to eat normal food with their families."

"To begin with, all the foods I bake with are natural foods. Second, if a person could eat your so-called normal food, they would, but when they can't eat normal food, they

can eat mine, and for a small moment in time feel normal."
I leaned forward into her face.

"I think you've gone a little too far, bless your heart."
Sharon leaned back and looked down her nose at me. "I
believe I have some work to do in the back."

"What do I do if I want research materials?"

She reached down and slid me a chunk of scratch paper
and a tiny pencil. "Put your request in writing and I'll get
to it when I can." With that she turned on her heel and
walked into her tiny windowed office and slammed the door.

I scowled, not at her ridiculous behavior so much as at myself
for letting her draw me into it. When I came into the room I'd
had the upper hand, but then I'd let my temper get in the way.
Blowing out a long breath, I looked at the blank sheet of paper
with words printed on the back. It was clear they were recycling
by taking old printed pieces and cutting them up for scrap.

I picked up the paper and the pencil and sat down at the
small desk in the center of the room. The setup reminded
me of the reference desk at the library. There were two desks
sitting face-to-face where people could thumb through index
cards with descriptions but no materials, and all the materials were kept behind the locked gate and in the hands of the
watchful historian.

Glancing up, I could see her watching me through the
glass. I wondered if she thought I'd give up and walk out.
She would be wrong. There was a computer screen in front
of me and I wiggled the attached mouse to unlock it from
its screensaver. It took a while for me to figure out the system. I was stubborn, and I'd be darned if I was going to let
her get me to ask for help.

Once I figured out that I had access to a listing of all
the files in the public domain, I went back to the 1950s

and skimmed for anything that might have Lois's handwriting on it. Unfortunately, a lot of the information was scanned in and not all that legible. I stuck the pencil between my teeth and used both hands to type into the search box.

First I tried looking for documents involving Homer Everett. There were too many to count. So I tried looking for documents that were assigned by Lois. That's when I hit the mother lode. It seems that from 1955 until 1959, Lois signed most of the county's documents. Wherever Homer was at that time, it wasn't in the office.

Curiously, it was Lois who signed for the courthouse remodel. Lois met with the architect on the wiring and wall placement. Why would Lois want to add a phony wall to the courthouse? What was her connection to the judge whose office was remodeled?

I pulled up the document. Judge Elmer Radcliff had held those offices during the remodel. I scribbled down his name and those of the papers authorizing the work. Interestingly enough the contractor doing the plaster work was Lois's brother, Edward Striker. There was a paper with both signatures on it. I wrote down the document number and went over to the partition and rang the bell.

Sharon didn't budge, so I rang it again and waved at her. She pretended not to notice. It was clear she did notice, as the corners of her mouth turned up in a sly smirk.

Fine. I hopped over the three-foot partition and headed toward the files.

She was out of her office faster than a bee on sugar water. "You can't be back here."

"Oh, I'm sorry, was there a sign?"

"A sign?"

"You know, one that says I can't be back here. Because I didn't see it."

"Everyone knows you can't be back here. Why, the lock on the gate should be the first clue."

"There's a lock on the gate?" I glanced over my shoulder. "Huh, so there is. My bad. Since you're here and all, would you mind getting me a photocopy of this document?"

I showed her the number I'd scrawled on the paper.

"In a minute," she huffed. "I'm in the middle of something." She turned on her heel and stormed back to her office.

"No biggie," I said to her retreating back. "I'll help myself." I turned to the wall of filing cabinets. "Now, if I were document 00-9876, where would I be? How about file cabinet 00-9700 through 00-9900?" I went over and pulled out the file drawer, only to have Sharon hightail it over and wham the door closed.

"I said you can't be back here, and if you can't be back here, you certainly can't be in the file drawers. Do I make myself clear?"

"Crystal." I gave her a little salute. "Since you're here and all, why don't you make me a photocopy of file number 00-9876? . . . Or I can do it. . . ."

"I'll do it. It's my job." I saw her eyes flash a funny green color.

"And so it is." I stepped aside, waving toward the cabinet. "Please, feel free to do your job."

"Fine." She opened the cabinet and thumbed through the files. She licked her finger and pulled out the file marked 00-9876. "What do you want a copy of the courthouse remodel project for? This was done in the 1950s. We weren't even born yet."

"I'm making a chocolate model of the courthouse for a customer," I lied through my teeth, trying not to think too hard about the fact that I'd gotten to be quite the liar and thief in the last few days. I promised myself I'd turn over a new leaf as soon as I left the courthouse.

"Oh, really? Interesting. Are you going to display it in the window of your bakery? It would be a nice draw . . . maybe for Homer Everett day. You could even do a chocolate copy of the statue." She made a photocopy of the document and handed it to me. "Oh, I'll get you a copy of the specs for the statue. It will help with your recreation."

She scurried off, looking so pleased with herself. I felt terribly guilty. I could feel my mother looking down on me with a deep frown.

"Here you go," Sharon said, any mean thoughts she might have had about me lost in her excitement over a chocolate display. "I love those cooking shows. Especially the ones where the cookie bakers recreate scenes from their hometowns. This is going to be an awesome window display. I can't wait to see it. Why, I'll call Helen right now and tell her." She touched my forearm. "You have no idea how tickled she'll be. I'm sure half the parade will want to check out the replica."

She bustled off to her office and I slunk back across the tiny gated area and out the door. I studied the paper she had given me with Homer's dimensions. A small shudder went through me. I'd better get back and get started on that replica. Knowing Sharon and Helen, everyone in town would be by to see it. And no one would forgive me if it wasn't there.

CHAPTER 19

"That's it. Lois's signature on this old document looks a lot like the handwriting in Homer's journals," Grandma said with glee. She sat in my office. The journal photocopies were spread out across my desk, where she was comparing Lois's signature from the original property map to the handwriting in the journals with her giant magnifying glass.

"I knew that handwriting analysis class would come in handy someday," Phyllis said. She stood behind Grandma and looked over her shoulder.

I would have done the same thing, but there wasn't enough room in the closet office. "You know," I said, "it's too bad Lois didn't keep her own journal. I would have loved to read it and see if she did have a child and then give it up to Homer for adoption."

"That is a brilliant idea!" Phyllis's eyes lit up.

"What is?" I could feel my eyes grow wide as I thought over the words I'd just uttered.

"Going over to Lois's house to find her journals." Grandma slapped her hand on the desktop. "I knew you were a genius. You had to be—you're my granddaughter."

"Wait!" I held out my hand like a stop sign. "Isn't Lois's house off-limits?"

"I don't see why." Grandma hauled her girth up out of my chair. She wore a pink skirt with bedazzled butterflies on it, athletic socks, and blue athletic shoes. Her tee shirt was white with a giant silver glitter butterfly across the chest. "Lois wasn't murdered there. If anything, the police checked it and then let her family know they could go in to clean out her things."

"Which reminds me," I piped up. "What did the police say when you showed them the pictures?"

Grandma shrugged. "They thanked me and moved on. They're not likely to use them. It's not like they are official photographs."

"They just thanked you and let you leave?"

"Well, we did get a lecture from the chief about tampering with a crime scene," Aunt Phyllis said.

"You should have gotten more than a lecture," I groused. "I have a feeling I will."

"Why?" Grandma asked. "You're not the boss of us."

"Fine." No sense in arguing with Grandma. "When is the funeral? Did you at least send flowers?"

"No one needs flowers when they're dead," Grandma said as she held her back in an attempt to try to stand straight. She made a loud grumbling noise and gave up, grabbing her walker and leaning into it. "You should give a person flowers while they're still alive to enjoy them."

"It's true," Aunt Phyllis said. "It's why I sent your grandma flowers when I heard of Lois's passing. It's kind of a thing with me now. I hear of someone dying and I send flowers to someone I know who's still alive. I don't know whose idea it was to send flowers to a funeral. Seriously, have you ever noticed how alike funerals and weddings are? There are flowers, seats up front for the family, someone cries, and afterward we all eat cake."

I tried to follow her train of thought, but then gave up. I stepped out of Grandma's way before I got run over. Grandma was as wicked with her walker as she was with her scooter. "Where are you going?"

"To Lois's house to find her journals," Grandma said as she rolled her walker toward the door.

"How are you going to get there? The police have your scooter and Aunt Phyllis's van." I crossed my arms over my chest and tried to gauge which door she was headed toward so I could cut her off at the pass.

"We can walk." Aunt Phyllis put a dark green beret on top of her golden bob. It sat jauntily to the side. If it were on my head it would have slid off after five seconds.

"I'm calling Bill; he'll pick us up."

"It's six o'clock in the evening," I pointed out, waving my hand toward the clock. "And completely dark out."

"And we'll be out of your hair." Grandma beamed at me. "Unless you want us to wait until nine P.M. when you close so you can go with us."

"I'm not breaking into another building in the dead of night," I stated firmly. "And neither are you."

"Is that your door bell?" Grandma asked and moved out to look through the door toward the counter. "You have a customer."

"How convenient for you." I squeezed between her and the counter to get out of my office. "Don't go anywhere. We'll talk about this when I get back."

"Hi, Jack." Grandma waved. "You're here late."

"Hey, Ruth. I'm picking up some dessert." Jack peered around me and waved at Grandma. Jack Rickman was one of my faithful customers. He stopped by rain or shine every morning to purchase two danishes and two coffees so he could have breakfast with Sarah Hogginboom, the Oiltop police dispatcher. He was fast becoming a friend and had been asking me what I thought Sarah would want for a proposal.

It was dark outside. The end of November brought shorter days. "Hi, Jack," I said. "What can I get you?"

He looked over the dwindling selection in the cabinet. "Anything except pie," he said. "Sarah's working the late shift tonight to make up for the holiday. I thought I'd take her something nice for her break."

"Aren't you the sweetest," I said. "How about chocolate-dipped cream puffs? They're filled with vanilla bean cream."

"Perfect," he said as I boxed two up in tiny individual boxes and tied them with string. There was something nice about a pink-and-white bakery box wrapped in string.

"How are the proposal ideas coming?" I asked as I rang up his order.

"I've got a date set. I told Sarah it was a charity event to raise money for the animal shelter."

"Oh, what are you going to do if anyone else wants to know more about it?" I frowned, worried that his plan would be discovered.

"I have her family in on my plan," he said. "It took a while. First I had to ask her father for her hand. Then her mother helped me come up with the idea. They're going to hide while I ask and then surprise her with a big party. We want you to cater, of course."

"Wonderful." I gave him his change. "When is the date of this elaborate affair?"

"December fifteenth," he said. "Sara's mom is supposed to e-mail you all the details."

"I'll look forward to it." I waved him good-bye and hurried back to the silent kitchen. "Grandma?"

How come those two old women could move so fast and so quiet when they were doing something they shouldn't? I rushed through the kitchen to the back door, but the back parking lot was empty. "Great."

I decided then and there that if they got arrested again I was not going to rush to their defense. Mystery aside, I needed my sleep.

Six thirty A.M. until nine A.M. was the busiest time of the morning for the bakery. Saturday was no different. I'd had a rocky night of sleep wondering about Grandma and Aunt Phyllis. I kept checking my phone, but neither had called, and this morning neither had barged in for coffee. I didn't know if that was a good thing or a bad thing.

I tried not to dwell on it as I poured coffee and boxed pastries. Meghan came in at seven to help out. Today she wore a flirty pink tulle skirt with a black top. Her regular black combat boots and torn tights had grown on me until I thought they looked cute on her when she had on the shop's pink-and-white striped apron.

Today her usual fifties-style makeup was a bit darker. Her brown gaze was a bit pensive and thoughtful.

"What is going on in your head?" I asked. "You haven't heard anything about Grandma Ruth being arrested, have you?"

"What? No."

When she didn't take the hint and bare her soul, I pushed. "You aren't leaving me, are you?"

"Huh? Oh, no, no," Meghan said, then went over to the coffee carafes and lifted them to check how full they were.

"I'm good." She left one and brought another back to refill from the perked coffee in the back.

"Are you sure?" I wiped down the countertops and did a quick check of the customers still in the bakery. "Let's go in the back." I pushed her inside the kitchen and stood near the door. "You look odd—are you okay?"

"I was wondering. . . ." Her fingers had black nail polish with pink tips. She played with the coffee carafe while I waited. Part of being a good boss was listening. "I was thinking about what Uncle Sam said yesterday about going to CI. . . ."

My heartbeat picked up a bit. "Are you wanting to start sooner than next year? Because I understand if that's what you want." Meghan was a dream come true for an employer, but she was also very good at what she did. Standing in the way of a young girl's dream was not on my to-do list. If that meant that Meghan would leave me sooner, then that's what it meant. No harm, no foul. Baker's Treat was my dream, not hers.

"No." She looked up at me through mascaraed lashes. "Sort of. I mean, CI is in like Chicago and that's a long way from Oiltop and Baker's Treat."

"But it's your dream, right? I mean, if you're getting nervous, don't. You'll meet a lot of great people there, and Chicago is a city with so much life and so much for a person your age to do—"

She made a face. "I was wondering, and it's not because I'm scared of leaving or anything like that, but I think I want to start school part-time next semester. Haysville has a decent program in creative food arts. I could get my associate's while I work here, if that's okay with you, I mean. I think that having a few years of experience here plus an associate's degree would give me a better foundation for

CI . . . and I could start in January, you know?" She looked at me, so uncertain and yet filled with hope. "I guess I want to feel like I'm getting somewhere instead of all the waiting."

"I didn't know Haysville had a cooking arts associate's. It sounds like a good deal if that's what you want."

"Yeah, they won the state battle of the chef's contest last year." Her eyes lit up. "It's, like, a really good program and I feel like I'd do better in Chicago if I could, like, work while I went to CI. An AA would mean I could be hired as a sous chef and keep developing my skills. You know?"

"Yes, I know. It sounds great. Why were you afraid to tell me about it?" I played with the damp rag in my hands.

"I was afraid you'd be disappointed in me or something. When I told my mom, she said that if I settled for Haysville, I'd never go to CI. But, like, I know I'm going to go."

"Of course you're going to go." I put my hand on her shoulder. "Your mom was probably thinking about the experiences she had in her life. Perhaps she wanted to go to someplace like Chicago, but then got sidetracked. Maybe she wasn't saying you couldn't follow your dream; maybe she was simply worried that you would repeat what happened to her."

"I'm not my mom."

"I know you're not, honey, and she knows it. What you're thinking is smart. It will be a few years before you can declare yourself independent and get more financial aid. Going to Haysville while you work here will help you get a two-year degree and years of experience. As far as I can tell it's win-win."

Her face lit up and her energy picked up. "That's what I thought. I'm so glad you agree. So, it's okay with you if I keep my job for a few years?"

"Okay with me? I'd be blessed." I hugged her. "Remember, if you change your mind at any time, let me know. Don't ever feel trapped because of me or Baker's Treat. Deal?"

"Deal."

"Good. Now, let's pack up more of these pies."

CHAPTER 20

"So, tell me, what have you learned in your investigation into Lois Striker's death?" Todd Woles, the owner of the only men's store in town, came into the kitchen carrying his coffee and sat on a stool. "Spill."

"I am not investigating Lois's death." I could feel my tone of voice rising with my frustration. My hands kept busy folding boxes for the afternoon's delivery. "Why does everyone think I am?"

"Because you solved the last murder so nicely." Todd sipped his coffee. "We are all certain you are also looking into this one."

"We?" I stopped folding and gave him a meaningful stare-down. "Who is 'we'?"

"Me and the mouse in my pocket, sweetheart," he said, ignoring my stare. "Seriously, the entire town is on pins and needles. All of the downtown stores are working on their floats for the Homer Everett parade. No one can get anything done with the specter of Lois flying over our heads." He waved his hand in the air in a sad imitation of swatting at a flying Lois.

Todd and I had met during my last investigation. We had become fast friends. When you lived in a small town like Oiltop and you were a little—how shall I put it . . . different?— you tended to find the others in town who were different and stick together.

It helped that Todd's store was down the block from mine. He had made it a habit to come down for coffee and a tasty treat on his morning break.

"I also noticed you seem to be done decorating yours."

"Yeah, I've been busy in my kitchen with orders. What do you think of ours?" I know the question sounded suspiciously as if I were fishing for a compliment. Todd had a good eye for design. If the float was a complete disaster, he would tell me.

"It could use a good edit," he admitted. "Once you do that it will look fine."

"Okay to be in public fine, or might challenge the Rotary club for first place kind of fine?" I raised an eyebrow and put my hands on my hips.

"That depends completely on the edit," Todd said.

"Right." I chewed on my bottom lip. "Would you come and edit it for me?"

"Oh my god, I thought you'd never ask." He slipped off the stool and dug his tiny calendar out of his pocket. Thumbing through the pages, he stopped on this week's page. "I can make some time today at four P.M. Shall I meet you at the fairgrounds?"

"Yes." It felt as if a huge weight were lifted off my shoulders. "I'll be there. Text me if I'm not."

"Oh, trust me, honey, if you care about your float at all,

you will find the time to meet me today." He took a small pen out of the spiral of his notebook and wrote down a note. "For the first time, I do believe your float might stand a chance of winning. For a while there I thought you would have to have a dead body on it. . . ."

"Don't say that!" I went back to my stack of dessert boxes. "I want people to come for the tasty baked goods, not for dead people."

"They would come for both if you catered funerals." Grandma Ruth came rolling in the back door, clearly pleased with herself, Aunt Phyllis behind her.

"And I'm out of here." Todd jumped off his stool and brushed a kiss on my cheek. "Thanks for the coffee and donut."

"You're welcome every day," I said as he sauntered off. Todd wore a gray Armani wool suit, pale pink shirt, and hot-pink-and-white striped tie. At first I had been afraid for him to come into the kitchen in such nice clothes, but Todd had reassured me that nothing would dare touch his Armani. I shook my head as he reached the doorway, his clothing as clean as if he'd come straight from the dry cleaner. How did he do that?

My own clothes were covered in rice flour and glazes of all flavors.

"I expect to see you at four," he said, and with his back to me, waved his hand in a good-bye gesture as he left.

"What are you doing at four?" Aunt Phyllis asked as she picked up a white mug and poured herself coffee.

"Todd has agreed to come over and edit my float so that I have a chance of winning."

"Why would he do that? Doesn't the men's store have a float?"

"Not this year." I puffed out a breath, sending my bangs flying out of my eyes. "Todd promised to help me instead."

"Be careful." Grandma scowled. "That man has an agenda."

"What?" I scoffed. "Todd does not have an agenda. He's a good friend. I won't have you talking about him like that."

"Agenda or no agenda"—Aunt Phyllis sat down at the table with a good bit of groan and tasted her coffee—"you need help with your float."

"You'd better not edit me out of it." Grandma Ruth sat down with a great deal of slow-motion effort. "I've been looking forward to it all year."

"I won't edit you out," I said, a bit perturbed. "As long as you stay out of jail. Where have you two been since I spoke to you last night? I was up all night expecting a call from the police."

"You'll be happy to know we did not break into Lois Striker's place," Aunt Phyllis announced.

"Wonderful," I said. "So, what, you slept in this morning? Did you take Bill out to breakfast? Stop at the Y for swim class? Take those journals to Chief Blaylock?"

"No, no, no, and hell no." Grandma pulled a paper napkin out of the holder on the table and set it down in front of her. She snatched one of the day-old donuts off the rack behind her. "Chief Blaylock has no idea how to conduct an investigation. He'd take these journals and lock them up—not read them."

"Besides, we need them to compare to Lois's diary." Phyllis pulled a tattered book out of her tan suede shoulder bag. She leaned back and opened the pages.

"I thought you said you didn't break into Lois's house." I walked over to see what the book was and possibly discern where she got it.

"We didn't," Grandma said with her mouth full of donut. "Didn't have to. The door was open."

"Grandma! Don't tell me you walked into someone's house and went through her things."

"She's dead—what does she care?" Grandma shrugged and licked her finger, then picked up the crumbs from the table and ate them.

"It's not right." I put my hands on my hips and glared at them both. "You both know better than that."

"It's okay, dear." Aunt Phyllis patted my arm. "Someone else broke in first. As far as we were concerned, we were looking to see if anyone was hurt or bleeding."

"That's right." Grandma nodded and gave me her most pious look. "We happened to find the diary while we were ensuring no one was hurt."

"Hmmm." I tightened my mouth into a single line. "Where was the diary?"

"In a secret cubby between her bathtub and the closet wall." Aunt Phyllis was back into the book, thumbing through the pages.

"Oh, my . . ." I shook my head and didn't finish the thought. Those two were hopeless.

"No worries, we were wearing gloves," Aunt Phyllis said absently as she slowed her page-turning.

"And we called the police." Grandma snagged another donut. "Barney Fife came and took over the scene."

"Stop calling him that."

Grandma shrugged. "Why? You have to agree that he is a bit of a self-important nitwit."

"Because someday you are going to call him that to his face and he's going to press charges for slander."

"Not a jury in the world would convict me," Grandma said and defiantly bit into another donut. This one was apple spice with maple frosting.

"Wow, listen to this." Aunt Phyllis adjusted her reading glasses and lifted the book to eye level. "November tenth: That nosy Ruth is investigating again. Why can't people just leave us alone?"

"Us?" Grandma asked.

I leaned over to see the book. "What year is that? For all we know it was written ten years ago and has nothing to do with her murder."

"It's this year." Aunt Phyllis put her finger on the page and closed the book to show me the year embossed on the cover. "It seems Lois was a regular journal writer. She has each day noted. This is the first one that doesn't list what she ate and who she talked to that day."

I frowned. "But why would she hide her journal and not write in it the last two days of her life?"

"The better question to ask is who broke into her house and what they wanted." Grandma Ruth sat back in her chair. "Why did she hide this journal and not the other twenty piled on her bedroom floor?"

"Right." Aunt Phyllis nodded. "This was the only journal in her hidey-hole. Whoever broke in must have been looking for it." She glanced at me. "The place was tossed. There was stuff everywhere. The pictures were even crooked, as if they knew about her hidey-hole and were looking for it."

"Wait, her house was not only broken into but ransacked? And you two waltzed in and found her stashed diary?" I was aghast. "Whoever broke in could have still been inside."

"We were careful," Aunt Phyllis said.

"Plus, we called the cops," Grandma said.

"After you found her cubbyhole," I pointed out and shook my head. "You both could have been hurt or worse. Neither of you do me any good if you're dead."

"Worried about your float?" Grandma asked. "I'm sure your Lucy would take my place should I die."

"I told you, Lucy is leaving for New York tonight so that she will be there to watch the Macy's parade." I snatched the diary out of Aunt Phyllis's hands.

"Hey!"

I flipped through the pages. "How do you know this wasn't planted?"

"For us to find?" Grandma narrowed her blue eyes. "Who would do that?"

"Better yet, who would know we were going to be there to look?"

"Maybe it wasn't hidden for you, but for whoever should be investigating," I said and thumbed through the pages. "Is there anything in here that no one else would know?"

"How would we know that?" Grandma asked.

"Exactly," I said. "Which is why you should have turned this straight in to the cops. We have no idea if this is even really written by Lois. It could have been planted."

"Yes, we do." Aunt Phyllis pulled out Grandma's sample of Lois's handwriting as an old woman. "The handwriting is a match. See?" She held up the papers.

I took one and placed it on the book next to the carefully written entry for October thirtieth of this year. The handwriting was a little shaky, but Phyllis was right. It was a dead-on match.

"Okay, let's just say that Lois wrote this current journal. What exactly does that mean?" I asked and sat down on one of the stools in the kitchen.

"It means that Lois was a regular journaler. Not only did she write her own journal but she wrote Homer's as well. We all read where the woman who wrote Homer's journal had

Homer's child," Grandma said smugly. "Which means that Hutch is Lois and Homer's child, not Homer and Susan's."

"That explains why she stuck around," Aunt Phyllis said and sipped her coffee. "She wanted to be close to her love child."

"Wait, Homer's wife knew Hutch was Homer and Lois's love child when she adopted him. Why did she tolerate Lois's presence in town?" I asked.

"Good question," Grandma said. "Why would you tolerate Lois's presence in town?"

"Maybe she didn't," I suggested.

"Susan's been dead for ten years," Aunt Phyllis said. "She couldn't have killed Lois, my dear." She patted me on the knee.

My head hurt. Small-town politics were crazy and part of the reason I'd run off to Chicago in the first place. Sure, Chicago was notorious for its politics and gangsters, but at least they were honest about it. People in Oiltop acted as if they were simple small-town people with Midwestern values, and all the while they were scheming in the background.

"So wait, let's start from the beginning." I rubbed my temple. "Grandma, you were investigating Homer Everett, right?"

"Yes, dear." Grandma snatched a third donut.

"And you suspected him of murdering his best friend, Champ Rogers."

"Yes," Grandma said. "We know that Champ was killed and that no one ever found the murder weapon. We also know that during that time the courthouse was mysteriously renovated so that there is space between the walls in the judge's chambers.

"I merely surmised that Homer was involved and that Lois knew the truth." Grandma leaned back in her chair.

"When you went to Lois with your suspicions, she denied them," I said.

"Of course she did." Grandma ran her hand over the table. "I expected her to, which is why I had a private investigator follow her."

"You what?" I straightened up. "Who is the private investigator, and why am I only now learning about him?"

"You mean her," Grandma said. "The private investigator is a her."

"Grandma, why are you investigating if you hired a private investigator?" I rubbed my temples.

"Because I don't want her to have all the fun." Grandma shrugged.

"Do you hear yourself?" I said. "You sound as crazy as this scheme."

"Oh, come on, you have to admit you're hooked. You want to find out who killed Lois, and why, as badly as we do."

"What I want"—I slipped off the stool and put the diary on a high shelf—"is to know that you two are safe. Why don't you go to the senior center and play cards or go swimming at the Y? Something safe and normal for people your age?"

"Old people are boring." Grandma put her hands on her hips.

"Besides, the private investigator had to go home for the holiday." Aunt Phyllis sipped her coffee.

"Who is she?" I asked. "Can I hire her to keep an eye on you two and report back the minute you decide to do something foolish?"

"Hi, guys." Meghan walked in the back door, the wind ruffling her fauxhawk. "What's up?"

"My granddaughter is being a stick in the mud," Grandma muttered, and dragged herself to a standing position. "I'm going home and taking a nap."

"I'll drive you," Meghan offered and handed Grandma her walker. "I've got deliveries in your neighborhood anyway."

"Fine." Grandma took in a deep breath and let it out slowly as she leaned on her walker. "I'll go out to the van and wait."

"Oh, stop being so dramatic," I said and opened the back door for her. "You know I'm only looking out for your best interests. Someone is out there killing old ladies. I don't want you to be next." I kissed her dry cheek. "I love you."

"Of course you do," she replied. "I wouldn't have to do this if you investigated, you know. . . ."

I didn't dignify that comment with a response.

Aunt Phyllis pulled her shoulder bag over her head and followed Grandma out. "I'll keep an eye on her," she said. "It will give you time to figure out who killed Lois."

"I don't—" I closed my mouth. After a while, my protests started to sound as foolish as Grandma's schemes.

CHAPTER 21

"Get a big trash bag," Todd ordered as he eyed my flowered float.

"Is it that bad?" I pulled a large black bag from the box that sat on the shelf near the door to the 4-H building where the floats were being stored.

"Hmm, like I said, it needs to be edited." Todd walked around it. "Did you design this?"

"Yes?"

"It does have a certain sensibility about it." He cupped one elbow and drummed his fingers on his chin.

"Can you make it look like it can compete with that?" I waved at the Elks club float Brad had been working on.

"Only if I tore it all down and started over from scratch," Todd commented. "Right now it looks like a tissue craft project gone bad."

"I was afraid of that." I dropped my shoulders in defeat. "Tell me what to do."

"Let's start by removing every other flower." Todd jumped up on the float. He had taken off his suit coat and tie and rolled up his pink shirtsleeves.

I started on the front left and picked off every other flower, carefully tossing the crumpled tissue in the bag. I had over two hundred dollars in tissue invested in the project. Maybe I could give the flowers away in a promotion of some sort.

The 4-H building was empty except for Todd and me. The parked trailers looked like an odd flotilla of Homer Everett statues, as if he himself were a one-man army. I suppose you had to be an Oiltop native to truly understand.

"You've lived in Oiltop your entire life, right?" I asked.

"Yes. . . ." Todd didn't stop removing things from my float. The bag was filling up fast.

"What do you know about Homer Everett—I mean besides the fact that he was a war hero and a football hero?" I handed him the bag.

"He was mayor of Oiltop for like twelve years," Todd said. "Everyone, including my grandmother, was half in love with him."

"Everyone?"

"Yes, everyone." Todd straightened. "You should ask your grandmother. She might have fancied him, too."

"Grandma Ruth thinks he was a murderer."

"What?"

"She's been investigating the possibility that Homer killed his best friend, Champ Rogers." I handed him the bag and went to get another off the shelf. "We just can't figure out why yet."

"No. Not *the* Homer, hero of my Grandma's stories. She made him out to be some kind of caped crusader when I was growing up." Todd tied up the first full bag. "There has to be some kind of misunderstanding. Besides, if Homer did kill Champ, wouldn't he have told someone? There are too many heroic stories about him for him to have died without admitting the truth."

"Didn't he die of a sudden massive heart attack in the Chamber of Commerce parking lot?" I continued to pull off tissue paper flowers.

"Right. I suppose there wasn't time for a deathbed confession." Todd attacked Grandma Ruth's throne with a tad too much glee. "I heard he kept detailed journals. If that is true, then he would have felt compelled to write it in his journals."

"That's what Grandma Ruth thought. She spent the last two weeks attempting to go through his journals for clues. It was an arduous project. The historical society will only let you go through a few pages at a time—with white gloves. So Grandma Ruth contacted Lois Striker. You see, Lois was Homer's secretary back in the day. She would know things that might not have been written in the journals."

"But Lois was killed last week." Todd stood on the float in a pile of tissue paper flowers and streamers that came up to his knees.

"Exactly." I shoveled the pile into the new bag I held.

"Wait, you think that someone killed Lois so she wouldn't tell what she knew about Homer?"

"Yes."

"Who would do that?"

"That is what we're trying to figure out." I glanced over the float. It looked bare and . . . better, much better.

Todd did some magic to Grandma Ruth's sitting area. It looked good—dare I say, almost professionally designed. For the first time I felt as if the float might actually be a finalist in the parade. That is, if Hutch Everett was fair in his judgment.

Todd jumped off the trailer and walked the circumference. "Maybe whoever killed Champ wanted everyone to think it was Homer. With Lois dead, no one would ever know. It would become a cover-up and people would write conspiracy books on the possibility of what happened without ever knowing the facts."

"Really? People would write conspiracy books on this? Why would anyone care about an unsolved murder in a small Kansas town?"

"Oh, honey." He shook his head. "There are true crime mystery fans everywhere. It's a huge genre. Seriously, don't you read?"

I drew my eyebrows together. "Who has time to read? I spend as much time as I can on my business, and then there's my family—"

"And your own investigations." He waggled one eyebrow at me.

I pursed my lips and gave him the stink eye. "I am not an investigator. I'm a baker."

"Riiight." He grinned at me and winked. "Seriously, if you read true crime you might learn a thing or two on how mysteries are solved. That could really help you in your investigations."

"I am not . . . Oh, never mind." I turned my attention back to the float. "Wow, it looks fantastic." I walked the perimeter, amazed at what he had done. "You are good."

"Thank you."

"No, seriously, you are really good. You should do this kind of thing for a living."

"I do, only instead of floats, I edit men, and trust me, honey, they are as bad as, if not worse than, your float."

I flung my arms around him and gave him a big hug. "Thank you, thank you!" I had a chance of being noticed by the parade committee. If I could make the final three floats I would be able to put a plaque in my store window. That meant that the town would take me seriously and expect even better next year.

That thought made me pause. I held Todd out at arm's length. "I'm hiring you to help with next year's float. I'll pay whatever you ask."

He laughed. "Don't say that, sweetie. I cost more than you can imagine. Let's agree that I will be on your float committee for next year. Okay?"

"Okay." I gave him a quick hug and then picked up the two giant black trash bags. "Do you have a need for pink tissue paper flowers?"

He gave me a look that was easily interpreted as not only *no*, but *hell no*. I laughed and raised the bags up. "You could use the tissue to pack clothes in bags."

"Honey, no cowboy will come into the men's store if I start packing their items in hot pink tissue paper."

"Oh, true." The door to the 4-H building opened and Hutch Everett and his wife walked into the building. Hutch was a tall, older gentleman with the jowl and belly of a man who sat behind a desk most of his life. He had brown eyes and gray hair that had thinned on top. He solved the thinning by combing it straight back. Not that it was a bad comb-over. It was clear that he had a good stylist who showed him what to do with thinning hair.

He wore the uniform of a professional: black dress pants, a pale blue shirt, and a red tie. Funny how men wore their politics around their necks these days: red ties for staunch Republicans and blue ties for Democrats.

His wife, Aimee, wore a neat little suit in maroon tweed with a crisp white shirt that had a Peter Pan collar. Her champagne-blonde hair was twisted up in a French knot. She held her finger to her nose as if she was afraid to breathe the air. I have no idea why. There wasn't anyone but Todd and me inside.

One thing I did notice as they came closer was the fact that Hutch's eyes were puffy and rimmed with red. Then I realized that, if our speculation was correct, Lois was his birth mother, and I remembered how hard it was when my mom had passed away.

I went over to where they stood studying the Elks club float. "Hi, Mr. Everett, Mrs. Everett." I held out my hand. "I'm Toni Holmes. I own the Baker's Treat bakery on Main."

"Yes, I know." He took my hand and gave me a proper firm shake. Aimee simply sent me a small smile and waved off my hand.

"I take it you're sponsoring a float this year?" Hutch's voice was at once quiet yet commanding.

"Yes." I waved in the direction of my pink-and-white decorations. "I think it's important to be part of the community."

"All the monies raised from the parade go to the free clinic in the hospital's west wing." His mouth moved into a brief smile. "There are so many underserved children and single moms in the area."

Perfect. He had led me right into the subject I wanted to talk about. Was he adopted? Was Lois his birth mother? Maybe if I hinted around the subject he'd tell me the truth. "So true. I heard you are head of the parade committee. Something I've always wondered—is serving children and single women a passion of yours or your father's?"

Aimee let out a small sound, her eyes alight with anger for a brief second before her superior expression returned to place. Hutch studied me for a moment and my heart pounded heavily in my chest. Did I overstep my bounds? Will he toss my float out of the running?

"In my youth, adoptions were closed," he said quietly. "Many people were hurt, and there was a huge stigma involved for young women who were not married but in the family way. I'm glad things have changed. I'm also glad the proceeds of the parade go toward helping those in need, which is the right thing to do no matter what your passion is. That said, I still support the celebration of my father and all he did for the community of Oiltop."

"Oh, of course, of course, wow—closed adoption. Sure glad that's changed. It is so important to know your family roots now, what with so many diseases having genetic links."

"Exactly. I know my genetic links, Ms. Holmes." He crossed his arms. "As does everyone in this room. It's a privilege to know your family history, and one of many reasons we promote open adoption."

The look in his eye was suddenly cold and predatory. I had to work at not taking a step back.

"So, um, speaking of family history—it doesn't bother you that your father's journals are available for anyone to read?"

"No, why would it?"

"Every family has its secrets." I sent him an innocent smile. "I'm not sure I would want my father's journals on display for the entire town to read. You are a brave and generous man. I'll be sure and tell my grandmother to put that in the article she's writing about your father. Do you want me to have her send you a copy before it's published?"

"No need. Your grandmother can't possibly say anything about our family that isn't already common knowledge. If she can, and if she has proof to back it up, then good for her. Do pass on to her that my lawyer will be reading her article closely."

"Oh, right." I tried to smile and made a point of looking at my watch. "Speaking of my grandmother, I have to go. She and my aunt are coming for dinner. It was nice to meet you both."

"Have a good evening, Ms. Holmes."

"Come down to the bakery sometime," I offered. "We have the best coffee in town, and the baked goods are tasty."

"We'll do that," he said with an implied *not*.

I picked up my trash and bustled off, my hands full of

bags. Todd waited for me by the door. He pushed the glass open and let me through first.

As soon as the doors closed behind us, Todd spoke up. "What did you say to them? They did not look happy."

"I asked him if single mothers were a passion of his."

Todd opened the back of my white paneled van for me. "That certainly took guts. What did he say?"

I tossed the bags into the back and closed the doors. The beep from my key chain told the world that the doors had been unlocked. Todd walked me to my van door. "He said his passion came from the closed adoptions of his age, and that knowing your genetics is a privilege. Although with my family, I'm not so sure that's true."

"So he didn't mention that he knew he was adopted?"

"Oh, he knew he was adopted, all right." I climbed into the driver's seat.

"But did he come out and confirm your suspicions?"

"No."

"Oh."

I started up the van and glanced around to see if anyone but Todd was there. The parking lot was empty except for my van, Todd's Lexus, and a Bentley that I had to assume belonged to Hutch Everett. "But his eyes were red-rimmed and puffy. I've seen that look before, and it doesn't come from alcohol. It comes from grief."

"Then common knowledge or not . . ."

"Lois Striker has to be Hutch Everett's birth mother. Or at the very least a surrogate. No one grieves like that unless someone close to them dies, and if Lois were simply Homer's secretary, there would be no need for tears."

CHAPTER 22

"You tried to get Hutch Everett to admit he wasn't Susan Everett's son?" Tasha stopped brushing her hair and stared at me. "What were you thinking?"

I fell back on her quilt-covered bed and stared at the sloped ceiling of my family home. "I don't know," I answered honestly. "I guess I was thinking that he might help me solve this mystery so that Grandma Ruth would stop getting arrested and I can sleep at night." I rolled onto my stomach and looked at Tasha. "I can't grow my business if I'm constantly trying to keep her out of jail."

Tasha sat at a white-painted antique vanity. Her makeup and perfume were neatly arranged in silver containers. The bedroom was part of the suite built in what used to be the attic of the homestead. When she moved in with me, she'd decorated it with a wrought iron bed, colorful rag rugs, and white linen curtains. There was little room for a closet, so she had put shelves and a clothing rack in the space under the eaves.

"You think someone is going to tell you something so personal when they first meet you? That's crazy, and a bit rude." She turned back and continued getting ready. Tasha had her first formal date with Officer Bright. *Calvin,* she told me, *call him Calvin.* It was difficult. He would always be Officer Bright to me.

I wasn't at all sure it was good to see her dating again. Unlike me, Tasha was a woman on a mission in search of a good man. The last man she'd dated had tried to kill us both. I think that's why she was attracted to Officer—Calvin. His occupation alone made her feel safe, and she deserved that. We all deserve to feel there is someone between us and the harsh world.

"What?"

"I'm glad you decided to see Off—I mean, Calvin. He seems like a nice guy."

"Yes, so did the last two men I dated," Tasha said. "At this point in my life I have to assume the worst of every man I date."

I drew my eyebrows into a *V.* "Then why date?"

She shrugged and turned to the mirror to apply her lipstick. "I am a romantic. I still believe that there is someone out there for me. Someone who will love me and Kip. Someone who will take care of me while I take care of everyone else."

I closed my eyes with a sigh. "You're better than me, because I don't believe anymore."

"What about Brad? He seems pretty reliable. I mean, he always comes when you call and has gotten you and your family out of some tight situations."

"He's my lawyer. He bills me two hundred dollars an hour. At that price, I'd come when someone called, too."

"Then there's Sam. He takes care of his elderly mother. He watches out for Meghan, and he's not even related to her. Isn't he her father's best friend?"

Images of both well-dressed, wealthy Brad and rugged handyman/cowboy Sam filled my head. I popped my eyes open to banish them. "Do I want a man that involved with his family? Or his friend's family? I mean, won't they always come first? I can't imagine what would happen if I needed something at the same time they did—or worse, I needed something they didn't support."

"You are a negative one, aren't you?" She stood and eyed her outfit in the vanity mirror.

"I've been trained by the best," I said and got up. "You look lovely. Very date-night." She did. Tasha had on a soft pink wrap dress made of jersey that hugged her curves in all the right places. She wore three-inch pumps that showed off her slender legs. Her blonde hair fell in soft waves around her shoulders.

"Are you going to be okay watching Kip tonight?" she asked.

"Sure, he'll spend all night with the puppy anyway." The "puppy" seemed to double in size every day. No one had reported a missing pet. If the dog remained unclaimed by Friday, he would be taken to the vet for shots and Aubrey would officially become part of the clan.

"It is probably foolish to start dating around the holidays," Tasha mused. "You have all those awkward family get-togethers, and then Christmas presents. Maybe I should cancel."

"Oh, no, you don't." I turned her toward her bedroom door. "You said yes. You go. Have a good time. You have my cell number on your phone. Feel free to call me anytime."

"I will," she said as I pushed her out the door and into

the small sitting room between the two bedrooms. My father had turned the attic into a living suite, thinking that my grandmother could live upstairs when the time came for her to let go of her home. He'd built the two rooms with a sitting area that included a small kitchenette and a full bath.

But Grandma had had her own ideas and instead had moved lock, stock, and barrel into the senior assisted-living apartments in town. "Don't want to be in any grown person's way," she'd said.

Then Dad had died and Mom had gotten cancer. Now I lived in the big old family home. It was nice to have Tasha and Kip living in the suite. That way, when family stopped by, I only had the three third-floor bedrooms. The two bedrooms on the second floor were really the giant master bedroom with en suite bath and the smaller ten-by-ten-foot study. It had been a nursery when I was a child, but with only me in the master suite, a study made more sense. I'd ripped off the nursery-rhyme paper and painted it a soft cream with gold trim. I had created a window seat that ran the entire length of the turreted windows. Then I added books and games. It made for a nice place to sit on a rainy day and look out and dream.

Tonight I had set up a game of chess. Kip liked routine. Tasha usually worked on Friday and Saturday night. When she did, I would watch Kip for her. We would have dinner and do the dishes, and then it would be bath time. The incentive for Kip to get clean was that once he passed inspection we would go into the study and play board games of his choosing until the cuckoo clock went *cuckoo* and the little dancers came out and danced. Kip was fascinated by the clock, as I was at his age. It had been in the family ever since my great-uncle had brought it home from his time in Germany during World War Two.

I followed Tasha down the staircase and into the foyer. The doorbell rang and I rushed ahead of her to open it. Officer Bright stood there. He was dressed in dark-wash jeans, polished cowboy boots, a white polo shirt, and a brown tweed jacket. His blonde hair was combed across his forehead.

"Hello," I said.

"Hi, is Tasha ready?" He stood there with his hat in hand and looked as uncomfortable as a sixteen-year-old on his first date.

"Sure, come on in." I waved him in. Kip came running down the stairs, the puppy following on his heels until they were a blur of arms and legs. Both boy and dog attacked Tasha at the same time.

"Mommy, are you leaving already?"

Ba-roo, ba-roo. The puppy jumped onto her dress. She reached down and roughed up the dog's head and leaned over to kiss Kip. "Yes, I'm going to have dinner with Officer Bright. We're going to a movie after and will be home late. So you take good care of Aubrey and Auntie Toni, okay?"

"Okay," Kip said solemnly.

"Come on." I held out my hand to the boy. "I need you to rescue me from some cookies in the kitchen."

"You do?" He veed his eyebrows. "Why? Cookies can't do anything to you."

"Yes, they can." I was as solemn as he was. "I'm allergic to gluten, you know. So if I eat too much, I could get very sick and possibly die."

"So could I," Kip reminded me.

"What then should we do with those cookies?" I asked him.

He cupped his elbow and drummed his fingers on his chin. "Maybe we can feed them to Aubrey."

"They have chocolate chips in them," I pointed out. "Dogs should not eat chocolate. It can make them very sick."

"Really?"

"Really," I nodded.

"I know," he said as Officer Bright took Tasha's dress coat from her and helped her into it. "We can take them to Mrs. Dorsky. She likes cookies."

"She does?" I tilted my head.

"Yes, she told me so one time. And she doesn't have any allergies like we do," he added.

"Good idea," I said. "Why don't you go into the kitchen and package up the six chocolate chip cookies left over from dinner?"

"Okay," he said. "Bye, mommy." He kissed her cheek and rushed off to the kitchen. The puppy followed at his heels, barking.

"You have regular cookies in your kitchen?" Tasha asked.

"Oh, no, they're gluten-free. But I know he likes to pretend. Besides, Mrs. Dorsky wouldn't take them if she knew they were gluten-free."

"So you let my little boy lie to her?" Tasha put her hands on her hips in mock anger.

"Certainly. If I lied to her she'd know." I pushed the front door open. "Go have fun, kids." I waved my hand toward the porch. "Don't stay out past curfew and don't do anything I wouldn't do."

"Good night, Toni," Officer Bright said as he stepped out.

"Good night, freak." Tasha gave me a quick hug. "Don't let him stay up late. He'll be hell to deal with tomorrow."

"Nine P.M., and we're both going to be upstairs in our jammies with a good book."

"You lead such an exciting life." Tasha took Calvin's arm. "Emergency numbers are—"

"On the fridge. I know. Go. Have fun." I shooed her off the porch and watched as Calvin opened the door for her and held it as she got into his blue sedan. He closed it and moved around the front of the car while I waved good night.

I certainly hoped Tasha had fun. She deserved it. No one was as dedicated to their kid as Tasha. Kip had Asperger's and could be a handful when he was having a bad day. Tasha took it in stride. She kept up a careful routine, rarely straying from a schedule that revolved around Kip's life. It was good for her to get out of it every now and then.

Their living with me meant I could watch Kip and help maintain his routine. In return, Tasha and Kip kept me grounded. Without them I wouldn't know what day it was, and my whole life could easily become all about the bakery. If there was one thing I learned from my dead marriage, it was that nothing, no matter how much you loved it, should ever take up your entire life. Because if you were to lose it, you'd look up and wonder who you were and what the heck you were supposed to do now.

CHAPTER 23

Sunday night I was hard at work creating cranberry mince tarts when the door to the bakery jingled. I had had a mirror system installed last month that allowed me to see whoever walked in. It wasn't much security, but it was enough so that I could grab a baseball bat and get the heck out. Sometimes time was the best defense when faced with a possible threat.

Not that I needed to worry. This time it was only Sam coming in the bakery door. The man had a bad habit of arriving close to closing time. He swore it was because he was doing a remodel in the area and wanted a late-night snack. But I suspected he worried about my ability to see myself home in one piece. Especially with it growing dark around four P.M. and there having been yet another unsolved murder in Oiltop.

"I'll be right out. Help yourself to coffee," I called. "The pot's fresh."

"Did you make this coffee fresh just for me?" He picked up the pot and raised it into the mirror so I could see the smile on his handsome face.

"Of course not," I called. "I made it for the last-minute shoppers." I finished crimping the piecrust tops on the small tarts and put them in the top oven. Then I washed my hands and wiped them on a hand towel as I went out to greet Sam. "There are some fresh orange cranberry scones. Do you want one?"

"Sure." He turned one of the café's black wrought iron chairs around and sat down on it so that his belt buckle was framed. He wore tight-fitting jeans, black cowboy boots with dust and paint on them, a plaid shirt with a snap front that looked like it would be easy to pop open, and a suede coat with a shearling liner. His cowboy hat sat on the table beside him. His dark hair was pushed to the side and his large square hands cupped the white mug of steaming coffee with great care.

He was a picture-perfect fall treat and my mouth was dry as toast. I pretended that my knees were not weak and my hands did not tremble as I dished up two scones. There was nothing delicate about my scones. I made them large for the men and added tiny cups of cinnamon butter to the plate.

I handed him the plate and turned back to get something for myself when he snagged my arm. "What?" I asked.

"I heard that Tasha was out with Calvin Bright last night."

"Yes, she was."

"Is she happy?"

I was warmed by his concern. "I think so, yes."

"So, she's over the incident last month and ready to date."

"Yes." My heart skipped a beat and I wondered if I read him wrong. If he was interested in Tasha—after all, she was so pretty . . .

His thumb caressed my arm. "Are you?"

"Am I what?"

"Ready to date again?" This last sentence was filled with smoke and meaning.

I told myself to take a deep breath. I told myself to count to ten. Think before I act. That's the drill. In the past, I always acted before I thought, then regretted it. This time I would remember to—

"Date?"

His smile was crooked and fast as lightning. "Dinner, maybe a movie, maybe a trip out to the spillway . . ."

Oh man.

The bakery door jangled open and a cold wind blew Phyllis inside. Her cheeks and nose were red and her eyes stark against her pale skin. "Toni, come quick, it's Ruth. She's hurt."

My heart leapt into my throat and I tore out after Aunt Phyllis.

CHAPTER 24

"What happened?" I managed to get the words out as I scrambled along beside Phyllis. I know I mentioned that she was fast for an older woman, but she was also spry. I was having trouble keeping up, and I had adrenaline going for me. "Where is she?"

"She fell." Phyllis's expression was grim. "She's in the town square."

"I'll call 911." Sam took his phone off his belt. "Where is she? I'll point the way."

"Near the statue of Homer Everett."

Phyllis could race-walk a marathoner. She shot out ahead of me. I turned to see Sam dialing his cell phone and wished that I had thought to call.

"Go," he said and waved me on.

He didn't have to tell me twice. I raced down the two blocks to Central Street and then the three blocks to the courthouse and town square. Phyllis, a glimmer of bright blonde hair in the streetlights, and I broke out into a jog.

There was a stitch in my side, and my heart pounded in my throat. I followed her around the statue to where the crime-scene tape used to be. There was Grandma Ruth sprawled out on the ground, her arms and legs at awkward angles.

"Grandma!" I rushed to her side and tried to remember basic first aid. Feel for a pulse—or was it check for breathing first? Darn it. I knelt down beside her. Her eyes were closed and her mouth open, her jaw slack. I put my cheek close to her mouth.

"Is she breathing?"

"I can't tell." I gently placed my fingers on her neck and held my breath. There was a pulse. It was weak but it was there. "She has a pulse." I glanced at Phyllis and realized that I didn't have my coat, but Aunt Phyllis had hers. "Give me your coat."

She stripped off the heavy suede jacket with the long fringe on the arms and handed it to me. I draped it over Grandma to keep her warm. Then I placed my cheek near her mouth again. "She's breathing, but barely. What happened?"

"We came back to go over the crime scene again."

"In the dark?"

"We had flashlights like they do on CSI." Aunt Phyllis rubbed her arms to ward off the chilled wind. Meanwhile I looked for bleeding. Grandma's right arm was at a terrible angle, clearly broken. Her fingers were swollen and purple. "Ruth thought she saw something on the statue. She climbed up to get a closer look, but the next thing I knew she was falling through the air. I swear it was the longest fall. I couldn't catch her." Aunt Phyllis's eyes teared up. "If I had tried to catch her, one of us would be dead."

"How high was she?" I glanced at the statue some five feet away. It stood on a three-foot-tall pedestal. The artist had taken creative liberty with Homer Everett's height. The statue was at least ten feet tall.

"I'm not sure. She was reaching behind his left ear when she slipped." Phyllis's teeth chattered.

"The ambulance is on its way," Sam said and took off his coat and put it over Phyllis's shoulders. "Here, put this on before you freeze to death." He knelt down beside me. "How bad is it?"

"Her arm is broken," I said, "and her ankle is swollen, so it may be broken, too. She's breathing and her heart is weak but she isn't conscious."

Sam checked Grandma over as well. There was little we could do but wait for the ambulance. The last thing we wanted was to move her and possibly hurt her worse. He shook her gently. "Ruth, can you hear me? It's Sam Greenbaum. Ruth?"

"She's not answering." Phyllis's mouth was a tight line, and there was worry in her eyes.

I checked Grandma's hands for circulation and noticed a slick clear substance on them. I rubbed some onto my fingers. "It feels like someone greased her hands." I looked at Phyllis. "Did you see her put anything on? Vaseline, hand lotion, anything?"

"No. I handed her the flashlight and her hands were dry." A tear escaped Phyllis's lashes. "I remember because I commented that she needed to take some vitamin E. She laughed it off and said she couldn't type with oiled-up hands."

The sound of sirens grew closer. Sam got up. "I'll flag them down."

I heard a faint groan and knelt down by Grandma's side. "Grandma, can you hear me?" I gently shook her shoulder. The last thing I needed was to make things worse. "Grandma, it's Toni. You fell. The ambulance is here. Hang on."

She made a faint moaning sound.

"Hang on, Grandma. They're coming."

Two EMTs in blue-and-white uniforms rushed up with a kit in their hands. One was a young woman with short curly hair and blue eyes. Her name tag said NEAL. The other was a young man with dark hair and dark eyes. His nametag said SHERIDAN. I didn't recognize either of them. "She's making moaning sounds." I stood to let them get close. "Her heartbeat is weak. I'm pretty sure her arm is broken, and her left ankle is swollen."

"What happened?" the girl asked as she knelt and took Grandma's vitals.

"She fell off the statue," Phyllis said, her teeth chattering.

"I think someone may have greased it," I said. "She has silicone-like stuff on her hands."

The guy glanced up at me. "Be sure and tell the police so they can get a sample."

I nodded and watched as they worked on Grandma, starting an IV, putting on a collar to stabilize her spine while they lifted her onto a stretcher. She moaned once loudly, and I grabbed her good hand. "It's okay, Grandma. They're going to take you to the ER."

I let go long enough for them to put her in the back of the ambulance. I turned to Phyllis, whose lips were a funny blue. "You should ride with her."

"Are you sure?" Her teeth rattled as she said it.

"I'm sure." I nodded, and the female EMT helped Phyllis up into the ambulance.

"Are you okay?" I heard the woman ask Aunt Phyllis. There was a muffled reply, then she added, "Let me check you out to be sure." Then the ambulance doors were closed.

Sam put his hand on my shoulder in a comforting way. "She'll be fine. She's in good hands."

It was then that the tears welled up in my eyes and my

throat closed up. I tried to take a deep breath but it came out in a shudder. Sam turned me into him and I rested my forehead on his broad shoulder and worked to collect my thoughts.

"I have to go to the hospital." I pulled away.

"I need to talk to you first." I turned to find Officer Emry walking toward me. He was so thin he had to hitch up his gun belt. He stopped and thumbed through his notebook. "So, what happened here?"

"My grandma Ruth slipped off the statue and fell." I collected my thoughts. "I think the statue was greased or something. There was a slick substance on her hands."

"Wait, back up, why was she climbing on the statue? It's against the city code to climb on Mr. Everett's likeness. That will be a one-hundred-dollar fine." He flipped through his book and made a note. "What time did she fall?"

"I am not going to give you that so you can write her a ticket." I turned to Sam. "Can you take me to the hospital? I want to be there when she regains consciousness."

"Certainly." Sam put his arm around me. I swear he glared at Officer Emry. If the officer had any sense he'd back off. But then again, it was Officer Emry we were talking about.

"I'm calling this in as criminal mischief," he said.

"Prove it." I kept walking.

"She'll pay the fine or she'll have to go before a judge." He raised his voice to ensure we heard him as we walked away.

"Whatever." I raised my hand in a dismissive wave.

Sam was warm against me. Neither one of us had a coat and his truck was a block away when I felt the ice in the air. My teeth started to chatter.

"Darn it," I said and nearly bit my tongue. I rubbed my arms and picked up the pace. Sam's expression was grim. He pulled out his keys and hit a button. The truck started up and the door unlocked. "Show off," I muttered.

My words had the right corner of his mouth lifting in a quick grin as he opened the door for me and helped me inside. Once he closed my door I turned up the heat.

"I called Meghan. She'll be here in five minutes to close down the bakery."

"Oh, crap, the bakery." I sat back against his seat and closed my eyes. "I still have to make up the dough for tomorrow."

"Meghan is good," he reassured me as he put the truck into gear and headed down the darkened street. "She can handle it."

I worried my bottom lip and opened my eyes as we passed the courthouse and the now two police cars parked near the square with their lights flashing. "I'll call her when we get to the hospital and give her instructions."

Sam's face was grim. "Do you think someone sabotaged that statue?"

I rubbed my fingers and still felt the slide of something greasy. "Yes, I do. I don't know if they meant for Grandma to get hurt or if it's a school prank, but that statue was slicked up."

"What was she doing up there, anyway?"

"I have no idea. Aunt Phyllis said that something about the statue caught Grandma's attention. I certainly hope it wasn't the sheen of whatever grease was on there."

"Your grandma may be a handful, but she's smart." Sam pulled into the hospital's parking lot. "She wouldn't have climbed up there if she thought for a moment that there was a slick coating on the statue."

"Then what caught her eye?" I wondered out loud. "It was creepy to see her lying there unconscious so close to the spot where Lois died."

"Your grandma isn't dead," he reassured me.

"I know, but knowing doesn't tell me anything. At her

age a simple bump on the head or a fall could be the beginning of the end."

"Oh, I think she has at least ten good years in her yet." He undid his seat belt and hopped out of the truck. I followed suit, meeting him in front of the vehicle.

"Not if I get my hands on her," I said. "I swear if she survives this, I'm going to kill her."

"Now that's the spirit." Sam chuckled.

I hurried into the building, dialing Meghan's number on my cell. It rang as I entered the building.

"Cell phones aren't allowed inside, dear," a crusty little man with a smoker's voice croaked at me. I glanced over to see that he was about five foot two and wore a blue smock over his tan dress pants, white pullover shirt, and stylish black athletic shoes.

"My grandma, Ruth Nathers, was brought in by ambulance. Can you tell me where she is?" I kept the phone on my ear and listened to it ring as I talked.

"Ruth?" the old man asked. "Ruth Nathers? What happened? Does Bill know?"

"She fell, and I haven't called Bill," I said as I heard Meghan pick up the phone. I held up my finger, gesturing to hold on a moment. "Hi, Meghan?"

"Yes, Toni, hi. I'm at the bakery and I have it all locked up. Don't worry. I'll clean up and prep for tomorrow."

"Thank you." I felt a tiny brick being lifted from my shoulders. "Make up the donut batter and put it in the fridge to rise overnight."

"Will do. Anything else?"

"That's it, for now. I'll keep you updated as I find out more."

"Sure thing." She hung up and I tucked the phone in my apron pocket.

"Are you Ruth's granddaughter? The baker?"

"Yes, can you tell us where to find her?" I asked again. His name tag said ED PRICE. "Please, Ed."

"Of course, follow me." He started down the hallway, his gait as slow as molasses in January. "Ruth brags about you all the time. Smart as they come, she says. So sad, I had no idea Ruth was in the ER. Does Bill know? Because you should call him. I hope she'll be okay for card night at the senior center. I really like to pit my wits against her in cards. Crafty as a fox, your grandmother is. Sweet lady, too."

I let him rattle on. I mean, he was a nice guy, but I was really worried and a bit distracted. He was right on one thing, though. I did need to call Bill. Grandma's companion would be very upset if I didn't let him know she was down here.

"The ER waiting room is right through there." Ed waved at the door. "Jessica Sanchez is working the desk. Tell her I sent you and she'll take good care of you."

"Thanks, Mr. Price." I pushed the door open.

"Don't forget to call Bill," he said behind me. "But not in the hospital."

I hurried toward the desk area. Sam kept pace with me.

"Do you have Bill's number?"

"Yes, Grandma made sure I put him in my contacts. Leave it to Grandma to date a man who lives two blocks from the hospital."

"Give me your phone and I'll go out and call Bill," Sam said.

"Thank you." I handed him my phone and stopped at the front desk. "Hi. Mr. Price said you would be able to help me."

Jessica looked up from her work. She was a pretty young girl with olive skin, dark curling hair, and big brown eyes. "Are you hurt?"

"No." I shook my head. "My grandmother Ruth Nathers was brought in by ambulance."

"Oh, yes, Ruth. I should have seen the resemblance." Jessica stood up. She came up to my shoulder and wore blue scrubs that tried but failed to hide her petite body. "Come with me." She moved around the desk and down the hall on the right-hand side. I hurried after her. My baker's shoes squeaked on the tiled floor, while her nurse's shoes were quiet and confident. "Ruth is in area three waiting on X-ray results."

"Is she conscious?"

"See for yourself." Jessica opened a curtained area at the end of the hall.

Grandma was on a hospital bed with her eyes closed. Her arm and leg were splinted. She was dressed in a hospital gown. A big purple bruise rose up on her forehead. Her left-hand index finger was clamped into a plastic finger clip connected to a pulse and oxygen monitor. An IV bag was on her right and the sound of her heartbeat rang through the tiny room.

Aunt Phyllis sat in a chair beside the bed. She looked tired and worried. Someone had given her a warming blanket.

"How is she?" I asked in what felt like an appropriate whisper.

"I'm alive," Grandma said in her gravelly voice. "I could use a cigarette."

"Ruth, you know there's no smoking in the hospital," Phyllis chided her.

I took Grandma's hand, and she opened her blue eyes and winked at me.

"Got myself in a real pickle this time," she said with a wry smile. "Ow."

"What were you thinking climbing up on that statue, anyway?" I was relieved and mad at the same time. It was hard to figure out what to do with the rush of emotion.

"I wanted to look at the crime scene from a different vantage point." Grandma stuck out her bottom lip. "I didn't know it would be slick."

"What could you possibly learn from a higher vantage point?" I squeezed her hand. Her skin was warmer than usual. "Do you have a fever?" I put the back of my hand on her forehead.

"Her temperature is up due to the fall," a female voice said behind me. I turned to see a tall brunette with light brown skin and tilted, exotic eyes. "Hi, I'm Doctor Nadir." She held out her hand.

I shook it firmly. "Toni Holmes. Ruth is my grandmother. How is she?"

"She had a bad fall," Doctor Nadir said. Her words held a slight accent. "Her right arm is broken and needs to be casted. Her right leg has a hairline fracture. We'll cast that as well."

"Okay."

"Her CT scan shows a concussion, which is not good for a woman of her age. We'd like to keep her overnight for observation."

"Fine."

"No!" Grandma said in unison with my "fine."

I turned to her. "Grandma, you will be here most of the night anyway while they cast you. You might as well stay in a comfortable room."

"I agree," Bill said behind me, and gently but firmly pushed me out of the way. "Ruth, what have you done to yourself?" He leaned over and planted a kiss on her frown. Then he took her free hand and patted it.

"I'm sorry, but she can only have one visitor at a time. The rest of you will have to go out to the waiting room." This news came from a large woman in nurse's scrubs. Her hair was steel gray and tightly curled, her nose prominent and hawklike, her chin set as she gave us the glare of a woman in charge.

"I'll stay," Bill said firmly. "She'll listen to me," he added, and I knew he was right.

"Come on, Aunt Phyllis. I'll buy you a coffee." I put my arm around her thin shoulders and walked her out. Sam had come in with Bill, and the three of us stepped out into the hall while the nurse closed the curtain on Bill and Grandma.

"How bad is it?" I asked Doctor Nadir.

"Not bad, considering all factors. She's lucky. There is no bleeding on her brain," the doctor said. "But, as I said, we'd like to keep an eye on her."

"With her arm and her leg, she'll need a wheelchair," I noted.

"She may also need physical therapy." Dr. Nadir wrote a note on a clipboard. "Six weeks in a chair will mean her muscles will be weak."

"They weren't that good to begin with," I muttered, thinking about the scooter she used on a regular basis. The very scooter the police had in custody.

"I'll write her a scrip for PT," the doctor said. "She lists Dr. Procter as her internist. She'll need to see him next week for a follow-up to see how she's doing."

"Of course—wait." I remembered the float and the parade just a few days away. "She's been excited to ride on my float for the Homer Everett Day festivities. Will she be okay to do that?"

"That depends. She certainly won't be able to walk the parade route."

"No, she's going to be sitting," I reassured the doctor.

"Then I don't see a problem. But if I were you, I'd make sure she was strapped down. The last thing she needs is to take another fall."

"I'll see she's buckled in," I said. "Thank you." Then I took Aunt Phyllis and walked her toward the waiting room.

"I tried to stop her from climbing up there," Aunt Phyllis said, her bright blonde hair mussed. "You know how she is. She gets an idea in her head and there's no shaking it."

"What was it that made her want to see the spot from a higher vantage point?" I asked. "It's dark out there. What did she think she could see?"

"I have no idea." Aunt Phyllis shrugged. "I thought she saw something on the statue. Sometimes she can be so close-mouthed. Especially if she thinks she might be on to a good story."

"It's not like you were going to beat her to the story." I was perturbed by Grandma's behavior. I swear, sometimes she acted more like a teenager than a grandmother.

I got Aunt Phyllis ensconced in a comfortable chair and went to the coffee service and poured her a cup of coffee, careful to add the right amount of cream and sugar.

"It's this whole Lois thing," Aunt Phyllis said as she took the Styrofoam cup I offered her. She sipped briefly and wrapped her blue-tipped fingers around it. "We really need to solve this before Ruth gets herself killed."

I sat down hard in the plastic seat across from her. "I know. What do you want me to do?"

Sam sat down beside me and put his arm around my shoulders. "Is this still about Lois Striker's murder?"

"I'm afraid so," Aunt Phyllis said. "Ruth has been like a bloodhound on a trail with it. There's no shaking her loose."

"Aren't the police looking into this?" Sam asked.

I turned and looked into his eyes. "Chief Blaylock says he is, but they aren't releasing any information to the public. I swear they're worried it will interfere with the Homer Everett Day proceedings. The police are biased. Chief Blaylock has to report to the City Council, and they all have a financial stake in the parade and the festival."

"Blaylock may be feeling some pressure from the City Council," Sam said, "but he also has to keep the community safe. If there's a killer out there, then he needs to find them, and quick, or heads will roll—and trust me, his will be first."

I'd forgotten that Sam came from a wealthy family with political connections in the county. His mother belonged to the country club crowd and often met with the most influential people in the state of Kansas. If anyone had insight into the politics of the region it was Sam.

"Lois's memorial service is set for Tuesday at nine A.M. One of us should go. It might help to see who shows." I chewed on my bottom lip.

"I'll go," Phyllis said. "Although I'm not all that sure I'll be welcome. I didn't exactly run with her group of friends."

"I should go along," I said. "Two pairs of eyes are better than one."

"It's Thanksgiving week," Sam reminded me gently. "Will you need extra hands at the bakery?"

I frowned. "Probably." I cupped my right elbow and drummed my fingers on my chin. "I'll call my cousin Lucy and see if Kelsey and Kallie can work a few hours." Kelsey and Kallie were Lucy's twins. They turned twenty-one this summer and were always looking for work to help pay their cell phone bills. "As long as someone is covering the bakery counter, I can bake the orders. Meghan can deliver them. Thank goodness I cut off delivery time at ten P.M. on Wednesday."

"They took Ruth off to her room," Bill said as he came

through the waiting room door. He looked ten years older than usual. His hair stood up and his shoulders sagged a bit. "She's not hurting now; they have given her some powerful painkillers. But I imagine she'll be a mess tomorrow."

I stood. "Do you want some coffee?" I hated emotion-filled scenes, and the worry in the waiting room was palpable. My instinctive reaction was to feed everyone, but since my bakery was closed, the coffee machine was as close as I could get.

"No, thank you." He gave me a small smile. "Ruth asked me to send you all home. She's fine. Go home, get some rest." He looked straight at me. "Especially you, Toni. We know you go to work in a few hours. You need your rest. She's sorry for scaring everyone."

"The doctor said she'll need PT once her bones heal," I told him.

"I'll see she gets there and does her work." His expression was grim. "I want to see her fully recover. Meanwhile, there is a nurse in our apartment complex. I'll make sure they come in and check on her a few times a day."

It was going to be hard to see my very active grandmother slowed down, but that is why she moved into assisted living. So that she could stay in her home should the time come when she needed extra care.

Grandma'd told me once, "No one wants to live in a nursing home if they don't have to." She was right, of course. My mind went to Lois Striker. She was Grandma Ruth's age. So who had she counted on when she needed looking after?

CHAPTER 25

Twenty gluten-free pies later, I was showered and dressed in my only black dress. It was a wrap dress with long sleeves and a poufy skirt that landed below the knees. My black pumps were shiny and my unruly hair was pulled back in a tight no-nonsense bun.

"There aren't very many people here," Aunt Phyllis whispered.

"Maybe her family is still in the vestibule," I whispered back. A glance around the funeral home chapel told me that five people besides Aunt Phyllis and me waited in the folding chairs that were carefully lined up in the small room to face the casket.

"She didn't have any family," Aunt Phyllis said low. "She never married, and her only sister died three years ago of cancer."

Poor Lois; not only did she have to give up her only child, but she lacked the crazy love of my big family. While I would never have ten children like my aunt, there was something to be said about being related to literally hundreds of people. Surely a few more than five of them would attend my funeral service.

"Who took care of her when she got sick?" I asked, thinking about Grandma and her apartment in assisted living. My mind's eye compared the apartment to Lois's old bungalow. When the oil refineries came to town, they brought with them a population boom, and so rows of bungalows, like the two-bedroom one Lois had lived in, were built and occupied.

But as the oil boom slowly disappeared, so did the people in Oiltop, and those bungalows were left to the old and then young. The homes blistered and warped over the years of exposure to the heat of Kansas summers and the wild cold of the winters.

"Lois had a full-time nurse," Aunt Phyllis said. "It was so odd, too, because everyone knew she didn't have the money to pay for a nurse like that. One of the mysteries of life, I suppose."

"I suppose." I sat back. Or maybe it wasn't such a mystery, I thought, as Hutch Everett and his wife and son walked into the room.

Hutch looked dignified in a charcoal-gray suit. His shirt was white and his tie a classic black-and-white. His wife, Aimee, wore a gray sheath dress with a fitted short jacket, hose, and gray shoes. Her hair was the champagne color that most women of a certain age and status had. It was carefully combed into a straight bob and sprayed to within an inch of its life.

Harold Everett was fourteen years old and heavyset, and he sulked as they came into the room. He grabbed the aisle seat in the very back and slouched with his hands in his pockets. It was pretty clear he didn't want to be there. The kid pulled out his phone and began texting or something. What do kids do with their phones that their heads are always down and their noses in them?

I noted that the handful of people present didn't include any of the nurses I knew. So if Lois had a nurse companion, the relationship had not extended into friendship. Hutch's gaze landed on me, and I sent him a small smile. He gave me a short nod, then he put his hand on his wife's back and guided her into a row across from us in the middle of the room. In my experience, no one ever liked to sit in the front seat of a church service. But sitting in the very back was rude and made it appear that you were ready to bolt at any second.

Aimee snapped her fingers, made eye contact with her son, and motioned to the empty seat beside her. She did it again but still the boy didn't move. Finally she turned around and ignored his defiance.

That would not have happened in my family. If Mom or Dad didn't come down and pinch your ear and drag you where they wanted you, then Grandma did. Trust me; it hurt more from Grandma Ruth—most likely because she would tell you how it hurts her more than you.

I turned my attention away from the sullen teen to the flowers that surrounded the casket. There was a black-and-white portrait of Lois that must have been shot in her twenties. She had been a pretty woman then, her hair dark and curled in a pageboy cut around her shoulders. Her face was thinner, her chin sharper, and her eyes sparkled as if she had a secret no one else knew. Maybe she did. Maybe she'd been pregnant with her lover's child when the picture was snapped.

If there had ever been any doubt that Hutch Everett knew his birth mother, it was squashed the second he walked into the chapel. There was no reason for Hutch and his family to be there unless they had some deeper connection to Lois.

A movement in the back caught my eye. I turned to see

the sullen teenager panning his phone as if he were videoing the affair. He pointed it right at me and studied the screen. Then he looked up, grinned, and put his phone down.

There was something creepy about being videotaped without your consent. If you didn't know you were being filmed, how could you object?

The service was short and sweet. When the director asked if anyone wanted to come up and say a few words, no one budged. And so in fifteen short minutes, the funeral was over and Lois was carted off to the cemetery.

"Shoot me if my service is that awful," Phyllis whispered to me as we stood to leave.

"Don't worry." I put my hand on her shoulder. "You're a Nathers now. The one thing we love most after weddings and babies is a good funeral. I'm certain the room will be packed with grieving Natherses who can't wait for the open bar at the luncheon after. Nothing like a good wake to bring the family together."

She smiled at the thought, and so did I. The Everetts left without a word to anyone, and I wandered over to the guest book to see if anyone else suspicious had signed it.

That's when it caught my eye. Hutch Everett had signed the book *Hutchinson Champ Everett.*

Why would Homer name his son after a man he'd murdered months before Hutch was born?

Maybe the answer was in Lois's journals.

"How was the funeral?" Meghan asked when I walked into the kitchen of the bakery.

"Short." I hung my coat up on the hooks in the back, then reached for my apron. "There weren't many people there, and it was done by the funeral director. Not in a church."

"Funny, I would have thought Lois would have been active in her church." Meghan consolidated the trays of donuts down to one colorful tray.

"She didn't have any family to speak of." I pulled down the ingredients for cupcakes. With everyone having pies for dessert on Thanksgiving, I had planned fresh cupcakes for the afternoon bakery rush. On today's menu were apple cinnamon, carrot cake, and pumpkin spice. "There wasn't anyone to coordinate a church service. When that happens they usually add it to the funeral expenses and keep it small."

"Sad," Meghan said, and took the full donut tray out to the front of the bakery.

It *was* sad, I thought. Family was the only real legacy you left in the world once you died. Maybe a good reason for me to reconsider the possibility of having a man in my life.

I followed her out to check on the number of baked goods and to help estimate what would be needed for the rest of the day.

A few small groups clustered about our black wrought iron tables. One was the usual group of knitters, undeterred by the impending holiday. I picked up the coffeepot and walked over to freshen their cups. "Good morning, ladies." I poured the coffee. "What are your holiday plans? Do you have family coming?"

Francy glanced up from the pale blue baby blanket she was knitting. "Dinner is at my house this year," she said. "I'm making the turkey, and everyone else is bringing sides and desserts."

"You're lucky to have family in the area," Julie said with a sigh as she worked on a deep-green-and-white blanket. "My family is all in Wisconsin, and no one could make it down this year."

"You should go up," Mary said as she put down her pale pink angora blanket and picked up her coffee cup to sip.

"I would if I had the money, but things are tight this year, what with Sean having to take off work for six weeks after his neck surgery," Julie said.

"How's Sean doing?" I asked. He'd had cervical spine surgery, and I'd taken a plate of gluten-free cookies to her home.

"He's good, back at work." She didn't miss a stitch as she spoke. "He said the pain went away the moment he woke up from surgery."

"Good, I'm glad to hear it," I said and straightened. "I went to Lois Striker's funeral service this morning."

"Oh, dear, poor Lois." Francy shook her head. "I'm surprised anyone went. She had a tendency to lord it over people."

"Lois wasn't nearly as bad as Aimee Everett," Julie said. "I went to a Chamber of Commerce coffee once to promote my Mary Kay business, and Hutch's wife acted as if she were the mayor's wife or something. Her nose was all up in the air, and she practically sneered at my shoes. When I found out she was a regular at the coffees, I quit the Chamber and never looked back."

"It didn't hurt you any," Mary said. "You still have your pink Cadillac parked in your driveway. Which reminds me, I need to order some of your mascara. I'm out."

I decided I'd learned all I could learn from that group and moved on to the next. This table was a couple of ranchers who came in weekly and spent an hour or two playing checkers and enjoying the bottomless cups of coffee I offered.

"Hi guys," I said. "Coffee?"

"Sure." Mr. Andrews scooted his cup my way. He jumped three pieces and took them off the board.

"Drat," Mr. Brooks muttered. "You can fill mine, too, while you're at it, young lady."

These two old guys had lived in Oiltop their entire lives. Surely they would know Lois, and might even be aware of her secrets. "Did either of you know Lois Striker very well?"

"No one like us knew Lois," Mr. Brooks said as he studied the board. "That woman was after the rich and famous."

"You know, for as hard as she worked to catch Homer Everett's attention, she sure ended up alone and broke, didn't she?" Mr. Andrews said.

"I thought she had a live-in nurse. If so, she must have had money. Live-in nurses are not cheap," I pointed out.

"I can't say as to where she got her money." Mr. Brooks jumped his checker over two pieces. "But she and Everett were in cahoots over something. If she ever needed anything she got it. His wife didn't complain either."

"Makes me wonder if they were a threesome," Mr. Andrews said with a cackle. "Although no one would believe it to look at her."

"Right." I walked away. So Grandma Ruth wasn't the only one who hated Lois. Maybe she wasn't killed because she was going to spill her secrets. Maybe she was killed because she had said the wrong thing to the wrong person one time too many. It was something to consider.

But who was it that greased up Homer Everett's statue and almost killed my grandmother?

"Hey, Meghan, have you ever known kids to grease Homer Everett's statue?"

"What? No, they might egg it. Heck, they've tried to tar and feather it. But why would they grease it?" She shrugged her shoulders. Today she wore a black peasant blouse under a black corset, with black pants and her customary thick-soled combat boots.

"Maybe it's the Everetts that greased it," Mr. Andrews said.

I spun on my heel. "Why?"

"To keep the blasted thing clean," he stated. "Didn't you hear the girl? The kids are always trying to deface the thing. I heard the Everetts were trying out this new silicone solution that would protect the bronze from damage and yet be invisible to the eye."

"Didn't they hire Charlie Handon to treat the statue with that stuff?" Mr. Brooks asked. He looked at me, his hazel eyes serious. "He said it was slick as snot, pardon my language."

"They need to put a warning on it, then." I frowned.

"There is," Mr. Andrews said. "Got a sign right beside the statue that says, 'Danger: Do not climb. Violators will be ticketed.' I ought to know; I made the sign. Right nice. Poured brass. One of my best, if I say so myself."

The bakery door opened with a jangle of bells. "Hi, Toni, how's your grandma doing?" Brad pulled his sunglasses off his nose, revealing electric-blue eyes full of worry.

"She's doing better." I put the coffeepot back on the heater. "Bill is taking her home this afternoon."

"What happened to Ruth?" Mr. Andrews said.

"She fell and broke her arm and her leg," I said. "She bumped her head as well, so they kept her overnight at the hospital to keep an eye on her concussion."

"Ouch," Mr. Brooks said. "How'd she fall that bad?"

I shrugged, not wanting to admit she was climbing on Homer Everett. "You know how easy it is to fall at her age."

"Don't we know it." Mr. Andrews went back to his checkers game.

"That's what got my wife, Eliza," Mr. Brooks said. "She fell in the bathroom and did all kinds of damage. You tell your grandma we're pulling for her."

"I will, thanks." I walked behind the counter. "What can I get you, Brad?"

"How about a couple of those bear claws and some coffee?"

I plated two gluten-free bear claws and he poured his own coffee. "Why don't you come on back?"

He followed me into the kitchen, where Meghan was boxing up the cooled pies. "Hey, Meghan."

"Hi, Mr. Ridgeway." She batted her eyes at him. I didn't blame her. The man was gorgeous. Every female from one to ninety flirted with him. It was something to consider when I started dating again. I had a bit of a jealous nature. I'd have to be able to handle the fact that he could have anyone he wanted.

"Will Grandma Ruth be able to ride on your float?" Brad asked as he sat down at the small table in the back room and sipped his black coffee.

I put the bear claws down in front of him and poured my own coffee. I added plenty of cream to mine. I love the taste of coffee, but I like it to have more body to it. Cream adds that. "The doctor said she could, if she felt up to it. I'm going to add a seat belt to her chair. I don't want her falling out and hurting herself even worse."

"Smart." He nodded and bit into a pastry. "How much sleep did you get? I heard through the grapevine you were at the hospital until after midnight."

"I'm running on about two hours." I raised my coffee cup and gave him a wry smile. "I think I've had three pots of coffee so far this morning."

"Tell me you won't be working all night tonight." His concern was touching, really.

"I won't be working," I reassured him. "The bakery closes at seven and we're closed for Thanksgiving."

"And the deliveries?" He pointed at the stack of boxes Meghan had made.

"I'm doing those, Mr. Ridgeway." She turned to us. "I won't let her drive on two hours of sleep. It's bad enough she's baking."

"Good girl," he said.

I, being exhausted and decidedly not in control of my emotions, stuck my tongue out at her. Meghan laughed.

"I hope you'll let me drive you home tonight," he said. "The last thing I need is a phone call telling me you've been in an accident."

"I'm fine, really. I don't live that far. This is Oiltop. Nothing is very far."

"As your lawyer, I have to take you. If anything happened I might be liable because I knew you were impaired." He said it with a straight face and sipped his coffee.

"What a bunch of hokum," I muttered.

"I heard you went to Lois Striker's memorial service." He smoothly changed the subject.

"Yes. I was surprised by how few people came."

"Lois might have been an influential pillar of the community, but she wasn't well-liked."

"I'm learning that." I lifted my mug and a thought occurred to me. "Did you know that Hutch Everett's middle name is Champ?"

"I might have seen it somewhere. Why?"

"Doesn't it strike you as odd that a man would name his son after another man he's suspected of murdering?"

Brad frowned. "I hadn't thought of that."

"I think it puts a great big monkey wrench in Grandma's theory that Homer killed Champ."

"True." Brad finished off his pastry. "So if Homer didn't kill Champ, who did?"

"Maybe Lois did," I said, thinking out loud. "I mean,

maybe Champ was going to tell everyone about her affair with Homer." I shrugged. "It's motive."

"And what, Homer hid the gun for his lover? I don't think so. Wasn't it Lois who signed off on the permit?"

"They say good friends hide the body," I stated.

"That only works if you think lovers can be good friends." Brad's eyes twinkled.

"Or that good friends can be lovers," I said. "Doesn't usually work that way."

"Hmm, sex messes everything up," he said. "Maybe that's why Lois gave Homer her son. Maybe Homer black-mailed her into it."

"Now that is an interesting thought," I said. "There's one way to find out."

"How?"

"If I tell you, you'll try to talk me out of it."

"Then it's my duty as your lawyer to inform you that if you are thinking of doing something unlawful, I have to advise against it. I may in fact have to tell the police that you did it."

"I'm not thinking of doing anything unlawful," I said. "Just . . . wait. What happened to lawyer/client confidentiality?"

"You mean doctor/patient privilege?"

"No, the one with your lawyer." I stood. "There has to be some sort of rule that you can't tell on me or crooks would never tell their lawyers anything."

"You got me there." He stood and put his coffee cup in the sink. "Thanks for the snack. I'll be here at seven to pick you up. Don't do anything today. You're tired and you may do something you'll regret later."

Darn it. He was right. I watched his Armani-covered backside walk away and tried not to sigh. I knew then what I needed to do. I needed to speak to Hutch Everett and ask him if he knew who killed Champ. It was a long shot, but if Lois had shared her deed with anyone, it would have been her son—not my grandmother.

I looked at the ingredients I'd gotten out for the cupcakes. Maybe I needed to make a delivery to the Everett household. When someone died you brought the family food. Right?

CHAPTER 26

I didn't drive to the big square limestone home of Hutch Everett. I walked. It was only about a mile, and I needed the brisk walk to help keep me awake. Okay, that was a stretch, but almost everyone would believe me.

I carried a box of fresh-baked gluten-free cupcakes. I'd picked apple cinnamon with maple frosting and carrot cake with cream cheese frosting. If nothing else, Harold would eat them. From what I heard, that boy would eat about anything, especially if it had frosting.

The Everett house was an imposing foursquare with thick columns in the front and a wide porch. I remember as a kid being fascinated with the old-fashioned carport attached to the side of the house. The drive swept elegantly up to the house, where the sturdy limestone columns held a thick roof that shielded the driver from the weather. I could imagine a butler jumping out of the side to open the car door for the ladies, then taking the car back to the garage while the man and woman of the house went inside.

Today the house windows were dark. The porch steps were painted light gray. I straightened my dress and rang the doorbell. The porch held dark rattan furnishings with blue-and-white striped cushions. I counted to twenty and pushed the doorbell a second time.

This time the front door opened. An older woman in a gray dress wearing an apron answered. I assumed she was the Everetts' housekeeper. I didn't think people had household help anymore, but if anyone did, it would be the Everetts. "Yes?"

"Hi, I'm Toni Holmes. I saw Mr. and Mrs. Everett at Lois Striker's memorial service this morning. I wanted to bring them some food and express my condolences for the loss of their friend."

"I'm afraid you're mistaken," the woman said with a sour look on her face. "The Everetts didn't have anything to do with that Striker woman. I would know. I've worked here for over forty years."

"Oh."

She started to close the door, but I stopped her before she could finish by putting my hand in the doorjamb. "Wait."

"What?"

"I brought cupcakes. The least you could do is take them. I'm sure Mr. Everett wouldn't mind. They're apple and carrot cake." I held up the pink-and-white striped bakery box.

"Who is it, Carla?" Hutch Everett's voice sounded behind her.

"It's a Ms. Holmes," the older woman stated, not taking her eyes off me, as if I might steal something from the front porch. "She's under the mistaken impression you are grieving over Lois Striker's death."

"I brought cupcakes." I raised the box when he came up behind her.

"Thank you," he said. "Carla, let the woman in."

I pushed the box into Carla's hands and stepped into the cool, rich foyer of the house. She took the cupcakes and muttered as she moved through the formal dining area toward what I assumed was the kitchen.

"Why don't we talk in the living room." He waved toward the formal parlor across from the dining area. The house was built with four classic rooms and stairs to the side. There were a formal living room, a dining room, a family room, and a kitchen. Each room had thick walls, wood floors, and sumptuous rugs. The walls were painted in soft pastels to show off the thick dark woodwork that ran through each room.

"Thank you so much for seeing me." I sat down on the edge of a pale cream couch with soft floral pillows. "I wanted to express my condolences for the loss of your friend."

"Lois was more than a friend, but I suppose you already figured that out." He went to a small bar and picked up a short, squat crystal glass. He opened a silver ice bucket and used tongs to put ice cubes in his glass. "Drink?" He held up the glass as he asked.

"No, thank you," I said. "I'm working on too little sleep to indulge."

"Ah, yes, I heard about your grandmother Ruth's accident. Is she okay?"

"She has a concussion and a couple of broken bones, but she'll get to come home today."

He took a sip of the amber liquid in his glass and studied me. "That is regrettable."

"She should have known better." I paused. "There's a

rumor you all coat the bronze in silicone to keep it clean. Is that true?"

"Hmmm, as far as I know, no. We don't overly concern ourselves with the cleanliness of the statue—except to spiff it up for Homer Everett Day." He walked over and sat down in the striped, winged-back chair in front of me. "How about we talk about why you're really here?"

I tried hard to keep my expression neutral and waited for him to tell me what he meant. It was hard. I hate awkward silences. I really wanted to jump in and ask him about his birth parents. But instead I simply waited for him to expound.

He took another sip of his drink, drawing out the silence. "You want to know about my birth parents."

"Yes." I kept my answer simple.

"Lois Striker was my birth mother. I always knew. It was—how to say this—delicate. But my father believed in absolute honesty in the family. Lois wanted for nothing. It was the agreement . . . and no, I don't feel as if I've been sold. You see, single motherhood was unthinkable when I was born. Lois and my father were in love, but he died before they could marry. So Homer stepped in. You see, he felt responsible. He'd introduced them."

"Wait—Homer wasn't you birth father?"

"Oh, god, no, I thought you knew. Champ Rogers was my father, and Homer's best friend."

I sat back and tried to digest this new piece of information. It did make sense. Why else would Homer's wife allow him to adopt Hutch?

"Can I ask you another impertinent question?"

His lids half lowered and held a glimmer of danger. "I suppose you will whether I let you or not."

"I'm sorry; it's important. Do you know who killed Champ? Er . . . your father?"

"No," he said. "Proof that money doesn't buy everything. I've had a reward out for years on any information that would lead to Champ's killer."

"Did you know that my grandmother thinks the gun is hidden in a false wall in the judge's chambers?"

"No." He swirled his drink and tossed back a swallow. "I'll have to look into that. Is that all, Ms. Holmes?"

"One last thing—Lois?"

"When my mother, Susan, died five years ago, I let Lois fill the void. She needed a nurse companion, she got one. She was allowed run of the Chamber of Commerce. Even when her, shall we say, lack of education showed, it was overlooked because of my family. You see, Ms. Holmes, we Everetts understand the meaning of family."

"Of course," I said, my mind roiling with ideas. "It's why I came . . . to express my condolences for your loss. If it had been a member of my family, I would be grieving, too."

He sent me a wry smile. "I understand our families grieve in different ways."

I let out a small laugh. "Indeed we do." His family grieved with quiet dignity. Mine grieved with big, sloppy, emotional noise.

He stood. "Thank you for coming by and for the baked goods."

I knew I was being dismissed. I rose and headed out. "You're welcome. I hope that you understand how much your adoptive father meant to Oiltop."

"Oh, I do. It's why we have the parade. It's why we host the carnival on the fairgrounds." He stopped at his front door. "There's something to be said for knowing one's ancestors. I'm sure you agree. Wasn't it your great-grandparents who founded Haysville College?"

"Yes, it was." I left it at that. Academics were never paid

enough to live in houses big enough to need a staff. The homestead might be large, but that was purely out of necessity. On any given day, my house was overrun with boisterous family members. Which reminded me—my family was coming for dinner tomorrow, and the two twenty-pound turkeys thawing in my kitchen needed to be prepped. Not to mention the house needed to be dusted and the linens ironed.

I glanced back at the Everett family home. Maybe having a household staff wasn't a bad idea.

CHAPTER 27

"You look dead on your feet, no pun intended." Tasha sat on the rolling stool in the bakery kitchen.

"I'll be fine." I stuffed the second turkey with a gluten-free apple/cornbread stuffing and basted it with herb butter. I had gotten Meghan to bring the turkeys from the house to the bakery. The ovens here were big enough to bake both turkeys at the same time. It was family tradition to bake them the night before.

"I dusted and vacuumed the house. I swear that puppy sheds three times its body weight every day."

"What did the vet say? Do we know what kind of dog it is?" I lifted the heavy pan and Tasha popped up and opened the second oven door for me.

"Yes. There's good news and bad," she said.

"Okay . . ."

"The puppy is a happy and healthy twenty-six pounds."

"Good." I nodded.

"And about five weeks old." Tasha waited for my reaction.

"You mean five months, right?"

"Nope." She shook her head. "Five weeks. He still has puppy teeth."

"But he's twenty-six pounds. . . . If he's only five weeks, that means . . ." I had a hard time wrapping my mind around how big he would get.

"He's a Great Pyrenees. Fully grown, Aubrey will run about one hundred and twenty pounds."

"Holy crap, he'll be as big as you." I had to sit down.

"I know. It means I won't be able to rent an apartment. The vet said they are a great family breed, but they need a house and a yard."

"Isn't Kansas too hot for the breed? I mean, think of how much hair they have. He'll die when the temps hit one hundred or better."

She shrugged. "I'll need a good air conditioner." She leaned against the wall and looked at me. "It's not like I can send him to anther home now. The minute Kip found him I was stuck."

Kip could not adjust to change well, and once he decided on something, there was little Tasha could do.

"I don't suppose you could tell Kip that Aubrey would be happier on a farm . . . a big farm, say in Colorado, where it's cooler."

"Not unless I move them both to a farm, a big farm, say in Colorado." She mimicked me because we both knew how hopeless the situation was.

"Then Aubrey will simply have to stay at my house. I have good air conditioning and a yard."

"And when we move out?" She sent me a look that showed she was unsure if she was crossing some boundary of friendship.

"He'll stay with me," I said. "I live close to school. Kip can come before and after to see him. I trust him to lock up. The kid follows directions to a tee."

"Yes. That can be a good thing and a bad thing." She hugged me. "Thank you. I can't tell you what your friendship means to me."

"How'd your date go with Calvin?"

Tasha blushed and poured herself some coffee. "I think I'm in love." She turned to me, spoon in hand. "What is wrong with me? How can I be in love so quickly? I mean, just last month I was in a really bad relationship. We know how that crush ended."

I touched her hand. "There's nothing wrong with you. It's not like you're marrying him this week. Right?" I raised an eyebrow.

"No." She laughed. "I'm not marrying him this week. Next month."

"What?"

"Just kidding." She laughed. "You are so easy."

I pushed her out of the way. "Go, sit down. Stop messing with me when I'm so tired."

"But it's so much fun." She sat down at the table. I went over my to-do list to make sure that I had all my orders filled and things ready for dinner the next day and for the parade. "Have you heard from your grandma?" Tasha asked.

"She's recovering. Complaining about how uncomfortable the casts are and how she hates having to rely on others to get around."

"Did you tell her that's what happens when she does foolish things?" Tasha waggled her eyebrows over the top of her coffee mug.

"Boy, would I love to," I said. "But I think she's smart enough to already know that."

"Is she going to be able to ride on the float?"

"Yes. I had Brad add a seat belt to her chair. There's no keeping Grandma Ruth down."

Tasha smiled. "I bet she told you she expected to ride on the float even if she were dead."

"Yes." My eyes grew wide at the ridiculousness of it all. "She said if she died I was to put sunglasses on her and have a machine hoist her hand in a pageant wave."

Tasha spat her coffee. "Oh, my, now that was an image I didn't need in my head."

We had a good laugh, I think because I was so tired that I laughed a bit more than was called for. My stomach hurt and my eyes watered.

"I guess I'm late to the party," Brad said as he walked in from the front of the bakery.

"Oh, I didn't hear the door bells." I wiped the tears from my eyes and tried to catch my breath.

"I locked the door and turned the sign for you," he volunteered as I passed him. "Why don't you tell me what's so funny."

"Toni was telling me about her Grandma Ruth's last wishes." Tasha giggled.

"Yes, nothing is keeping her from the parade," I added and took a deep breath.

"I think that's an image I don't want to know about." Brad was dressed in a cashmere navy sweater, white shirt, dark blue dockers, and boat shoes. Why men wore boat shoes when they didn't have a boat was beyond me, but it was a look that Todd would like. "You're still dressed for the memorial service."

I glanced down at the black dress, covered in one of my giant pink-and-white striped aprons. The apron was covered in baking splash back. There was evidence of pie filling, muffin batter, cupcake frosting, and turkey basting. I know it sounds nasty, but it made me happy to know how much work I'd gotten done. I pulled the apron over my head and threw it in the basket I kept for laundry. "I put the turkeys in the ovens. I think that's all I have to do tonight."

"I'm off. Kip is spending the night with his grandmother, and I've got a puppy to take care of." Tasha poured her coffee in the sink and rinsed out her cup. "Nice to see you, Brad."

"You, too, Tasha."

She tugged on her jacket and grabbed her purse. "See you in the morning, Toni."

"Right, Thanksgiving," I said. "Be at the float by eight A.M. Tell Kip he can bring Aubrey."

"Oh, he's planning on it. 'Night, all." She left out the back. The silence in the bakery made me very aware of being alone with Brad. I told myself I shouldn't feel this kind of tension. The man was my lawyer and a good friend.

I tried to act casually and checked on the turkeys, which didn't need checking on, since I had just put them in.

"How long will those turkeys need to cook?" Brad asked. He leaned against the doorjamb, looking every bit the *GQ* cover model.

"These will cook all night. I'll pull them out right before the parade and bring them to the house."

"They look pretty heavy. Are you going to be handling them yourself?"

"I've got a house full of family. One of the guys will come over and take care of it."

He reached over and took my hand. "I can come over and take care of it, if you want me to."

Oh boy.

"I figured you'd be busy with the Elks club float and your own family dinner."

"There are plenty of people taking care of the float," he said, low and soft. "And as for family, they'd take one look at you and understand."

"That's a nice line," I said, trying to pretend that the spit didn't dry up in my mouth. "Everyone knows that Thanksgiving is for family. My family would have a conniption if I tossed over Thanksgiving with them for some guy I was dating."

"That is one of the things I admire about your family."

"What? That we're loud, creative, boisterous, and have a tendency to need a lawyer?"

"Maybe you should think about how much you need a lawyer in your family." He raised his eyebrows, and his smile would have melted butter. Lucky for me my knees were stronger than his easy charm.

"Not dating." I think I said this out loud, as he backed off, if not physically, at least mentally.

"I haven't forgotten," he said, paying attention to his cell phone.

"I'm good, you know. You don't have to see me home." I picked up my purse and grabbed my coat from the hook near the back door.

He was beside me in a second, taking the coat from my hands and holding it out for me. "I'd feel better knowing you were home safe."

"I promise not to fall asleep at the wheel. Seriously, I've had about a million pots of coffee today."

"Are you afraid someone might help you, or are you afraid of me?"

I stopped and stared at him. It was a good question. "Maybe both."

"At least you're truthful." He cocked his head, his blonde hair falling across his eyes, and he brushed it away. It was a terribly endearing thing for him to do. "Come on, I'll follow you."

We stepped out into the floodlight I'd installed behind my building and I locked the back door. It was quiet out— that fall silence after the first frost when the bugs have hunkered down to sleep for the winter and the birds have moved onto warmer climes. The gravel of the back parking lot crunched under our feet and I noted that he had parked his Cadillac next to the bakery van.

"I talked to Hutch Everett today," I said as I stopped by the van and unlocked the door.

"Okay." It was not a question, but a declaration that I had his full attention.

"Did you know that Lois Striker was his birth mother?"

"I guessed as much."

"And his father was Champ Rogers." I studied Brad's face for the surprise I hoped to see. He had a great poker face.

"Interesting," was all he said.

"Grandma Ruth thought that Lois knew something about Homer Everett. She speculated that Homer killed Champ." Brad grunted and I figured he knew something I didn't.

"What?"

"Where's your motive? Weren't they best friends?"

"That's what Hutch confirmed," I said. "You don't kill a man and then adopt his son as your own. Do you? Unless you couldn't give your wife a son—they had been trying for ten years."

"So what? When he couldn't give his wife a child and learned that Champ had gotten Lois pregnant, he what? Killed his friend in a fit of rage?"

"Maybe," I said. "And maybe guilt is what drove him to adopt Hutch as his own."

"Wow, you have a good imagination."

I gave Brad a dirty look. "Okay, so blackmail and/or a fight over a woman doesn't do it for you—what does?"

Brad laughed. "I prefer not to speculate before I see the evidence."

"I told Hutch about the courthouse wall."

"What good did you think that would do?"

"He said he's had a reward out for information on Champ's death for years. If anyone can get the police to cut a hole in the judge's wall, it's Hutch Everett—Homer's son or not Homer's son."

"And you're certain of this?"

"Yes, aren't you?"

"Why would I be?"

"Because your family runs in the same circles as Hutch. Because they have a vested interest in his political connections."

"I don't remember having a vested interest, and I know nothing about Homer—or Champ, as he died before we were even born." Brad crossed his arms.

"I know. I thought maybe you remember stories your grandparents might have told."

"My grandparents rarely talked about anything but what my parents were doing and how I needed to go to the right colleges." He tilted his head. "What did your family talk about?"

"My family talked about what sports my brothers were into, who my sisters were dating, and what the professors at the college were doing." I blew out a breath, realizing he hadn't been asking about my family but was making a point. He was right. I suppose I was still trying to investigate and making a hash of it. I blame the fact that I was running on two hours' sleep.

I climbed up into the van, and he closed the door for me.

I put on my seat belt, and he made a motion for me to roll down my window. I did as he asked.

"Keep your windows open to let in the cold air. I'll be right behind you," he said. "If I see you weaving too much I'm going to honk."

"I'm really not that . . ." A big yawn came over me, and he raised a thick blond eyebrow. "Fine. I'll keep my window open."

"Good." He pounded his pronouncement on the side of the van. "I'll be right behind you."

I started up the van and waited for him to get into his car and pull out. Then I gently drove through the parking lot and out into the street. It was only seven P.M., but the entire town had closed up. Most people were at home entertaining family or preparing for tomorrow's feasts. My thoughts turned to Grandma. What was she really looking for when she climbed the statue? I'd asked Hutch straight out if they siliconed the statue, and he had said no. So how did the silicone get there? And worse, I still didn't know who had killed Lois, or why. Time was running out.

CHAPTER 28

"How do I look?" Grandma Ruth's voice was rougher than usual. "Pretty, aren't I?" She laughed, low and rumbly. Her eyes were bright, and there was a big fat bruise on her cheek. Her arm was in a pink cast. Her leg was in a white cast. Instead of trying to get her in her float throne, we had created a makeshift ramp out of two boards and Bill had pushed her wheelchair up onto the float. The wheelchair was closer in appearance to the scooter than the throne was and more people would recognize her.

"You look lovely, Ruth," Tasha said as she carefully combed Grandma's orange curls back and pinned a white tissue flower behind Grandma's left ear.

"Is it left for single and right for married, or vice versa?" Grandma asked.

"You mean the flowers? I think left for married and right for single, like your rings," I said as I carefully tied her chair into place on the float. Grandma wore a red, white, and blue sweatshirt and a bright red skirt with white stripes. Bill tucked a blue throw blanket around Grandma's knees. It was supposed to be a sunny day, but the high was only fifty degrees. Too chilly for a woman in her nineties who was still recovering from a concussion—but Grandma would not hear of wearing her coat.

"This little heater runs on a battery," I said as I set the small area heater near Grandma's feet. "That way even if it gets knocked over it won't set anything on fire."

"How about my tablet?" Grandma asked with a gleam in her blue eyes. "Will I be able to watch the Macy's parade? I have a grandson marching in that parade, and I don't want to miss it."

"Lucy's taping it, Grandma," I said as I adjusted the final decorations on her part of the float.

"I don't want to see it taped, I want to see it live. You said you would get me one of those new-fangled tablets to watch it stream online."

"I didn't have time to buy one," I said with a sigh. "I had to make thirty dozen cookies to give away on the parade route." Not to mention a chocolate display for the window.

"How am I going to give away anything strapped in this chair?" Grandma frowned at me.

I had to bite my tongue not to tell her that she should have thought of that before she tried climbing the statue. But I didn't. "It's okay, Grandma. Kip and Aubrey are going to do the giveaway for you."

"Who's Aubrey? Did I have another grandchild without knowing about it?"

"Aubrey is Kip's puppy," Tasha said. "Remember, Kip rescued him from a well in the park."

"Oh, right. Cute sucker." Grandma sat back. "Sorry. Must be the pain meds going to my head. Did you say you had one of the tablets for me to stream the Macy's parade?"

"Are you okay to ride in the parade?" I asked and put the back of my hand to her forehead.

She pushed my hand away. "Of course I'm okay."

I put my hands on my hips and tightened my lips into a straight line. Grandma crossed her arms and glared at me. Tasha stepped in to break the tension.

"I have your Gluten-Freedom sash, Ruth," she said as she gently pulled the sash over Grandma's head and adjusted it around her.

"How do I look?" Grandma asked and posed.

"You look lovely," I said, my worry dissipating.

"I bet someone has a smartphone and you can stream the parade on that," Tasha suggested. They both looked at me.

I raised up both hands. "Don't look at me. I don't have an unlimited data plan." Truth was I didn't have time to go online and figure out which plan was best for me. I simply bought the least expensive phone from Walmart and still didn't know how to use half the features.

"I have a phone you can use." Sam stepped up onto the float. "Hello, Ms. Nathers. You look fetching today." He brushed a kiss on grandma's dry, freckled cheek.

Grandma blushed, then sat up straight. "See, Sam understands how important it is for a grandma to see her grandson on television." She took the phone Sam handed her. "How does this work?"

There was a tap on my shoulder, and I turned to see Aunt Phyllis. She looked better today. The color had returned to her cheeks. Her eyes sparkled and her bright hair swung around her jawline. "Oh, Aunt Phyllis, you look good." I hugged her. She hugged me back and then, with a glance at Grandma, pulled me behind a nearby pillar.

"So what did you learn?"

"What do you mean?"

"I heard you went to the Everett house. Did you confront Hutch Everett? Did he know anything about his father murdering Champ?"

"Shhh." I glanced around to see if anyone heard her excitement. Lucky for us they had opened up the side of the building and people and floats had started the slow procession out to the parade route. "Yes, I talked to Hutch. Yes, he knew that Lois was his mother, but he told me that we had it wrong."

"What did we have wrong?" Aunt Phyllis frowned.

"Homer wasn't his father."

"What? Why did he adopt the boy if he wasn't the father?"

"Because Champ was Hutch's father. It's in his name: Hutchinson Champ Everett."

"Oh." Aunt Phyllis's eyes grew wide. "Of course. That makes perfect sense."

"It does?"

"Yes. Champ was a known womanizer. It would make sense that he would knock up Lois."

"Aunt Phyllis!"

"What? It's what he did. He probably told Lois to get rid of it. It wouldn't surprise me if she shot him."

"Who shot who?" Sam stepped around the pillar.

"No one," I said. "At least not in a long, long time. Thank you for taking care of Grandma. She's on pain meds and I'm not at all certain I would have been able to calm her down."

"Hey, Phyllis," Grandma bellowed from her side of the pillar. "Did you see my sash?"

Aunt Phyllis stepped out from behind me. "Very nice, Ruth. You look like you won a beauty pageant. Do the wave thing. You know . . . elbow, elbow, wrist, wrist, wipe a tear, and blow a kiss."

"Your aunt is a lot of fun, isn't she?" Sam was dressed for the chilly morning in a jean jacket, a plaid snap-front shirt, tight-fitting cowboy jeans, and boots. He had a pair of leather gloves tucked in his back pocket and a black Stetson on his head. His gray eyes twinkled.

"Like I told you, there are a lot of characters in my family."

"I like character." He winked at me, and I blushed.

"Hey, Baker's Treat, you're next in line." Chief Blaylock was in full uniform directing the floats.

"I have to go." I headed to my brother's red pickup. He'd let me borrow it when I had mentioned that I was going to use the bakery van to haul the float trailer. The men in my family proceeded to inform me that that was all wrong. Only a fool would do that.

Before I knew it, Tim had gotten a trailer hitch put on the back of his pickup and I was given keys. Tim would have driven it himself, but he worked the night before and didn't think it was safe to drive in a parade on less than two hours' sleep.

So it was me climbing up into the big cab of my brother's pickup and slowly pulling Grandma on the back of a float out into the bright, cold sunshine. Tasha and Kip walked beside the float with boxes of cookies ready to give away to the parade watchers. Aunt Phyllis climbed up on the float to be with Grandma Ruth and ensure that she didn't get so busy watching Sam's phone streaming video that she forgot to smile and wave to the citizens of Oiltop.

In all the hustle and bustle of the morning, I forgot to ask Grandma Ruth what it was that she wanted to see so badly that she risked life and limb to climb up on Homer Everett's statue.

At this point, nothing made sense to me. Would Homer have killed his best friend, then raised his son as his own? Wasn't that a bit twisted? But if Homer didn't kill Champ, who did? And more importantly, why did they do it?

Means, opportunity, and motive were the three parts of

any murder investigation. What we had were two murders: Lois and Champ. The two had been lovers whose son was now the most prominent person in Oiltop. Who killed them, and why? Were the two deaths even connected?

Right now there was nothing to go on. Grandma was striking out. First strike: the police refused to dig into the courthouse wall and look for the murder weapon because Grandma Ruth's evidence was weak. Second strike was investigating Homer's journals for evidence of him killing Champ and not finding it. The third strike was thinking that Lois was Homer's longtime mistress. Grandma had tried to bully Lois into telling her the truth about Champ, only for Lois to end up beaten to death near the foot of Homer's bronze statue.

What I did know was that within months of Champ's murder the courthouse was remodeled and one wall in the judge's chambers was built out by a square foot. That was deep enough to hide not only a gun but a body. But we couldn't get Chief Blaylock to even investigate the wall without any concrete proof.

Lois Striker was indeed Hutch Everett's birth mother, but Champ, not Homer, was the father.

I was at a terrible dead end. I glanced in my rearview mirror. Grandma Ruth practiced her pageant wave on the kids along the parade route. Aunt Phyllis sat beside her, feet dangling off the float, eating cookies. I suppose I could let it go, let Chief Blaylock continue the investigation, except for one thing. I suspected that someone, perhaps Lois's murderer, was out to get Grandma Ruth.

Why else would they kill Lois and leave her close to where Grandma was supposed to meet her? Why ensure that there were incriminating scooter marks at the scene?

And why silicone the statue? Surely it was too crazy to think Grandma would climb on it. So why do it?

While the fall didn't kill Grandma, it did hurt her badly enough that she wouldn't be investigating anything for the next couple of months.

Long enough for the case to grow cold.

Didn't they say the best time to solve a murder is in the first forty-eight hours? It had been close to two weeks since Lois was killed. That meant the case was already cold. Sigh. Right now, Chief Blaylock led the parade in his slow-rolling squad car. The lights on the black-and-white flashed red and blue at the head of the parade.

Officer Bright wasn't in a big hurry to do anything but date Tasha, and Officer Emry was . . . well, Officer Emry. That didn't leave a lot of room for investigating.

It didn't help that Lois had been elderly and controlling. Most people spoke of her death as if she'd tripped and hit her head. "Oh, well," and "too bad" and "bless her heart" were muttered. Then life went on. Parades were watched and turkeys served. Whatever undercurrent of murder and mayhem ran through Oiltop was ignored and soon forgotten.

But there was one thing the killer didn't plan on . . . me. I refused to let anyone harm my family and get away with it. Some people might think Grandma Ruth was funny on pain pills, but every time I looked at her casts my blood boiled. I was determined now more than ever to find out who did this to her. The best part about Thanksgiving was that I had twenty-four hours free from the bakery to figure out who that was.

I scanned the crowd and the long line of floats. Someone in this very parade route was a killer, and it was up to me to figure out who and bring them to justice.

CHAPTER 29

"Congratulations on your third-place finish in today's parade." My sister Rosa came in carrying her famous sweet potato casserole.

"Thanks." I gave her a quick hug and cleared a space for her casserole dish on the old buffet in the formal dining room. "It was a collaboration. Tasha helped with the flowers and the decorating, and my friend Todd did a fabulous job of editing. But I think the real ace in the hole was Grandma Ruth and Aunt Phyllis. They were a real hit with people."

"I know—the announcer called Grandma the Grand Dame of the parade."

I giggled. "She was so high on painkillers she practically floated on top of the trailer."

"Are Joan and Eleanor here yet?"

"Joan and her kids are in the den. Eleanor said that Rob got called into work so they'll be late."

"I don't know how she puts up with Rob working like that. Sometimes your family should come first. Right?"

"Right."

"What's right?" My brother Rich stepped into the kitchen to snatch some cheese and crackers off the platter I planned to put out.

"It's what's not right," Rosa said and smacked Rich's hand.

"What? It's pre-turkey food and this is pre-turkey time. . . ."

"Take that out to the den," I said. "There are appetizer plates on the table near the wall."

"Yes, Mom . . ." Rich teased as he grabbed up the giant platter. Rosa smacked him for his sassy comment as he left the kitchen through the swinging door.

"Two turkeys this year? Do you think that's enough?"

"They are twenty pounds each." I lifted the foil that was tented over the birds to show off their perfect golden skin.

"The rule of thumb is three pounds per person. That means there's enough turkey for thirteen people." Rosa pursed her lips. My sister's hair was a lovely shade of auburn with the perfect skin and bright green eyes that came with the pretty red. "There are the six of us, plus spouses and kids. . . ." I could see her counting up everyone who was coming. "With Grandma Ruth and Bill—"

"Don't forget Aunt Phyllis." I crossed my arms and leaned against the gray granite countertop of my Victorian kitchen. "Then there's Tasha and Kip."

"I thought Tasha was going to her parents' place today."

"Her parents had the chance to take a last-minute cruise. So they celebrated on Sunday."

"I hope you don't mind, but I invited Calvin." Tasha came in carrying a large pan covered in foil. "He had to work tonight and his family lives in Kansas City."

"Calvin?" Rosa asked.

"Officer Bright," I said and waved Tasha toward an appropriate-sized spot on the counter. "Tasha's started dating again."

Tasha put down the roaster. "I think this time I might have a real keeper."

"Today will be the test," Rosa said. "If he can hang with our family, then he'll be okay. But if he takes one look at the bunch of us and runs the other way, then he wasn't worth dating in the first place."

Barking erupted down the hall, accompanied by the sound of multiple sneakered feet. Kip and my niece Leah and my nephew Joshua came screaming into the kitchen with Aubrey barking and jumping at their feet.

"Outside!" Rosa said with the commanding tone of a mom. She pointed at the back door. "Take that puppy with you."

"Aw, but we're hungry."

"I wanted to see what the turkeys looked like."

"Do you have any tofu?"

"Out!" my sister bellowed.

I grabbed a plate of cookies and handed them to Leah with a wink. The kids shot out the back door with a bang. The puppy, fast on their heels, barely made it out before the door slammed.

"As I was saying, two turkeys, even twenty-pound turkeys, are not enough to feed this bunch." Rosa was thin as a rail. My sister Eleanor used to complain that Rosa could eat anything and never gain an ounce. Meanwhile Eleanor had that pleasant curviness that came from Grandma Ruth.

"That's why I brought in roast beef." Tasha lifted the foil on her roaster to show off thin slices of roast beef resting in au jus. "My boss gave me permission to use the hotel's oven as long as I cooked up a pan for his family, too."

"Looks fabulous," I said and went over to the sink where

I had been peeling potatoes before Rosa knocked at the back door for me to let her inside.

Tasha grabbed an apron hanging on the hook by the back door and wrapped it around her waist. "When is Grandma Ruth getting here?"

"She was happy but exhausted after the parade." I handed Tasha a peeler and we stood side by side preparing a mountain of potatoes that would be boiled down, then whipped into fluffy mounds of mashed potatoes. "So Grandma went home to take a nap. Bill said he'd see she was up by four P.M. Dinner is set for an early five."

A roar came from down the hall. "Somebody's football team scored." Rosa pulled up a stool, took our peeled potatoes, and cut them into cubes and placed them in a pot of cold water.

"Thanks for the hard work on the float," I said to Tasha. "Third place is pretty decent for our first time."

"Especially since you were over at Hutch Everett's house poking around," Rosa said. "Honestly, Toni, have you no sense of politics? The whole town thinks you bought your vote."

I drew my brows together. "How did you know I went to the Everetts' yesterday?"

"Oiltop is a small town," she said smugly. "You've been in Chicago too long if you don't remember how small towns work."

"You live in Augusta," I pointed out. "That's twenty minutes from here."

"Facebook is not just for kids, you know." She raised an eyebrow at me.

"My visit was discussed on Facebook?" I was a bit appalled. The social media site was a trend I still expected to end any day.

"Sheila Hamm saw you take over a plate of cupcakes. She thought maybe you were buttering up the parade judge."

I rolled my eyes. "I was not buttering up the judge. Hutch Everett lost his birth mother. I was simply extending my condolences."

"And trying to find out if he knew who might have murdered Lois Striker," Tasha said as she worked the peeler in short, even strokes.

"Tell me you did not go over there and accuse one of the most prominent men in Oiltop of murder." Rosa's face was pale with disbelief.

"I didn't." I sent Tasha a look of betrayal. "I went to extend my condolences." I waited a heartbeat. "And to find out why Hutch's middle name is Champ."

"Maybe because Champ was his father's best friend." Rosa rolled her eyes at me.

"Grandma Ruth thought that Homer was the one who killed Champ," Tasha said.

"What? That's ridiculous. Homer was a hero."

"A hero with secrets," I said.

"That hasn't been proven yet," Tasha reminded me gently. "If he did have secrets, then Susan and Lois took them to the grave," she added. "It's all about family."

"It's all about family. . . ." It hit me then that family connections were usually made and kept by the women in the family. "When did Homer's wife Susan die?"

"Gosh, I don't know . . . a few years ago," Tasha said.

I put down my peeler. "I'll be right back."

"Where are you going?" Rosa called after me.

"Finish the potatoes," I answered with a wave and headed up the stairs to my sitting room. I passed the den filled with men intent on the flat screen television and their football teams. The living room was filled with kids playing video games and board games.

I loved it when the house was full. I loved the noise of it, the ribbing, and even the fights that occasionally broke out. We were family, after all. At the end of the day we'd take a bullet for each other.

My study was not empty. My niece Michaela was curled up on the yellow-and-white settee reading a book.

"Hey," I said as I entered. "Why aren't you downstairs with the rest of the family?" My laptop was open on my desk, and I wiggled the mouse, waiting for the browser to pop up.

"It was too noisy," Michaela said with a sigh. At twelve years old, she was the oldest and my sister Joan often worried that she was too reserved.

"What are you reading?" I asked as I typed into my search engine.

"*The Hound of the Baskervilles*," she said without looking up.

"A classic." I straightened. "Do you have to read it for school?"

"Naw," she said and turned a page.

"Then you like mysteries?" I had my hands on my hips. Michaela shrugged. "I like books. This one's not bad."

I turned my attention to the search engine and typed as I sat down. Susan Everett popped up several times in my search. "Huh."

"What?" Michaela was beside me looking at my screen.

"Nothing," I said and closed the browser.

"Why were you searching skeet shooting?" She blinked at me. Her hair was not the family red; instead she had her father's black tresses. What she did inherit was our pale skin, freckles, and blue eyes. She was tall, already five foot seven, and gangly as a new colt.

"I wasn't searching about skeet shooting. It came up in connection with my Homer Everett research."

She rolled her eyes and plopped back on the settee. "If you ask me, this whole Homer Everett thing is for the birds."

"Uncle Rich took out a plate of appetizers, if you're hungry," I said and stood.

"I'm fine." Michaela curled up on the settee, becoming immediately engrossed in her book.

I barely remembered when life was so simple. Another roar echoed up the stairs and Michaela let out a long-suffering sigh. I grinned. Like I said, I loved a house full of family. One never knew what would happen next.

CHAPTER 30

Thanksgiving dinner was not a sit-down affair at my house. Instead it was a chaotic buffet. The fancy linen–covered table groaned with enough food to feed an army. The meal was officially served at five, but the feast continued into the night, with a second table laden with desserts.

Family came and went. Everyone had at least two affairs to go to, ours and their spouses'. Everyone, that is, except me, which is why all holidays were held at my house. Grandma came to my house because it was bigger than her apartment at the senior assisted-living building, and so aunts and uncles and as many of my fifty-two cousins as possible stopped by to eat, drink, and visit.

Then there was the yearly tradition of the "holiday reveal." Homer Everett Day aside, Thanksgiving was the beginning of the Christmas holiday in the Nathers family. The reveal always began with the telling of the story, then the procession, and finally the reveal. What had started as a joke, Grandma had made a tradition.

The cuckoo clock in the den struck eight P.M. and the kids all jumped up to mob Grandma Ruth.

"Tell the story, Grandma."

"It's eight o'clock."

"Okay, okay." Grandma held out her good hand and hushed them with an up and down motion. The kids sat down as she cleared her throat. "Way back in 1972—"

"That was a long time ago," Emma said, her blue eyes wide.

"Way before your mom was born," Joan said with a smile.

"Stop interrupting," Grandma Ruth commanded. The room grew still. "As I was saying, back in 1972, my daughter—your grandma—decorated the basement with the finest Christmas decorations money could buy. They were so fine, in fact, she saw no reason to take them down once the New Year came."

"Imagine Christmas year-round," Rosa told the kids. "All we had to do was go down to the basement and there it was."

"Until the years passed and your grandma got tired of dusting them, so she cleverly covered the decorated silver aluminum tree with black plastic. It remained covered all year, and was then uncovered for the Christmas season. Each year when a new child was born, a new stocking went up on the wall to wait for Santa."

"I have a stocking up there," Emma said. She was four and wanted everyone to know how much she, too, was part of the family. "When Auntie Crystal has her baby, the baby will get a stocking, too."

"That's right," Grandma Ruth said. She adjusted her hips in her wheelchair. "This went on for some time, until your uncle Rich got tired of the decorations always in view. He wanted to bring his friends over to play video games in the basement. So he took sheets and tacked them up on the walls, completely covering the walls and the lovely decorations.

At this point the entire family gave Rich the stink eye. He took it in good humor and crossed his arms and shrugged.

"This lasted for two years," Grandma went on, "until your uncle Tim announced the big reveal would happen at precisely eight P.M. on Thanksgiving Thursday, and that first year we had no idea what the big reveal was. So we all gathered in the living room at precisely eight P.M. to find out what Tim was talking about."

"And then he led you all in a procession into the basement," Emma said, clapping her hands excitedly.

"Yes, he did." Grandma Ruth waved her hand and Tim stood and good-naturedly led everyone to the basement. We followed him down the hall through the kitchen and down the stairs into the soft glow of the single-bulb overhead light.

We waited while Grandma was helped down the stairs. It had been decided that Rich and Calvin would take Grandma down in a fireman's carry because the house elevator didn't go into the basement—whoever had installed it hadn't thought about having it go down there. Dad had considered extending the elevator to the basement, but there was a structural issue, so he had decided we would make do with stairs just like all the other people in the neighborhood. Thankfully the men were strong enough to manage more than two hundred pounds of grandma with her leg and arm casted. She refused to miss the big reveal.

"If this doesn't make Calvin run, then he really is a good guy to date," I whispered to Tasha as the two men, red-faced, sidestepped down the ten stairs.

"Oh, he deserves some extra TLC after this," Tasha agreed with a grin.

Once Grandma was ensconced in the dusty, old Barca-lounger near the stairs. The kids gathered around her again. "We all came down and Tim told everyone to sit."

She nodded at Tim, who said, "Sit."

All the kids hit the floor. The basement had been remodeled in the seventies, which meant a painted concrete floor with large rag rugs. The walls were paneled and currently covered in sheets that had motifs of everything from the Backstreet Boys to Star Wars to pale pink roses.

"Dim the lights," Tim said with ceremony. The overhead disco ball light was dimmed with the dimmer switch my father had installed one year when my sister Rosa wanted to have a boy/girl party. "Man your stations."

My brothers and sisters and I each had our duty stations. Tim, Rich, Eleanor, and I were to yank the sheets from the wall. Rosa was to pull the plastic off the tree, and Michaela, being the oldest grandchild, was to plug in the extension cord, which ran the entire light show.

Boyfriends, girlfriends, and, in my case, husbands, came and went, but blood always attended the family reveal.

"Begin the countdown," Tim bellowed, and everyone started: "Ten, nine, eight, seven . . ."

When we hit zero, the sheets and plastic were yanked off and the lights were plugged in and the entire room was plunged back in time to a 1972 Christmas, complete with giant, groovy, multicolored lights, plus a train that never failed to chug around the track at the bottom of the tree. The air was filled with must, dust, and the *oohs* and *ahhs* that were the magic of Christmas in the Nathers family.

Yes, I know, Grandma was the only one with the last name of Nathers, and that was the only thing she'd kept of the man she'd married. But Nathers we were and would always be, no matter what our last name was.

"They do this every year?" Calvin asked Tasha loud enough so I heard it.

"Every year," Tasha said. "Our entire life, right, Toni?"

"Remember the first time you were here for the reveal?" I asked her.

She giggled. "I was thirteen and my mom and dad had said I could come over as long as I did all the Thanksgiving dishes."

"All of them?" Calvin raised an eyebrow. "All by yourself?"

"All of them," she acknowledged. "I think they hoped it would deter me. But I was insistent because I wanted to get to see the reveal in person. Toni had talked about it her whole life."

"Not my whole life," I said. "Tim had only started it two years before."

"It's a sight to be seen," Calvin agreed.

The noise level in the basement precluded being able to hear yourself think. Rich had started a fire in the potbelly stove. The basement wasn't exactly heated, so when my father had envisioned a family room in the seventies, he'd thought it wise to put in the stove. For the most part, it worked wonders. Over the years furniture came and went, but the rugs remained the same, along with the decorations. My mother never spoke of another renovation. I wouldn't be able to do one either, now that she was gone. The reveal was one of the few things we had left of her.

"You okay?" Tasha bumped me with her hip.

I wiped the tears out of my eyes. "Yeah. Thinking about Mom."

"There is so much of her in this room," Tasha agreed. "It's kind of cool, because she was the foundation of the family, wasn't she?"

I looked around the room at all my relatives. Tasha was right: Mom was the foundation.

"Now you are the foundation." Tasha hugged me. "I'm glad you moved back."

"Hey, where is everyone?" My assistant, Meghan, stuck her head through the open basement door. "Wow!" Her eyes were nearly as wide as little Emma's. She came clomping down the steps in her skinny jeans and thick boots, silver chains, and full-on piercings. "Awesome!"

"Welcome to a 1972 Christmas," I said and waved my hand.

"You missed the big reveal," Tasha said.

"It was big," Calvin agreed with a glint in his eye. Someone had put a Christmas DVD in and the big screen television was now playing *Rudolph the Red-Nosed Reindeer*.

"Oh. My. God. I haven't seen that since I was a kid." Meghan moved in to sit beside my nieces.

"Speaking of dishes"—I headed up the stairs—"a foundation's work is never done."

I said I liked the noise and chaos in the house, but like Michaela, I was rarely part of it. Maybe that was my creative nature. While Michaela always had a book in her hand, I was always in the kitchen trying something new.

While in the kitchen I heard the doorbell, which was odd. No one in my family ever rang the bell. Even Brad and Sam knew to just walk in. With the number of people in the house, all you had to do was holler as you came inside. There was always someone there to greet you.

I wiped my hands on a dish towel and went down the hall. There was a young man at the door. I recognized him as Hutch Everett's son, Harold. "Hi, Harold," I said as I opened the door.

He seemed taken aback by my familiarity. I saw a

moment of uncertainty in his eyes and then a strange light. It lasted only a second, and then the heavyset, pouty young man was back.

"I brought over your prize," he said and shoved a holiday tin in my hands. "See ya." He turned and headed down the stairs.

"Thank you," I called after him. He waved his hand and got on his bike and peeled off.

I studied the tin. It had a turkey motif. Opening it, I found homemade chocolate chip cookies. Nice try, I thought, then put them down on the dessert table. I'm pretty certain they weren't gluten-free. I'd let the kids eat them.

CHAPTER 31

"Aunt Toni, come quick! Something's wrong with Aubrey!" Kip's cry struck fear in my heart. I rushed into the dining room as Tasha raced down the stairs.

When I got there Kip was making a mournful sound as the puppy lay on his side panting hard, his little eyes glazed over. Beside him was the tin of chocolate chip cookies. The dog had somehow gotten them off the table.

"Oh no," I heard Tasha say.

I picked up the dog, who only let out a small pitiful whimper that made Kip start screaming.

"I'll get him to the vet, you calm Kip down." I had to shout for Tasha to hear me.

"Take a cookie with you," Michaela said and handed me a cookie. "The doctor might need to know what's in it." Her blue eyes were too wise for her age.

"It's probably the chocolate," I said. "Aren't dogs allergic to chocolate?"

"Smells like almonds." Michaela opened the back door for me. "It could be cyanide."

I placed the puppy in the passenger seat of my van and hated the fact that a twelve-year-old would know what cyanide would smell like.

It was only another three minutes to the emergency veterinary clinic. Thank goodness Oiltop was surrounded by ranchers. It wasn't every town that had access to emergency animal care.

I burst through the door with the puppy in my arms. "He ate something bad," I said as I rushed him into an open examine room. Aubrey was panting hard, his tongue hanging out.

"Do you know what it was?" The vet tech pulled out her stethoscope.

"He got into a tin of homemade chocolate chip cookies. My niece put one in a bag." I lifted the bag.

The tech frowned. "How many did he eat?"

"I don't know, not that many if even a whole one," I said thinking back on how big the pile was in the tin.

"A couple of chips in a cookie won't make a dog this sick. Has he thrown up?"

"Yes."

"Did you bring in a sample?"

"Um, no, but I can get one."

"Do," the vet tech said. Dr. Peter Bekany walked into the room. He was in my brother Tim's class in high school and was the resident veterinarian.

"What's going on?" he asked and quickly assessed the situation. "Get a blood draw."

"Yes, Doctor."

"Thank goodness you're here, Dr. Bekany," I said. "There's a young man with Asperger's who is very attached to this puppy. You have to fix him."

"Do you know what he ate?"

"Some cookies." I lifted the bag. "My niece said it smells like almond, but they are chocolate chip cookies. She thought maybe they had cyanide in them."

Peter helped the vet tech administer IV fluids. "Let me see that bag." He took the bag and sniffed it. "She's right. It could be cyanide. Okay, little guy. We're going to do our best to make you well." He petted the pup and looked at me. "Why don't you step out for a few minutes while we figure this out."

"Should I leave him?"

"He'll be fine." The vet nodded toward the door. "Go get that vomit sample and comfort the boy."

"Okay." I hated that my adrenaline was working overtime. It was so hard to feel calm and in control when your brain was screaming as loud as Kip had been when I left the house. Thank goodness for Michaela. I would have never thought to bring the cookie.

I hit my sister Rosa's cell number. They were all still at the house watching holiday movies. "Pick up, pick up!"

"Toni, what's going on?" my sister asked as she answered the phone.

"Rosa, did anyone eat any of those cookies? The chocolate chip ones in the turkey tin?"

"No, I don't think so. I'll ask."

"It's important." My stomach was in my throat. I paced the linoleum floor of the vet's waiting room. I would have driven back home to get the sample, but I was shaking too hard.

"No, no one ate them."

"Not even a crumb?"

"What's going on? Are you worried because the dog got into them?"

"They may be poisoned."

"What?"

I pulled the phone off my ear as my sister's tone rose three octaves. "Michaela, get away from those cookies."

"Michaela knows," I said. "She suspected the minute she saw the dog. She might have saved his life."

"Okay, okay. I'll get them cleaned up."

"Vacuum as well. I don't want any of the kids getting crumbs on their hands."

"Not a worry," Rosa said. "Where did they come from? I mean, you wouldn't bake poisoned cookies."

"No, gluten is poison enough for me. Harold Everett stopped by after the reveal. He brought them. He said they were part of my finalist prize."

"Holy Moses, Toni, why would Harold Everett bring you poisoned cookies?"

"I don't know." I pulled the hair off my forehead. It was a hot mess of wild curls. "Listen, call the cops on this and don't let anyone get near the cookies."

"Not a problem. Once the cops get here, I'm pitching the entire dessert table."

"I don't think you have to go that far," I said as I paced.

"Would you want to eat anything off that table?"

"Um, no, okay, toss it all—once the police say you can. Too bad Calvin left already."

"Right? I'd have him go over to the Everett place and kick that kid's butt. I swear, if he thought this was some kind of joke, I'm going to give him a piece of my mind."

"I don't know what he thought." I sat down hard. "Did Tasha get Kip calmed down?"

"She managed to get him calm enough to get in the car. They're on their way."

"Okay. Listen, I need a sample of the vomit if you can get one. Wear gloves."

"Oh, I'll be wearing gloves and a face mask." Rosa loved to exaggerate. But this time I couldn't tell if she meant it or not.

"Thanks Rosa—and thank Michaela."

"Thank goodness for that puppy," Rosa said. "Can you imagine what would have happened if it had been Emma?"

That was something I didn't want to think about.

CHAPTER 32

"The puppy is going to be all right," the vet said as he came out to the waiting room. "He's sleeping. Do you want to go see him?"

"Yes!"

"Kip." Tasha's tone brooked no disobedience.

"Yes, please," Kip said. His face showed his worry and exhaustion, but now his eyes held hope.

"Come with me," the vet tech said and put out her hand. "My name is Shelly."

"I'm Kip." He took her hand. "Is Aubrey a hero?"

She glanced at us. "Yes," she said with a definitive nod. "He is."

"I knew he would be." They disappeared into the back room.

"Clinical observation tells me it was most likely cyanide poisoning," Peter said. "I've sent samples to the county lab for testing, but from the thick smell I'm certain the cookies were heavily laced with it."

"Where would someone get cyanide in the first place?" Rosa asked as she stood next to Tasha.

"It's common in insecticides."

"So someone baked cyanide in chocolate chip cookies and gave them to us?" Tasha said. "That's attempted murder, isn't it?" We all looked to Calvin, who had come back over the minute Tasha called.

"There's a strong case for it, yes," Calvin said.

"Why else put it in a human cookie?" I said.

"Do you know who did it?" Peter asked.

"The cookies were delivered by Harold Everett. He's down at the station now, but his father has hired a lawyer," Calvin said.

"Which means we have to wait before we have any idea," Grandma Ruth said. Even in two casts and a wheelchair she looked madder than a wet hen.

"What about Aubrey?" Tasha said, concern on her face. "Will the puppy live?"

"Yes, I wasn't lying for the boy's sake," Peter said. "Toni did the right thing bringing him in right away. With the cookie and the sample of vomit Rosa brought, we were able to determine an immediate cause. We put him on dialysis to get it out of his blood and we also got any remaining cookie out of his digestive system. His blood work shows that his liver and kidneys are holding up. We'll have to keep him a few days until he fully recovers."

"Be prepared to have a little boy with you until he does," Tasha said with a deep sigh.

Peter lifted a corner of his mouth. "Not a problem. You'd be surprised how many people stay for their pets. If it's all right with you, we can put up a cot next to the puppy's crate."

"Kip has Asperger's. . . ."

"It's okay," the vet said, his brown eyes calm. "My son has special needs. I know what to do. If it will make you feel better, you can stay."

"I have to work, but yes, I'd like to be here when Kip is here."

"With any luck, we'll have the pup out of here by Monday." He winked. "In time for life to return to normal."

"How much is this all going to cost?" Tasha said weakly.

"Don't worry about that," Peter said. "I'm sending the bill to Hutch Everett. It's the least he could do, even if it was only supposed to be a prank."

"Not a funny prank." Calvin's eyes were flat and seriously coplike.

"I'm going to write a piece on the dangers of punking," Grandma said, her blue eyes narrowed. "If it's more than punking, I'm going to dig around in that kid's life until the entire world knows everything he's ever done and will ever do."

"Come on, Ruth, you've had a long day." Bill undid the brake on her wheelchair. "Let's go home."

Aunt Phyllis shook her head. "Someone needs to take an old-fashioned belt to that kid," she muttered.

"Aunt Phyllis, I thought you were into peace, not war," Rosa said as she walked out with Phyllis.

"Perhaps there were some things my generation got wrong."

Tasha and Calvin and I were left in the bright light of the vet's waiting room.

"What a day." I dropped my chin into my hands. The

bright plastic seats were easy to clean but far from comfortable.

"Those cookies couldn't have been meant for you," Calvin said as he sat down beside Tasha and took her hand. "Everyone knows you don't eat wheat."

I looked over at him. "The kid handed them to me. He said they were part of my prize."

"Do you think he didn't realize you couldn't eat them?" Tasha asked. She rested her head against Calvin's shoulder. He put his arm around her. It warmed my heart to see that my family's antics hadn't put him off of dating Tasha.

"It could be he was so caught up in his 'joke' "—I used finger quotes—"that he didn't think things through."

"One thing's for sure," Calvin said. "Kip is right. Aubrey is a hero."

"Yes," I agreed. "Aubrey will always be a hero in my eyes. I imagine my family will keep him in steak for the rest of his life."

Exhausted, I walked out of the house to my van. It was four in the morning, my usual time to go to work. I had managed to crawl into bed at midnight. Rosa and her family crashed at my house. Tasha, Kip, and most likely Calvin were all still at the vet's office with Aubrey.

"Good morning. I brought you coffee. It's not as good as yours, but it's hot. Two creams, right?"

I started at the sound of Sam's voice. The man had this nasty habit of sneaking up on me. Though I guess I can't say it was nasty if he brought me coffee. "You scared me half to death!" I had my hand on my heart and I'd stopped in my tracks.

"That wasn't my intention," he said gently and pushed a

large coffee cup at me. "My intention was to ensure that you didn't get scared on your way to work."

I took the coffee and stepped around my van. "You heard about Aubrey." It was a statement, not a question.

"My mom is on the direct gossip pipeline." He gave me a weak smile. "I figured if someone was trying to poison you, then perhaps you shouldn't be going to work by yourself in the dark like this."

I leaned back against my van. The man was right. It had crossed my mind that those cookies were meant for me this time and that the entire town knew when I went to work. It wouldn't be that hard to jump out at me when I was this tired. Sam had proven that himself. I sipped the coffee. It wasn't half bad. Neither was the man who brought it. He crowded me and my heart rate sped up—but not because I was scared.

He wore his cowboy hat low. Today he wore a suit coat and a blue dress shirt under it. His classic jeans were gone. In their place were dress slacks—but he still wore his boots. It made my tired mind wonder what he looked like with just the hat and boots.

"Are you doing okay?" he asked, his voice gravelly, as if he'd picked up my thought waves and liked their direction.

I straightened. "Yes, thanks for the coffee and the company."

"You must be tired."

"Why?" I opened the van door and put my purse and coffee inside.

"Because you thanked me for being here. Usually you're all bristly when I try to be a gentleman."

"Maybe it's because I carried a dying puppy in my arms yesterday." I paused. "All I could think of was what if it had been Emma or any of the kids."

"Don't go there," he said gently and pulled me into his broad, warm chest. "It didn't happen, and going there will only hurt you."

I let myself find comfort in his solid warmth for a couple of heartbeats. Then I backed off, threw him a small smile, and climbed up in my driver' seat. "I'll take the usual route."

"Good." He turned toward his pickup.

"Sam—"

"Yeah?" He paused and looked at me.

"Did you hear anything on why he did it?"

"Nothing yet."

"Okay. I didn't think so." I closed my van door and started it up. It crossed my mind then that maybe we were looking too hard for Lois's killer. Maybe he was right under our noses.

Even if he was, it didn't explain why. Or who killed Champ Rogers.

CHAPTER 33

In typical small-town manner, bad news brought people into town. Thank goodness they tended to gather, and the bakery was the best gathering place at this time in the morning. It was six A.M. The coffee was hot and plentiful. I kept the baked goods simple, figuring correctly that most everyone had had their fill of rich food the day before.

My biggest seller for the morning was my bacon breakfast muffin. It was less sweet than a fruit muffin and yet the hint of maple with the bacon and corn bread structure gave it the taste of a sit-down farmer's breakfast. The next was my potato fritter with apple and ham.

"I'm headed out, Toni," Sam said as I refilled the coffee carafes. "Is someone going to see you home?"

"I'll get Rich to see me home," I said, knowing he'd balk if I didn't name names. "Thank you for all your time today."

He lifted one corner of his sexy mouth. "You're most welcome. Call me. I'll be there."

"Thanks." It made my heart do a little flip. The idea that there were two men I could count on. That idea had followed me my whole life. Watching my Dad be there for my mom, helping her without being asked. He seemed to always understand when she came home from the store that she needed help with groceries. He knew she shouldn't be carrying something heavy. When she asked for the lightbulbs around the house to be checked and changed, she meant to check them right then. As an adult I realized he did it out of respect and love.

It was something I'd assumed Eric would do, but my ex had disappointed me at every turn. "Take me as I am," he'd said. "Or leave."

Eventually I'd left, but not until he'd flaunted his cheating in my face. When I made a commitment I made a commitment. It was why I needed to take time before I dated. To remind me how easy it was for me to believe the best in a man. How strongly I commit to a relationship after a handful of dates. To remember that, for me, it was never just about a good time.

"Heard about the boy's pup," Jack Rickman said. "I hope they throw the book at the Everett boy. It wasn't right."

"Thanks, Jack. I'll tell Kip how you feel. It helps."

"I'm going to talk to the mayor about getting some kind of hero award for that pup," Jack said. "As far as I'm concerned, he saved lives."

I leaned on the glass counter. "I agree. How was your Thanksgiving?"

"Good. I spent it out at the Hogginboom place with Sarah. Lots of good food and good company." He patted his stomach.

"Can I get you your usual?"

"Thanks. And Sarah sends her thoughts your way."

I wrapped up the bear claws and put in a couple of the potato fritters. "On the house."

"Man, you gals are going to fatten me up past reason," he muttered and paid for his breakfast.

"It's winter," I said. "You have to have something to fight the cold."

The morning went that way. My regulars came in with words about the Everett boy and then went home to their families or back to work. Until ten A.M., when the door bells rang and I came out of the kitchen to find Hutch Everett and Harold standing in the middle of the bakery.

"Can I help you?"

"I'd help them out the door," Meghan said from the doorway.

"Everyone who comes in is a customer," I reminded her gently. "We don't discriminate."

"We came in to apologize," Hutch said, his voice deep and serious. He pushed his son forward. "Apologize."

Harold Everett glanced at me. Again I saw something that made my skin crawl, and then it was gone, leaving only a fourteen-year-old boy in its wake. "I'm sorry about your dog."

"Harold will be paying the entire vet bill and any further bills that come up later due to this . . . prank."

"He's darn lucky one of the kids didn't eat those cookies," I said. "The vet told me they were deadly."

"Yes, Harold will be in counseling until he turns eighteen. We've also agreed to serious community service hours for the next two years. He'll be on probation, and there will be no further incidents."

"I would hope so," Meghan said behind me, her hands on her hips and her chin high.

"Poison is not funny," I said to Harold. "What made you think it was?"

He kept his gaze on the floor and shrugged. "It was stupid."

"It was more than stupid. It could have been deadly," I said.

"Again, we apologize," Hutch said, looking down his nose at me as if his explanation of punishment was enough. "Should you so desire, we'll get you another dog."

"Another dog! You think that's going to make up for what he did?" Meghan stepped forward, and I put my hand on her shoulder to stop her.

"There's no need for another dog. Aubrey is the only dog we need."

"Then we won't trouble you further. Good day, Ms. Holmes." Hutch turned, and Harold sneered at me before his father pulled him along. It was then that I noticed the boy's piercings. Like Meghan, he had piercings in his eyebrows and in his upper lip. His studs were bigger than hers, more in-your-face. They looked like spikes. All except one. One was a simple, round dog bone.

I waited for them to leave, then I turned to Meghan. "Is it common to wear spikes and a dog bone piercing?"

She shrugged. "The dog bones are usually for new piercings. They are pretty standard. I don't know about the spikes. Not too many people have them."

A thought crossed my mind. I pulled off my apron and handed it to her. "Hold down the fort for a bit."

"Where are you going?"

"Don't worry, I won't be long." I headed out the front door.

The crime-scene tape was long gone. I studied Homer Everett's statue. "Was it you?" I asked. "Did you kill your best friend and raise his son out of remorse?"

He didn't answer, of course. I didn't expect him to. What I'd come back for was the shiny piece I'd seen in the leaves under the bushes. With the crime-scene tape gone I could search for it in the daylight.

I squatted down at the spot and peered under the bushes. The leaves and mulch were damp. Maybe it was silly to think that something I'd seen in the dark would still be there a week later—especially since the crime-scene guys had canvassed the area. I picked up a stick, then used it to dig around, turning over leaf after leaf.

Was it stupid to squat there in the square and dig under the bushes for a glint? Probably. Was I stubborn enough to keep going? Yup.

Finally, after what felt like two hours, and after two people stopping and asking if I was okay, I found it: a spike of shiny metal as long as the tip of my little finger. I pulled it out and looked at it, pretty sure it matched the ones Harold Everett wore.

I stood, not sure what it meant. Except that Grandma Ruth wasn't the only person at the crime scene. I frowned. I suppose he could have lost it any time before or even after Lois died. The tiny piece of silver didn't mean anything by itself. And worse, they could say that I planted the evidence.

What a waste of a good couple of hours. I shook my head at myself and curled the spike in my fist.

"You found it. I'd say that makes you smarter than your supposedly brilliant grandmother."

Harold Everett stood behind me. That look in his eyes was back and downright feral. "Excuse me?" I slipped my hand in my pocket and hit the first button on my phone. I hoped and prayed it was the right button.

Harold held out his hand. "My spike." He snapped his fingers as if I should hurry up.

That got my back up. How dare this teen speak to me like that? "I don't know what you're talking about, Harold."

"Oh, you do know," he said as he stepped toward me, contempt on his face. "Don't think I would fall for your little phone trick either. I read how you called the cops when that guy attacked you. I happen to have a phone of my own." He pulled out his smartphone and waved it in the air. I noticed it was an expensive phone—one capable of taking excellent pictures and video.

"Wow, cool phone," I said. "I bet it takes excellent pictures."

"Better than your ancient phone," he sneered.

"Really? Because I've got some good pictures with my phone." I unlocked my phone and brought up a picture of Aubrey and Kip. "Cute, right?"

"It stinks. Mine is way better."

"Really? I don't believe it."

"Believe it, lady."

"Prove it," I said with a jerk of my chin.

"I don't have to prove squat." He grew agitated.

"Fine." I put my phone back in my pocket. "If you can't prove it, then I say you're lying."

"I'm not lying." He rolled his eyes. "Give me my spike."

"Why'd you put the silicone on the statue?"

"It was a joke," he sneered. "Too bad about the old lady, but hey, she should read. Now hand over my spike."

"You know what would have been funny? If you had a hidden camera and greased the statue. Then you could film anyone who slipped on the silicone."

He narrowed his eyes. "Maybe it would have been funny. If someone had been stupid enough to fall for that old trick."

"You like to video things, don't you, Harold? I bet you have some really cool videos on your phone." I raised up my phone and pointed the camera toward him and turned it on.

"Turn that off." He reached toward my phone and I ducked.

"Silicone on the statue was a joke, right? Like putting cyanide in the cookies you gave me—how were you going to take pictures of that? Hidden camera?"

"Don't be stupid." He stood a foot from me. I could smell

the classic junior high body spray he wore. "I'm done yapping. Give me my spike!"

"Fine." I dug into my pocket. "I'll give you the spike." I took a step back and held out the spike in my palm. "You know, I really thought you were clever like your grandfather, but I guess you aren't, are you?"

He took a step toward me and reached for his spike; I was quicker and pulled it away. "Poisoning those cookies wasn't very smart," I said. "If you were trying to hurt me, you really failed. Everyone knows I'm gluten-free. I'd never eat a wheat-flour cookie."

"Do you really think I'd do something that stupid?" He raised a dark eyebrow.

That made me pause. Poison was usually a woman's trick. "It was your mother, wasn't it?"

"Wasn't what?" he sneered.

"She gave you those cookies to bring to me. She told you they were poisoned so that you wouldn't eat them. Did you go around the house and peer in the window to see where I put them? What did you think, that you could video the poisoning through my window?"

"You're crazy, lady."

"Do you have video of the poisoning on your phone?" Anger made my voice rise. "Were you laughing when that puppy got sick?"

"Give me my spike!"

Then it hit me. "You recorded it, didn't you?" I pushed. "On your phone. You had a hidden camera on the statue to watch for prank victims. Only instead of someone sliding off the statue, you recorded your mother killing Lois."

"I'm done screwing around. Give me my spike."

"Lois was going to tell us where the gun was that killed Champ. Aimee couldn't let that happen."

"Spike!" His eyes sparked and his impatience boiled. He looked like a giant two-year-old who was not getting his way. I half expected him to threaten to hold his breath.

"Why'd she do it, Harold? Why did your mother kill Lois? Was it to keep your family secret?"

He lunged at me. "Give it to me now!"

I didn't have two brothers for no reason. I'd learned early how to judge a boy's breaking point, and I ducked and dodged. He stumbled and hit the ground.

"Lois was going to tell us where the gun was. She was going to reveal to everyone that your father wasn't Homer Everett's son, that you are not Homer's grandson. Your mother couldn't have that. She could sacrifice her own standing in society, but she refused to sacrifice yours," I pressed as I waved the spike in the air.

He got up and charged me like a bull. Harold might be younger, but I was lighter. I dodged. This time he caught himself before he fell and reached out with a meaty fist. I saw stars.

He was on top of me. I raised my arms against his blows. Then as suddenly as it started it stopped. Harold was lifted off me.

Calvin had the oversized boy flat on the ground and cuffed him.

"Are you okay?" Sam reached down to help me up.

"I think so," I said. "Thanks."

"Sit." Calvin pulled Harold up and pushed him into a sitting position, then said to me, "I saw the whole thing. If you don't press charges, I will."

"Your face." Sam reached up and brushed my hair out of my eyes. "You're going to have a shiner."

I touched my eye. He was right. The shock had worn off, and pain blossomed. "Ouch."

"What was this all about?" Calvin asked.

"She has my spike," Harold said, pouting.

"Be quiet," Calvin and Sam said at the same time.

"He recorded Lois's murder," I said through the pain. "It's on his phone."

"Shut up!" Harold said.

Calvin pulled Harold to his feet and patted him down. He took the phone and flipped through it to bring up the video. Calvin's face grew stone-cold angry as he watched.

I turned away at the sound of angry words, a horrible crunch, then rock on flesh and terrible silence.

Sam stepped between me and the recording as if it could hurt me. "Let's get you to the ER."

"I'm fine."

"I'd prefer to get you checked out."

"Fine." I let Sam walk me out of the square. I glanced back to see Calvin calling in backup. Harold glared daggers at me.

"You have to stop getting into altercations." Sam's tone was gentle but firm as he put his hand on the small of my back and guided me to his pickup.

"How did you know what was going on?" I asked as he opened the pickup door and helped me inside.

"I had an eye on you." He closed the door.

I rested my head back and waited for him to climb in the driver's side. "Are you stalking me?"

"No, that would be illegal." He started the vehicle and pulled out into traffic. "Meghan called me."

"Ah." I watched the blocks roll by and tried not to think about how badly my face hurt. Harold might be a kid, but he was a big kid, and he could really wallop.

"People care about you, Toni." He pulled into the clinic part of the hospital. "You need to learn to let them."

For the first time in my life I thought he was probably right.

CHAPTER 34

"Your investigating is good for business," Meghan said as she refilled the coffee carafes for the third time. "It's usually slow this time of day."

I looked out at the group of people who sat around the bakery. Several made eye contact and smiled and nodded. My heart warmed. They were here to support me. Others came to see my shiner for themselves, while still others came because they wanted to be in the middle of the news. Hutch Everett had convinced the judge to open up the false wall in his chamber.

"We'll have to close when we run out of baked goods," I said and looked over the near-empty shelves. I'd had no time to do more than bake a few cupcakes for the evening hours, and those went quickly.

Candy Cole walked in the door and all conversation stopped. "They've found a gun in the wall. It looks to be the same caliber as the gun reported to have killed Champ Rogers."

Conversation ran like wildfire around the room—speculation on whose gun it was.

"They arrested Aimee Everett," Candy said to me and made a beeline for the coffee buffet. "She's not talking. Hutch has hired a high-powered lawyer out of Kansas City. So we may never know for sure why she killed Lois."

The crowd breathed a collective sigh of disappointment and went back to their conversations. Candy waved me into the back room and closed the door. "Sit. You look awful."

"Thanks, Candy, I can always count on your honesty," I said as I took a seat.

"I didn't tell them the real scoop, as I have to have something that will sell papers."

I tilted my head as she took the chair next to me. Meghan sent me a look as she washed dishes. I winked at her with my good eye.

I waited for Candy to talk. I'd learned early on that she hated silence and usually filled the space if I waited long enough.

"Okay, fine, here's the scoop." She leaned in toward me. "Lois was going to confirm Ruth's suspicion about the wall in the judges' chamber. Only it wasn't Homer that okayed the false wall. It was his wife, Susan. It seems that she had pull with Judge Jonas, who was in office for forty years."

"So did Homer kill Champ after all?"

"No." Candy shook her head and sipped coffee, allowing the silence to create tension.

"Then who?"

"I suspect it was Susan who killed Champ. We'll find out if there are any fingerprints or DNA on the gun."

"Why would Susan kill Champ?" Meghan asked. She faced us, her pink-dish-gloved hands held in the air so that they wouldn't get anything wet.

"I did some checking," Candy said. "It seems Champ was a real ladies' man, and Susan was in love with him. She even tried to seduce him in the hopes that he would give her the child Homer couldn't give her. But before her plan could come together she learned that Champ was head over heels for Lois, and the feeling was mutual. When Susan discovered that Lois was pregnant she lost it. Picked up Homer's gun and murdered him."

"And then Homer adopted Champ's son. . . ."

"And Susan got the child she wanted while keeping the man she loved from ever loving someone else."

"Creepy," Meghan said.

"Why did Aimee kill Lois?" I asked.

"Lois found out about the gun. She confronted Susan in front of Aimee. The emotions of fear, horror, and despair caused Susan to have a giant heart attack."

"She was dead on the spot—just like Homer."

"Exactly." Candy sipped her coffee. "Aimee was horrified that not only was the man she married not the man he claimed to be but her own mother-in-law had killed to keep the secret."

"She must have put the fear of God into Lois for Lois to keep this quiet for all these years."

"You forget," Candy said. "Both Aimee and Lois had a vested interest in Hutch maintaining his identity as Homer's son and heir."

"So they had a bond until Grandma pushed Lois toward confessing," I stated.

"Exactly. Aimee refused to let the truth come between her and her son's family inheritance."

I shook my head at all the wasted lives. "It seems the apple didn't fall far from the tree, right?"

"Right," Candy said. "Good catch on the boy, by the way.

They pulled video off his computer that showed he was well on his way to serial-killer status. He'd been murdering animals and videotaping the events."

"I hope he goes away for a long time," Meghan said and went back to the dishes.

The bells to the bakery door jangled. Meghan slipped off her gloves and went out to see if anyone needed help.

"I have to say," Candy said, a gleam in her eyes, "things sure have gotten interesting in Oiltop since you moved back."

"Is that a good thing or a bad thing?" I asked and touched my bruised eye.

"Oh, good, honey, all good. Now, where do you keep the yummy stuff? I've been too busy to bake and my family will be coming this weekend to celebrate a late holiday."

I got up. "There's two pies in the freezer. I hope you like pecan."

"Oh, honey, there's never been a pecan I didn't like, and the same goes for my family. They'll be thrilled."

I laughed. It seemed the desire to impress family was universal. I was glad to be back in the midst of mine. Because it was true, family was one of the most important things in life—even a crazy family like mine.

BAKER'S TREAT RECIPES

Gluten-Free Yogurt Blueberry Coffee Cake

1 package of gluten free yellow cake mix (Betty Crocker®
   sells a good one.)
¼ cup brown sugar
1 cup low-fat vanilla yogurt
½ cup applesauce
¼ cup water
¼ cup vegetable oil
3 eggs
2 tablespoons lemon juice
2 teaspoons cinnamon, plus enough to sprinkle on berries
1 ½ cups fresh blueberries
¼ cup confectioners' sugar

Preheat oven to 350 degrees F (175 degrees C). Grease and flour a 10-inch fluted tube pan (such as Bundt®).

Mix cake mix and brown sugar together in a bowl; add yogurt, applesauce, water, vegetable oil, eggs, lemon juice, and cinnamon. Beat on low speed with an electric hand mixer until blended. Scrape bowl and beat on medium speed for 4 more minutes.

In a separate bowl, toss blueberries with enough cinnamon to evenly dust each berry. Fold blueberries into the batter. Pour batter into the prepared pan.

Bake in the preheated oven until a toothpick inserted in the center of the cake comes out clean (55 to 60 minutes). Let cool in pan for 10 minutes, then turn out onto a wire rack to cool completely. Dust with confectioners' sugar.

Gluten-Free Raspberry Swirl Cheesecake

¼ cup milk

2 teaspoons gluten-free vanilla

2 eggs

¾ cup sugar

¼ cup gluten-free Bisquick® or your favorite gluten-free baking mix

2 8-ounce packages of cream cheese

1 cup raspberries

2 tablespoons sugar

Heat oven to 325 degrees F (165 degrees C). Spray bottom only of 9-inch glass pie plate with cooking spray. (Note:

Ensure your spray is gluten-free.) In blender, place milk, vanilla, eggs, sugar, and the baking mix. Cover; blend on high speed 15 seconds. Add cream cheese. Cover; blend 2 minutes. Pour into pie plate.

In same blender, place ½ cup raspberries and 2 table-spoons sugar. Cover; blend on high speed 15 to 20 seconds or until smooth. Drop blended raspberry sauce by teaspoon-fuls on top of cream cheese mixture. With a butter knife, swirl sauce into cream cheese mixture.

Bake 28 to 32 minutes or until about 2 inches of edge of pie is set while center is still soft and wiggles slightly. Cool completely at room temperature, about 1 hour.

Refrigerate at least 4 hours. Garnish with remaining ½ cup raspberries. Store in refrigerator.

Gluten-Free Party Fruit Dip

8 ounces whipping cream whipped until light and fluffy (can use whipped topping if you can find one gluten-free)
7 ounces marshmallow cream
3 ounces cream cheese

In a mixing bowl, combine the whipped topping, marshmal-low cream, and cream cheese. Mix until smooth. Add straw-berries or any of your favorite fruits—serve chilled.

Gluten-Free Peanut Butter Bars

1 cup butter or margarine
4 cups confectioners' sugar
1 cup peanut butter
1 ½ cups of premium semisweet chocolate chips
4 tablespoons peanut butter

In a medium bowl, mix together the butter or margarine, confectioners' sugar, and 1 cup peanut butter until well blended. (Hint: If it isn't thick enough add more confectioners' sugar.) Press evenly into the bottom of an ungreased 9-inch by 13-inch pan.

In a metal bowl over simmering water, or in the microwave, melt the chocolate chips with the 4 tablespoons peanut butter, stirring occasionally until smooth. Spread over the prepared crust. Refrigerate for at least one hour before cutting into squares.

Gluten-Free Coconut Lime Cheesecake with Mango Sauce

¾ cup sweetened flake coconut
¾ cup of crushed gluten-free gingersnap cookies
3 tablespoons of melted butter
2 8-ounce packages of cream cheese
1 10-ounce can of sweetened condensed milk
2 eggs

1 tablespoon lime zest
2 tablespoons lime juice
1 tablespoon coconut milk
1 teaspoon gluten-free vanilla
2 cups cubed fresh mango
1 teaspoon sugar

Preheat oven to 325 degrees F (165 degrees C). Lightly grease a 9-inch springform pan.

Combine the coconut, gluten-free gingersnaps, and melted butter in a bowl; mix until even. Press the cookie mixture into the bottom and slightly up the sides of the prepared pan.

Bake the crust in the preheated oven until browned and set, about 10 minutes. Set aside to cool.

Reduce oven heat to 300 degrees F (150 degrees C).

Beat the softened cream cheese in mixer bowl until smooth. With beater set to medium-low, slowly pour the condensed milk into the bowl, mixing only until just blended. Add the eggs, mixing one at a time.

Pour about half of the cream cheese batter into a separate bowl. Stir the lime zest and lime juice into the portion in the new bowl; pour the batter over the crust in the springform pan, smoothing into an even layer.

Stir the coconut milk and vanilla through the remaining cream cheese batter; pour over the lime-flavored batter in the springform pan, smoothing into an even layer.

Bake in the preheated oven until the top of the cheesecake springs back when gently pressed, about 45 minutes. Turn oven heat off, but leave cheesecake inside with oven door slightly ajar until the oven cools completely. Refrigerate until completely chilled.

Prepare mango sauce by pureeing the mango with sugar until smooth. If too thick, add one teaspoon of water at a time, using just enough to make pourable. Drizzle over cheesecake when plated.

Gluten-Free Berry Shortbread Bars

½ cup butter—cubed
1 ½ cups of gluten-free baking mix or gluten-free
    all-purpose flour
¼ teaspoon xanthan gum
½ cup white sugar
½ teaspoon salt
¼ teaspoon baking powder
1 egg yolk
1 teaspoon cold water if needed
1 ½ cups fresh berries

Preheat oven to 350 degrees F (175 degrees C). Place butter cubes in the freezer for 15 minutes.

Whisk together flour, xanthan gum, sugar, salt, and baking powder in a large bowl.

Cut in frozen butter using a pastry cutter until the butter pieces are about the size of peas. Mix in egg yolk and continue cutting in until thoroughly combined. Drizzle in ice water and stir to combine. Use enough water for the perfect consistency. Too much water and the dough will get tough. Not enough water and the dough will be dry. The dough should just come together when pinched between your fingers.

Pour about ¾ of the crumb mixture into an ungreased 9-inch by 9-inch baking dish. Press the mixture down firmly using the back of a spoon. Spread berries in one layer and sprinkle with remaining crumbly dough.

Bake in the preheated oven until the top is golden and sides are crisp and browned, 30 to 35 minutes. Cool completely before serving.

Gluten-Free Lemon Cake

3 cups of gluten-free flour—tapioca is great for this
¼ teaspoon xanthan gum
1 teaspoon baking soda
¼ teaspoon salt
6 eggs
2 cups sugar
1 cup butter, softened
2 teaspoons lemon zest
2 tablespoons lemon juice
1 cup of plain yogurt

Preheat oven to 350 degrees F (175 degrees C). Grease one 10-inch springform pan.

Sift the flour, xanthan gum, baking soda, and salt together. Set aside.

Separate the eggs. In a large bowl, beat the egg whites until soft peaks form. Gradually add ½ cup of the sugar, beating until stiff glossy peaks of meringue form.

In a separate bowl, cream 1 ½ cups sugar, butter, egg yolks, lemon zest, and lemon juice together until fluffy. Add flour mixture alternately with the yogurt to the egg yolk mixture. Gently fold in the egg whites and pour the batter into the prepared pan.

Bake for 50 to 60 minutes. Let cake cool in pan for 10 minutes, then turn out onto a rack to finish cooling. Serves 12.

For a fancier cake, slice cake in half. Frost bottom half with lemon curd. Place top of cake back into place. Frost with whipped cream. (Be sure to refrigerate.)

Chocolate Italian Cream Cake

    1 cup butter
    2 cups white sugar
    5 eggs
    1 teaspoon gluten-free vanilla
    1 teaspoon baking soda
    2 cups all-purpose, gluten-free flour (Better Batter is a
        good brand)
    ¼ teaspoon xanthan gum
    ¼ cup unsweetened cocoa powder
    1 cup of buttermilk (or almond milk with 1 tbs vinegar)
    1 cup shredded coconut
    1 cup pecans, chopped

FOR FROSTING:
    1 cup cream cheese
    ½ cup butter
    4 cups confectioners' sugar
    ¼ cup unsweetened cocoa powder

1 cup pecans, chopped
1 teaspoon gluten-free vanilla

Preheat oven to 325 degrees F (165 degrees C). Grease 3 8-inch round cake pans and dust with cocoa powder. Separate the eggs.

Cream white sugar and 1 cup of the butter together. Add egg yolks, one at a time, beating after each addition. Stir in 1 teaspoon of the vanilla.

Sift baking soda, gluten-free flour, xanthan gum, and ¼ cup cocoa powder together. Add alternately with buttermilk to the creamed mixture, beginning and ending with dry ingredients. Stir in the coconut and pecans.

Beat the egg whites until stiff peaks form and fold into the batter. Pour batter into the prepared cake pans.

Bake for 25 to 30 minutes. Let cakes cool completely before frosting between layers and on sides.

Frosting: Cream the cream cheese and butter together. Sift confectioners' sugar and ¼ cup cocoa, beating in a little at a time until well blended. Add 1 teaspoon vanilla and 1 cup pecans.

FROM *NEW YORK TIMES* BESTSELLING AUTHOR

Jenn McKinlay

Going, Going, Ganache

A Cupcake Bakery Mystery

After a cupcake-flinging fiasco at a photo shoot for a local magazine, Melanie Cooper and Angie DeLaura agree to make amends by hosting a weeklong corporate boot camp at Fairy Tale Cupcakes. The idea is the brainchild of Ian Hannigan, new owner of *Southwest Style*, a lifestyle magazine that chronicles the lives of Scottsdale's rich and famous. He's assigned his staff to a team-building week of making cupcakes for charity.

It's clear that the staff would rather be doing just about anything other than frosting baked goods. But when the magazine's features director is found murdered outside the bakery, Mel and Angie have a new team-building exercise—find the killer before their business goes AWOL.

INCLUDES SCRUMPTIOUS RECIPES

jennmckinlay.com
facebook.com/jennmckinlay
facebook.com/TheCrimeSceneBooks
penguin.com